THE LION'S DEN

BOOK 9
The New Life Series
By
Louise Bouck

PERMISSION

COPYRIGHT

This book is a work of fiction, any resemblance to events or persons living or dead is coincidental.

ACKNOWLEDGEMENTS

Thank you to all the people who have encouraged me and kept me in their daily prayers. A special thank you goes to Mary Koestner for her prayer support from the very beginning.

To my husband, Dale Bouck my editor, thank you hugs. He somehow manages to keep my computer running in spite of the monsoons. Thank you to Maureen Burge for working so hard at editing, smiling and giving hugs.

Thank you to all those who gave me technical help. A special Thanks to Ray Shaw for his time and patient repetition until I got it... Without his technical help in the beginning, this series of stories would still be files in my computer. Thank you to the people in the computer lab of the Show Low, AZ library. What would any of us do without the public libraries and the wonderful people that work there?

DEDICATION

This New Life Series is dedicated to Jesus, my family, those that have gone before me, those that are with me and those to come and to my brothers and sisters in Christ.

✝

INTRODUCTION

This is book nine in "The New Life Series." The Christian fiction in this series is written to offer the reader a wholesome entertainment, starting back in a simpler but not easier time. Their example of spiritual strength and "never quit" attitude is refreshing and inspiring. The adventurers follow the trail to a new land and challenges they never imagined.

In book one "More Than Survival", follow Benjamin Slater as he copes with the wild isolation of the new frontier and the lesson of self-preservation. He experiences the pain of loss and joy of accomplishments. He travels, "Life's Many Journeys," in book two and learns to appreciate the "Land's Heritage," in book three.

In Book four, you will find out "The Story of Sarah"

As you read the books, Ben develops into a man of physical and spiritual strength. His problem solving mind is challenged many times.

When Sarah, his sister returns to him, they are finally "Together," in book five. You will find out how her life affected the Indians that took her and how they became "The Blue Stone People," a chosen nation in book six.

A change of scene takes you to the camp of the Sentu and three survivors enter the story, in book seven "Teewahpanyee the Boy, Two Feathers the Man," Willow and Water Bug bring new strength and young blood to an old people. With Willow at his side in book eight he becomes leader of "The People of The Lion". They are chosen by the Lion of Judah to be rescuers, and are rewarded in book nine, by being allowed to discover "The Lion's Den."

In book ten, the land that Ben Slater's father chose has miraculously remained with the family as time has gone by and generations were born. In a day beyond today, the series skips to the final times after the rapture. A new heroine stands up bravely to the soldiers of the anti-Christ. She finds Ben's Bible, Mary Slater's journals and the gift of faith. Emily spreads the word and struggles to survive the time of tribulation as she finally realizes that this is "Just the Beginning" for those who believe.

TABLE OF CONTENTS

CHAPTER ONE
REASSURANCE

Father Bob shook David's hand and then gave him a big hug. He made the sign of the cross on Pili's forehead with his thumb before he kissed the sleeping baby goodbye.

"Goodbye Sarah, I will be eager to return to see the way you and David develop your land, but in the meantime, I know that you will be safe here."

David helped him to cross the slowly flowing river on the raft and they were soon on their way back toward the S. and J. Ranch to pick up Brother Tim's bundles and crates left under the trees at the crossing. Josh held the reins as Sundown pulled the smallest wagon toward home. Father Bob smiled at him thinking that this lad will grow up knowing how to handle almost anything that has to do with horses.

Tim had set a reasonable pace with the big work horses and knew that the job of pulling the empty freight wagon was an easy one for them.

Father Bob looked back and thought he would have liked to linger until late afternoon so that he could have seen the image of the lion above the cave once more. We have so much to accomplish this summer. The campaign against the Abalinah seems to have taken us the entire spring. I hope when Tim and I get back to the settlement, that Tom will have enough lumber cut at the lumberyard so that I can get another load right away, he thought. It was the right thing to do, to let David have my first load, but it means we will spend time getting some more before we can start working on the church and school at the Indian village.

Tim had pulled the team to a stop and was looking for food in his bag.

"Father Bob, do you have any food?" He sounded desperate.

"I am sure that I have something. Let me check." He pulled out a pack that held some dried beef and a small amount of oil coated, dark orange cheese. "There is food in the bundles we are picking up, but that will be a while yet. Will this help?"

"I just need a piece of that meat and a drink of water and I will be fine." Tim struggled to bite off a piece. It was very hard and dry.

Later, when they looked ahead and saw everyone from the ranch standing in the grass under the big oak waiting for them, they were glad to see the happy smiles.

"We pulled all your things back to this side to save you time. Beth and Mary have packed you a hearty lunch in this bundle. Your water bags are full of fresh water, too. Do you want us to empty your barrels and fill them with fresh water?"

"Thanks Ben, but the first one is still full. We should refill the second one. We used that for the horses at the halfway spot."

Ben lifted the dripping barrel up to Tim and held it steady as it was strapped in place.

Mary and Beth had spread a blanket and had settled the children on it for a picnic lunch.

"Ladies you have a special talent for making the mundane seem like a celebration. I always enjoy visiting with you. I wish that we didn't have to hurry on our way." Jed had led the new horse for Tim on a long lead and tied it to the back of the wagon.

Brother Tim jumped down from the wagon and went to Jack and talked softly to him and scratched his ears. He shook hands with Jed and Ben and thanked them again for agreeing to let him take Jack. He looked at Ben's face and could see the tight muscles in his jawline.

"Ben, we don't know yet what God is doing, but it's obvious that you and this beautiful ranch are part of it. Forget the pain and frustration of the last few days. Let it fade away. Just remember the love that has been expressed and the image that guards your sister and her family. You must accept that change is never easy. I have been traveling for a long time and I still have yet to see where I will be living and working, but I have met some wonderful people. God has blessed me and all of you mightily," said Tim.

With that he hopped up and tucked the big lunch sack under his side of the seat, grinning and teasing Father Bob. He gathered the reins of the ready horses in his hands as Father Bob laughed.

"That's for me, too," he said reaching for it and waving as the wagon slowly pulled out. The women were laughing at the way the two men had shown their appreciation for the lunch they had prepared.

*****

In the settlement, with Matt's help at the narrow bridge, they were able to continue straight down the main street to the mill. Tom and his crew had been keeping the saws singing later than usual, anticipating the summer season orders that would need to be filled. He was surprised to see Father Bob and Tim back so soon, but was able to accommodate their needs and the wagon was loaded before the mill closed.

They rested on the hay in Matt's blacksmith shop and were on their way as soon as it was light enough to see.

The trip back to the village was stress free. Tim took the team across the Silver and Father Bob knew that God was answering his prayers every step of the way.

10

As Tim approached the woods just beyond the big rocks, Growling Bear rode out of the trees to greet them.

"Hello, Father Bob, we have been watching for you. I have been working a little on the trail by the bluff and it is a good thing that I cut some of the branches that had grown out because your load is higher than the last one."

"Thank you Growling Bear, that was thoughtful of you. Let me introduce you to Brother Timothy Sunning. He was sent to us to help build the church and school. Tim, this is Growling Bear. He is my good friend, top hunter and warrior of the Blue Stone People and a baptized Christian."

"It is nice to meet you Mister Bear," said Tim pensively as he cautiously directed the horses on to the slim path through the trees. Growling Bear chuckled and decided that the young man had all he could handle getting the team and freight wagon through without incident, so he waited to correct him on his name until the wagon stood beside the church on the top of the sheep hill.

"You do a fine job of handling the horses. I really appreciate it Tim," said Father Bob stretching as he stood on the grass. "Well, this is it, your church and home. These people are our congregation and they will unload for us. They like to do it."

"You didn't lie, it is small and rustic!" Several men were carefully removing the white canvas that covered the load. They dragged it a short distance away and spread it out. Next as they lifted down each box or crate, they looked to Father Bob for directions on where it was to be taken. Tim found that his things were again in a stack under a tree.

"I'm sorry but we only have room inside to walk through to our beds. I think we should ask them to bring the lumber out of the church and let's leave the wagon load of wood as it is for now."

Chief Dark Wolf greeted him with a fond hand clasp and a slap on the shoulder.

"Chief Dark Wolf, this is my new assistant, Brother Timothy Sunning. He has been sent to help me build the new church and school. Tim, this is Chief Dark Wolf. He is the Chief of the Blue Stone People."

"It is good to be here and to meet you," said Tim.

"I am glad that you have come to keep Father Bob, company. Since the death of Father Peter he has been alone."

Growling Bear had heard the comment about leaving the wood on the wagon and was now orchestrating the careful removal of the lumber from the church. They had made a level area beside the wagon and were piling the lumber ever so carefully. All the men of the camp were impressed with the smooth surface of the boards and only Growling Bear and Singing Wind were there that had seen how it was made. They were making sure that no one made a nick or mark on it. Tim watched and was amazed at their helpful spirit.

"That is the last piece from inside the church," said Growling bear. Would you want us to move the boxes and crates in along the back wall now?"

"Thank you that would be very helpful. I don't want them to get wet." Tim picked up a crate of books and started in with it, but Growling Bear took it from him.

"We will do this, and you can call me Growling Bear. I am not a mister."

"Oh, I am sorry. I didn't mean to mess your name up." Tim was mumbling apologies and Father Bob couldn't hold in his laughter. Soon they were all laughing.

"The horizon has a dark line of clouds. Do you want us to put the canvas over the wood?"

"That would be a good idea Mister Bear," said Father Bob laughing again.

"I have a tent in that bundle there in the corner. If we split it open it may be big enough to cover the rest of the wood," said Tim.

"Don't worry Tim. We were just having fun with you and if your tent is like the one they sent with me, we will have to coat it with grease. Those things leak, but it might help to keep some of the wood dry."

It had taken quite a while to get things where they wanted them and covered securely. Tim had a soft bed pallet against the wall, where Father Pete's had been. The desk had been placed along the back wall of the church for now.

"Tim, what do you think of the place?"

"It's not what I expected. Neither are the people."

"What did you think would be here?"

"It's not that so much as they seem like regular guys and they have a sense of humor too."

"I hope that in a few days you will feel at home here. The women here are kind and you will find that they are very good cooks."

Father Bob poked through the boxes and bundles from the Trading Post and finally found what he was looking for. He started dumping ingredients into his biggest pan but stopped to find his new stick matches.

"I am going to make us a small cooking fire in here. I heard a little thunder a minute ago. No use setting up outside and having to carry it all in. Do you like coffee?"

"Yes, but what are you starting in that pan?"

"I have vegetables from the ladies at the ranch and some potatoes I'll toss in some of those. I have a lot of dried meat in our cache, I'll show you that in the morning, but tonight I am going to cut up this dried beef and add it. It will soften as it cooks." Tim looked around and smiled.

"This place feels good and I am hungry again. I have eaten a lot lately. I couldn't eat very much at the seminary. My stomach was always in a knot. Maybe now I will gain some weight."

"I think you and the Bishop made a good decision. You are going to find that all your natural talents will be used here and probably you will discover some you didn't know you had."

They sat near the small fire sipping the coffee and talking. So much had been going on since Tim arrived on the mail boat that they really hadn't had a chance to just relax and talk. Tim noticed the guitar hanging on the wall.

"That's a nice guitar. I didn't bring mine. I gave it to a friend before I got on the train."

"You can use that one anytime you want. It was Father Pete's. I don't play and I can't sing on key either. God should have made it a requirement in heaven before he called people to serve him. At least now if we sing Old McDonald had a farm, the children will know what a cow and a chicken are. Sarah and David brought those to the village their last visit."

"They are nice people and I could tell when I was around them that they are sensitive to God's guidance. Poor Ben, he was having a rough time accepting the change that Sarah and David were not going to live at the ranch anymore. He likes to keep everything close, safe, and where he has them under his vigilant eye. I could tell that right away. That's a beautiful ranch. His parents must have been prosperous," said Tim.

"Well, you are partly right. He is having a rough time with Sarah moving, but she was taken by the Winahatah Indians when she was a young girl and his parents were killed. He was wounded and left there where the crossing is now, with practically nothing. The Indians took the horses, and everything they thought they could use from the family's covered wagon. Ben built that place with his own effort and prayer. Jed came along at a time when Ben was injured by a mountain lion and helped him. They have been closer than brothers ever since, but we need to save their story for another time. It is late. Let's get some rest."

The next few days were surprisingly peaceful. Father Bob strolled through the camp greeting people. He stopped at the shade pavilion and looked at all the babies and children there, that the story mothers were caring for.

"Who is this pretty little girl?" He asked. He knew it was a girl baby by the many beads fastened in her hair. Smiling Moon nodded and gave a toothless grin. When he thought about it, he realized he had never heard her say a word. Blue Stone saw his attempt at communication with the adopted grandmother and she hurried over.

"Smiling Moon doesn't talk much. The baby is Clover's child. She named her Freedom. She was born just a few days after Sarah's baby."

"Did Chief Dark Wolf have a naming ceremony for her?"

"No, Clover named her the day after she was born. Father Bob, I think as time goes by we will see many breaks in our old traditions."

"Thank you Blue Stone," he said. Just as he turned to leave he saw Willow coming toward him.

"Hello, how are you Willow? And how is Two Feathers?"

"We are well. I just noticed that you saw Clover's baby. She is a cute baby, isn't she? Clover left her with them a little while ago and has gone to the woods to gather; with two other mothers. She doesn't let me take care of her and she didn't invite me to go with her. She acts like she resents me. She spoils Water Bug so much that he won't mind me anymore. She speaks to Cricket in Abalinah so I don't know what she is saying. She speaks our language but she hasn't taught Cricket one word of it. I feel like she is pushing me out and taking my family away. Father Bob, I don't know what to do!

They had walked almost all the way through the camp and were on the path to the church.

"Willow, do you still intend to marry Two Feathers?"

"Yes, I think so, but I am not sure how he feels about it now that we have our extended family. Maybe he has changed his mind. We have not had a chance to talk alone since he returned with the captives. I don't want to lose him Father Bob. I don't know what to do!"

"The solution is easy. Announce your intention to be married and then do it, soon."

"How can we do that? I don't know how he feels anymore."

"I will talk with him. Come back to see me tomorrow and smile Willow. It is going to be alright. You will see."

The next morning Father Bob strolled through camp with Tim at his side. They were talking about starting the construction of the addition to the church, but he kept his eyes open for Two Feathers.

The young men of the night guard were no longer required to stand their positions during the dark hours. Only two guards were used to secure the camp. One watched the northland on the far side of the north woods and one was stationed at the opening of the path through the big rocks.

Now they sat together under the trees near their row of tents and talked of a desire for better times, and hoping for challenges as exhilarating as the recent campaign carried out by the seasoned warriors of the people, against the Abalinah. They were eager for adventure. They wanted to prove themselves.

Father Bob greeted the young men enthusiastically and introduced Brother Timothy. Most of them had already met him, but he was making sure they all knew who he was.

"Before me, I see strong men sitting idle. Is there anyone here that is willing to work?" The men laughed and said they would be glad to work if there was something to do.

"There is! I have lumber and nails and hammers and a desire to see our church extended so that it will hold all our people with room to spare. I need help. You are all young and strong and this is a big important job. Tonight I want to have a communal fire and discuss the church and what we need to do to make it accommodate the needs of our people. Two Feathers I want to talk to you for a moment at the church if you would walk back with us. I would like the rest of you to think about what you would like to have in the church. It needs to be more comfortable during Mass, story time, weddings, or winter Baptisms. Tonight I will read from the Bible some of the things that God required His people to do when they built the temple for Him. You will be amazed. It is a story like no other. Two Feathers I need to stop and tell Chief Dark Wolf about the meeting and communal fire. Please come to the church in just a few minutes."

"Alright Father Bob, I'll be there soon."

When the priest left Chief Dark Wolf's tent, he was smiling.

"Tim this is going to be a fun meeting," he said. "Moonflower has sent messengers to all the tents to be sure that everyone will come and bring food. It will be a feast. The young men in this camp will no longer sit idle. The Chief is going to reveal a very important piece of news. You are going to see what sets these people apart from other Indian villages!"

"What is it? Tell me what you are talking about!"

"No not now. I must talk to Two Feathers. He is on the path coming. Take this board and mark in the grass a square two board lengths out toward the meadow and two back toward the sheep hill. The board is twelve feet long. That will make the addition twenty four feet by twenty four feet. That should give us room to wiggle." It will give us a small room on the back, and then we can extend the lean-to for the horses. Make sure it is square Tim."

"I will Father Bob. This will be fun." One of the young shepherds wandered over to watch what Brother Tim was doing and brought his twelve sheep with him. As he walked, the sheep did a good job of mowing the grass near the church. Tim smiled and suggested that he take them all the way around.

"Two Feathers, thank you for coming. This won't take long. Willow has said that you have asked her to marry. She wants to do it before the people leave for the summer meeting. I need to know if you agree. Do you want to marry Willow?"

"I asked her, Father Bob, on the night we were getting ready to leave on the raid of the Abalinah. So much has changed since then. I don't know what I should do. I love Willow, but I feel that I am obligated to Clover and our children. I think I love her, too, but in a different way. I know I love Water Bug and the baby is precious. I feel like she is mine. Cricket is cute but she is a puzzle. She won't talk to me."

"Sit down Two Feathers. The situation you find yourself in is an unusual one. You must realize that it is good that you have a loving and compassionate heart, but you have opened it so wide that you have left no room inside for a special place for a beloved mate. I would suggest that you go for a long ride out on the prairie where you can think. I want you to picture Clover in a separate tent, well cared for and happy. Then picture Willow in your tent, as your loving wife. If you could accomplish that, wouldn't it be the ideal thing?" You are attached and feel responsible. You have sympathy for Clover and all that she went through. We all care about Clover and Sylvia Warren, and Sky Fire's young children, but we can't change what happened to them or any of the rescued people. All we can do is try to head them down a path to a healed and happy future. Two Feathers, tell me something. Who prepares the meals at your tent now that Clover is well again?"

"I think Willow does that."

"Who cleans up the tent and after a meal?"

"Clover is usually taking care of Freedom or playing with the children."

"What does Clover do to bond the children into a family?"

"What do you mean?"

"Does she teach Cricket the words of the Blue Stone People or is she speaking in Abalinah to her? That makes her different and separates her from you, Willow and Water Bug, too. Is Clover pushing Willow away by not including her? Willow cannot thrive in a family where she is not wanted. She wants to marry you, but I am not sure if she should with things the way they are. She wanted to announce your intention to marry at the communal meeting. I can't approve until these issues are worked out. I want you to take a horse and go pray and think. Come back to me here, when you have some answers. I will let the Chief know that I sent you on an errand." Two Feathers stood up and his face was covered with a mask of trouble.

"How is it that you know to ask these questions? Does Willow speak her dissatisfaction to others? Am I not man enough to care for the people in my tent?" He hurriedly walked out to the gate of the meadow and placed a bridle and blanket on his brown stallion. His haste had unsettled the horse. It reared and nearly dropped Two Feathers to the ground. He rode recklessly through the herd and out the far gate; entering the path around the big rocks to the prairie beyond.

Two Feathers finally found that the horse was motionless just outside the rocks. With no direction it had slowed and stopped. It stood waiting, nibbling the grass. He walked the horse to the left until he could follow the trail along the bluff, to the spring and the pool at the bottom. It looked different now that the men had not been working there extracting the blue stones. The grass around the water was taller and undisturbed; the rocks had begun to grow moss again and between them ferns spread out. He had not been with the Blue Stone People before they found the stones, but he knew that this area was trying to go back the way it had been. He knew it couldn't. I can't go back the way I was either. Things change and not always for the better. I think I need to talk to Clover and Willow.

CHAPTER TWO
RIGHT AT HOME

David had placed rocks in a small circle near the base of the bluff intending to start a fire, but decided that the blustery wind made it unsafe and that the wind was soon bringing rain.

Instead he went into the cave just far enough to discover that the left wall jutted out and created a natural wind break.

"Sarah, I think I want to put a small fire here. What do you think?"

"It seems like a good place to me. I think we will want one when it starts raining outside. Besides we can use the light and save the lantern oil. David I am so tired that I think as soon as I can get a stew going in the biggest kettle, we should get some rest."

"Our little Kitten has snuggled in her crib. She doesn't seem to notice that we are not in the cabin."

"She is too small to care where she is, as long as she has her mommy and a dry diaper."

"David you are funny. You made it sound like I am an item on a menu."

"I think she figures that you are her menu, right now anyway." They laughed together.

"Listen David, I think it is raining."

"It sounds nice."

"I hope Woof and his sisters are dry."

"They are fine as long as they stay in that Den." David slid in the bed beside her and soon both of them were asleep.

When Sarah opened her eyes it was morning. David was outside and already marking out a possible outline for the house.

"Pili, you slept all night." She picked her up and changed her diaper and sat in a willow chair that Beth had placed near the wall. "After you are finished nursing, we can go see what Daddy is doing."

She stepped carefully out of the opening of the cave into the sunshine. The pine trees were still dripping but the sky was starting to clear. "It's going to be a beautiful day," she said walking out away from the cave and looking up. The image is not there now, but maybe this afternoon it will be, she thought.

"David, where are you?" She called out.

"I'm over here. I'm glad you are up. How's my kitten this morning?"

"She was starving! She slept through the whole night. That's the first time she hasn't gotten me up. She likes it here, too."

"That's a good girl. You knew your mommy was tired. Didn't you?"

"Look over here at this cove made by the pines. It is far enough from the river to be dry even when the river is a lot higher. I paced the land off twice and I think our land ends about there. If we put our house so the front of it faces the river, we would have room to add on each end eventually without cutting the trees. We could start building here for the main room now. Sarah I think that is all I can accomplish this year. It will be small and just one room with a fireplace."

"David I love it. The location is perfect. We are back away from the prairie line and even when the house is complete it will be far enough away from the church land and Tim's cave to be separate and private."

"The nice thing is that I won't have to cut down any big trees to start building." She could tell by his voice that he was excited.

"I'm going to go back and feed the pups and check on the horses," she said.

"I put the horses on Tim's land near the crossing, so they will eat the grass there and clear it a little for us."

"That's good. David, there is a big deer watching us from the other side of the river. Where is your rifle?"

"It's in the sleeve on my saddle in the cave."

"I hope I can go get it without the deer leaving." She returned to the cave and placed Pili in her cradle for safe keeping while she took the gun to David. He continued to mark the ground and measure the area, but when he looked up, the deer was gone.

"It's gone now but since we didn't do anything to scare it, maybe it will come back. Lean the gun against that big rock and see if you think this will be a livable size for the start."

*****

Ben and Mary had talked about it and they wanted to help David and Sarah all they could. Ben had ridden down to find the men just arriving and preparing to unload the first wagon of logs on the Parker place. He explained to the men that they had a change of plans and that he wanted both loads of logs taken up river to a different location. They agreed they would do it but since they would be gone longer, he would have to pay Tom for the extra time. Soon the logs were secured again and on their way to David's property.

When Mary realized that Ben would be going there to show them the location, she hurriedly put together a plan to take the small wagon, with all her boys, some fresh bread and two pies. She added a big tub that had set under the trees near Sarah's outside fire and picked up two well-seasoned cooking stones, too and added them to the wagon. I know there are other things that we have forgotten but I will have to get them next time, she thought. She scooped all the ingredients needed for a huge batch of beef stew into the tub. The dried vegetables and dried beef would be fine in there to travel. She covered it with the heavy lid, just as Ben rode up on the prairie side of the crossing.

She heard Johnny ring the bell twice and then three times. She quickly pulled the wagon to the crossing and waited while Ben changed horses and doused his face and hair in the river. He helped her ferry the wagon across. Natty was standing in the corner of the wagon, wearing a harness she had made for Eli when he was at this stage of reckless adventure. She had fastened him in and placed the big tub on one side and Adam on his other. She had thought to bring a sack lunch for them all and tossed in her apron full of blocks for the boys to play with at the last minute before leaving the house.

As soon as the horse was hitched and ready, they headed out. She knew that the wagons hauling logs would move slowly, but was anxious now to be there. Josh drove the wagon and sat beside her proudly.

"Mom did you notice that Dad put his saddle on Chaco? She is the horse that I was telling you about. She has long lean legs like Dash Away and she loves to run. She was with that last small bunch of mustangs that we caught, but Dad says she wasn't wild. He was riding her a week after we got her."

"I don't remember you telling me all that, but I did notice the horse he was on. It is a beauty. Did your dad check her all over for an owner's mark of some sort?"

"Yes Mom we did and Dad checked the ears and even inside her flanks. He said some people are marking their horses where it doesn't show. He said he is sure that Chaco is valuable and that he plans to put a notice in the Trading

Post just in case the owner is in the settlement, but he said they better have some papers that prove they own her."

"Josh your father is signaling for you to pull up under the trees."

"Hi Dad, are you alright? Your face is really red."

"Yes Son, I am alright but I need to talk to your mother for a minute."

Mary climbed down and felt concerned when she saw the look on Ben's face.

"What is it Ben? It's obvious that you are upset." He took her hand and walked toward the river away from the boys.

"Mary, what if we get there with the logs and she gets angry again? What if she thinks I'm trying to control the building of their house? I used to charge into things and get them done thinking that I was doing a good thing. Now I am second guessing myself and not sure of anything. Should we be doing this? He bought the lumber from Father Bob. It was enough to start, but not nearly enough to build a house."

"Ben I'm not sure what you want me to say. I think that now they are on their own place, they will see this as us just helping them to build their future on their land. Ben I really believe it will be appreciated." He knelt and dunked his head in the river again and tossed his hair back and tied it.

"One thing is for sure, it is a hot day!" He helped her back on the wagon and Josh had used the time to water the horse and they were ready to roll. Behind them on the trail, the two wagons bringing the logs could be seen.

Once they were moving, Josh voiced his concern again.

"Mom is Dad sick?"

"No son, but he is worrying that Sarah might think that bringing the logs is interfering. He doesn't want her to be upset with him again."

"Oh, is that all? She will be fine now that she is in the Lion's Den. It is so peaceful there. Mom, I wish you could have seen the image of the Lion when we did. I think He was telling her that everything was going to be alright. I hope we get to see it again."

"I would like to see it," said Mary, but somehow I think it was a very special thing and that it will be rare if it is ever seen again."

*****

Sarah had taken food and water to the wolf pups and then went back to their den carrying Pili in her arms. She sat down in the shade and watched them tumble and chew on each other, playing. One by one they ventured in her direction the few feet until finally she was looking down at her lap filled with four sleeping babies. The poor things miss the security and companionship of their mother, she thought. I will cuddle them for a little while.

Starting with the smallest one, she placed them in the leaves against each other and stood up. As pleasant as it is here, I can't sit holding all of you. I have a lot of work to do, she thought. She was smiling as she placed Pili in her crib and stirred the stew and pulled it away from the unfed fire. I guess I better check with David and see if he needs me before I try to make order out of any of this stuff.

The area where he had been earlier was empty. She walked around and saw the line in the dirt. He had expanded it.

When she looked up she saw Mary climbing down from the parked wagon on the other side of the crossing.

David had heard them coming through the trees on the church property and was there to ferry them across the river.

After hugs Josh and David went back and moved her wagon to the crossing and brought it across without a problem.

"We had a nice rain last night but it doesn't seem to have raised the water level much," said David.

"Did you see the lightening?" I was sitting in the bedroom on the windowsill watching it. It was beautiful, but a little scary too," said Josh.

"I didn't sit and watch the lightening but we listened to the rain from our bed. It sounded nice in the cave."

Ben rode Chaco across the river at the church crossing and David's face showed that he was surprised to see him.

"I thought you would be in town hiring some help for the ranch. It is good here Ben, Sarah is a different person. She is calm and happy."

"Good, I hope she stays that way when I tell her that two wagons of logs are almost here for your house."

"What? How did you manage that so quickly? Ben that's fantastic! I'll take any help I can get. I was pacing off the place for the first room. Come see."

"I think you better tell me how you want the wagons brought in here first. I can hear them coming."

"If we move the raft and the ropes, do you think the teams can come right across there?"

"Ben rode Chaco back to the crossing and walked him into the water. The bottom is stable but those logs are heavy. Maybe if we work on the banks a little more, and they get a good run at it, they can get them across."

Ben rode out to the edge of the trees and waved at the driver of the first wagon.

Stop here and take a walk with me. The two wagons were pulled into the shade and the rest of the men gave the horses a chance to drink and eat while they waited.

Mary had given the news to Sarah that the logs were there for her cabin.

"If you want to get upset at someone, it better be me, because I told Ben you were smart enough to know when help was being offered and that bringing cut logs isn't all the help David will need to get a place built and cozy by winter!"

"Thank you Mary. I am not angry. I am ashamed, at the way I behaved. Forgive me please. All of you have done so much for me. I do appreciate it, really I do. I don't understand why I acted that way, but now we are here I know this is where we were meant to be." Natty was dancing in the corner of the wagon, eager to be set free.

"Josh, please take Natty in the bushes while he is still dry and don't let him run around. There are a lot of things here that he can get hurt on. Keep track of him for me."

"Sure Mom, I will."

"He is such a help these days. He is growing up Sarah."

"Yes he is," Sarah agreed.

"Let's unload the wagon and figure out a good place for an outside campfire. We have men coming and we need to make some food. Adam I need you to take care of Eli. Sarah and I are going to be very busy. You can walk around with him but be sure that you are both safe. Don't go in the cave. The men haven't checked it yet and there may be places that are not safe to walk on."

"Is it alright if we go down to the edge of the river if I hold his hand? Dad is there with the man from the wagon." You should ask him if you can be there as soon as you arrive, so he knows you are there. If he sends you back then you will know that it isn't safe right now. Adam you are such a big help to me. Thank you for taking care of Eli for me."

"It's fine Mom. We will walk around and have fun. I hope the clouds go away so we can see the Lion on the rocks. Dad said that God uses the sunshine to make the picture."

"I hadn't noticed the clouds. I hope they go away. I would like to see it, too." Mary smiled at her son as she helped Sarah carry the big tub to the spot where David had started to make an outside fire.

"I don't want to make it here, Mary. The fire will discolor the rocks at the bottom of the bluff. I don't think we should do anything to change this place."

"Let's move the circle out a few feet."

"That's a good idea."

"If you are worried about disturbing Tim's land, we can look for a permanent spot to make one on your land. What do you think?"

"I like that idea better. Let's leave everything here and search for a good place," said Sarah enthusiastically. She showed Mary where David had marked the ground for the front wall of their cabin and pointed to the spot they saw the deer. Mary saw the gun leaning against the rock and said she thought that wasn't safe for her boys. She lifted it up and placed it as high as she could reach on a branch of a tall oak tree.

"They aren't apt to even see it up there. You will have to tell David where it is."

"I'm sorry, we wouldn't normally put a gun where the boys could reach it, but things are in such disarray yet, that we just didn't think of that."

"Sarah, look over there. That would make a perfect place for an outside oven. Which end of the house do you want to put your kitchen?"

"I don't know. David said he wants to put bedrooms on the ends the way you and Ben did so I guess the kitchen will be somewhere in the middle. That stick back there with the strip of cloth on it is the back of our land, so we can make the campfire anyplace back here and then I can just go out the back door to check what I am cooking."

"This land is beautiful, Sarah, but maybe we should move over there where there aren't any trees. It won't be as convenient but it will be safer."

"I think you are right. I like it. Across the river is where I thought I would ask David to put the garden. I would have to cross over to work in it but that would leave the rest of this part of the land for something else, like maybe a small barn or shelter for the horses."

"You won't get all this done in one summer, Sarah. You have only so much time and energy. Ben's ranch took him many years and he announces new projects every spring."

"Speaking of projects; what did Ben intend to do with the logs when he ordered them?"

"We were going to surprise the boys and build a small cabin in the woods by the spring. We can still do that. We have all the rest of summer and fall and Ben said that doing the well will be easy because of the spring right there. He will order more logs right away, when he goes in to hire help for the ranch. It would be nice to get a little family in the lake cabin again, or now that you have moved out, we could put them in your cabin. How would you feel about that?"

"That's a precious little cabin. They better treat it with respect," said Sarah laughing. You will need to put some furniture in there. I have everything that was in there. The furniture they made is so beautiful. Ben and Jed did a great job."

As the two women chatted, they had started to carry large stones and had a ring made to contain a campfire. They brought kindling and dry downed branches and it wasn't long before they were washing out the big tub and starting the stew cooking for all the men. The big tub straddled the edge of the fire, resting on four flat topped stones.

"That looks like it belongs there. It could have been there for years. Thanks Mary for helping me. You have always been my friend as well as my sister."

"I am glad that you have this place, Sarah, but it will be hard sometimes. I will miss you so much." Mary had tears in her eyes that she wiped away.

"I will miss all of you, but you will have room to stay here anytime you want and we will help each other when the gardens need many hands, and the boys can bed down on the floor or the hay in our barn, or Tim's cave once we see that it is safe. They will love that."

"Come on Mary; let's go see how they are doing at the church crossing." The driver from the first wagon was named Jake. He and Ben had enlisted the help of the rest of the men and they were hauling skids of gravel from downstream and grading the banks of the river to prepare for the heavy wagons pulling across. Ben and David were praying the whole time that none of the men would spot a sparkle of gold while they were there.

"We are going to need to cut that big tree down, in order to get a little momentum coming across. I don't want to get stuck halfway!"

"Sorry Jake, we can't give you permission to cut trees. This land belongs to Father Bob and the church. He particularly said that he wants to keep all the ancient trees and is designing a church to build that will tuck in between them."

David knew that he was putting Jake and the men in a difficult position, but he was trying to preserve Father Bob's vision for the land. Ben walked the path the smaller wagons had taken and he could see where Tim had stopped with the lumber.

"Jake, could you pull in over here and cut through to the crossing, if we remove this one little pine?" Ben asked hesitantly.

"He just said we can't cut the trees!" Jake was growling and angry. He was tired and hungry and none of this work was what he planned to do when he left the mill with the simple assignment to take the logs and deliver them on the Parker place near the spring.

"I will take the responsibility. It's just a little pine and I will cut it myself so no one else will get blamed if there is a problem." Mary could hear the tone of the conversation although she couldn't make out the words.

"It sounds like it is time to tell the men that we want to feed them. They need a break." Sarah and Mary spread the word that they would be serving lunch in five minutes over at the campfire. The news was received with smiles and glad comments.

"I don't know if we have enough bowls for all the men, but I will bring out what I can find." Mary sliced the two loaves of bread onto a huge platter and cut the big apple pies each into eight hearty pieces. They spread several blankets on the grass and Mary caught her boys and handed them each a cup containing the stew. They sat together in a huddle and she wondered what they had been doing that had been so entertaining. Even Josh seemed happy to be in his brother's company.

Ben had found the saw and while the others ate, he cut the small pine tree down and dragged it out of the way. After another walk down the depth of the land he decided that any good driver should be able to take that load across and keep right on going to the spot David had indicated.

He approached the fire just as several of the men stood up expressing their thanks.

"That was a mighty fine meal ladies. We sure do appreciate it," said Jake. He wasn't growling now. Ben chuckled to himself at the change that Mary's cooking had accomplished.

"Jake, I think that you will agree that this can be done now. I cut that little tree and it is clear now all the way to the crossing." Ben was walking with him and literally walked him into the river so he could test the solidity of the bottom and then up the other bank and out to the prairie on the intended path for the wagons.

"This all looks good now Ben, I think we can try it with the first load." The men responded by getting the first team back in place and ready to go. Jake turned the experienced team onto the church property and chucked the reins and started to whistle as they curved toward the crossing. He gave a harsh yell as they entered the water and they never gave a thought to the possibility that they couldn't make it. Up the new gravel bank they went, digging in their hooves and pulling with all their strength. Jake kept them moving until they were slowed and he stopped them right at the location where the logs were needed.

The entire group had watched the spectacle as the muscled team did their job. The women cheered right along with the men and boys.

"Jake that was an amazing piece of driving! You sure know how to get a team to do their best!"

"Thank you David, I know my horses and what they can do. I also know what they can't do and we need to fix those new banks again before we can bring the next load over. While some of the men unload these logs, let's go see what we can do to make it as stable as possible. I want to get both teams back across before the rain hits."

He was the only one that had noticed the heavy dark clouds hanging over head. The men worked quickly to unload the logs and were ready to remove the first team when Jake decided they could use the crossing. Two more skids of gravel were used and the banks were graded again.

"Let's do it," he shouted as he climbed up to the seat of the second wagon. These guys are a little nervous from waiting. I'm going to do a big circle and then come in, and so everyone stand back! Keep the children away and safe."

As he lifted the reins, he lifted his voice and shouted at the horses. They stepped into the harness and tightened it as if it was all their idea.

"God needs this load delivered you lazy beasts. You have been resting all day while the rest of us have been working our guts out! Let's get some muscle into it, before I tell Tom you are all wolf bait!" He was laughing inside but it didn't sound like it. The team moved out and dug in from the first step. The large circle on the prairie helped them build a smooth momentum as they entered the path and rounded the curve to the crossing.

"Go Joe, Go Jimmy, take it home," he shouted. His lead pair moved as one, entering the water exactly the way Jake wanted them to and at the perfect pace to take the heavy load through the muddy water and up the new soft bank. He directed them to the spot and stopped them where they needed to be. Jake didn't look at the people applauding the precision of his efforts. He walked to the front of his horses and praised and patted them all.

"It's always harder for the second team. These are the best horses I have." Josh and several others were scooping buckets of water from the river and bringing it to the horses. Their sides were heaving from the effort.

"Let's get these logs off so we can get back to the prairie sod before the river rises. It's raining up north."

The men did as they were asked and by nightfall, the logs were all off the wagons and the horses stood under the trees on the prairie side, eager to start back. Jake took a look at the sky and said they were going to bed down under the wagons. True to Jake's prediction, it was soon pouring rain. David and Ben carried the tub of stew into the cave and lit the little fire inside. Sarah stood chewing her lip and finally ran over to Ben, hugging him tightly and started sobbing.

In all the activity, Ben, had never gotten a chance to greet her or talk to her at all. She had interpreted that as deliberate; especially when he didn't come to eat when the rest of the men had. She was sure that he had thought about her leaving the ranch and that he was both hurt and angry.

Ben was dumbfounded. He stood there holding her and wondering what he should do or what he had done now to get her suddenly so upset. He raised his eyebrows and looked questioningly at David and then Mary, but there was no help coming from them.

"Sarah, what is the matter? Why are you crying like this?"

Ben decided he was not going to sympathize with her. She had to stop being so emotional and She just has to take my help whether she likes it or not, he thought.

"Why didn't you talk to me all day? Why didn't you come eat? Why are you so angry with me?" She wailed between sobs. "I can't stay your baby sister forever! I have to grow up!"

"Sarah, I am sorry that I didn't come to talk to you when we arrived, but the men arrived right behind us and I got so imbedded in the work that I felt I had to help get the stuff done. I didn't eat because I was cutting a tree that was in the way. I had to get it cut so that Jake could bring the first wagon through.

As it is now, the river is so high, that it will be hard to cross in the morning to go home. Jed probably thinks he has been deserted."

He stood there still holding her tightly and rocking her a little.

"Now if you want to feed me, I'll let you. I am starving!" Just then Pili chimed in saying she also wanted to be fed. Ben released Sarah and carefully picked up the baby.

"Listen little Kitten, I am your uncle Ben and I am very hungry. Your mommy is going to feed me before she feeds you." He cuddled her close and she was quiet just lying in his arms looking up at him studying his face.

"There that's nice. No women crying," he said to Sarah.

When he looked down at her again, Pili gave him her best smile.

"Now that was dazzling! She knows me. Sarah, David did you see that? She smiled at me! It would be nice if your mommy smiled for me."

Sarah brought a bowl of stew and a slice of bread.

"As lovely as she is, I am betting you will trade her for this," said Sarah jokingly. She looked around at the family gathered in the mouth of the cave, staying dry and laughing together and she couldn't help but smile.

"I love you Ben, don't ever doubt it. Thank you for the logs for our house and all the hard work. Thank you for coming today, thank you everyone. This is like our first party!

David had been watching the boys from the corner of his eye and knew they were entertained by something.

Eli giggled and finally their day's entertainment was made known. The pups were in the cave back in their newly enlarged crate.

"How long have they been in here?" David was trying to sound stern but the faces on the boys were showing that they knew he wouldn't put the pups out in the rain. Josh spoke up and admitted that it was his idea to make the crate bigger.

"We knew they were probably scared without their mother when it was storming and if they wandered back in the cave they would get lost, so we worked on making the crate big enough so they can use it when the weather is bad and this way Aunt Sarah won't have to try to keep track of them."

"Well that was very clever Josh. I am not sure they should be in here, but I guess it won't hurt to have them in when it is storming," David could see that Adam and Eli were bursting with joy at the news that their secret was out and they were not in trouble. Mary suddenly remembered David's gun that she had placed in the old tree.

"Oh, David I am afraid that I know of something that should be in here that isn't!"

"What's that Mary?"

"Your rifle, I put it up on a tree branch when I spotted it leaning against the boulder. I was concerned to have it there with the boys around. I am so sorry. It will take you hours to get it dried out and oiled so the rain doesn't damage it."

"Relax Mary, I found it when I went over there. The branch cleared my head in the morning, but when I went back, the branch brushed my hair. I looked up to see what had changed and there it was. I brought it in. It's back in my saddle holster where it belongs."

"That's good; I guess I should have brought it in when I found it."

"How are we all going to sleep in here?" Adam asked as if adults had a solution to everything.

"We will sleep wherever we can. I heard that there are men who sleep on a bed of nails, so I guess we should be comfortable on these soft rocks!"

"Uncle David, you are funny. Rocks are not soft, and nobody can sleep on nails."

Are you sure about that? Adam I am guessing that you will find a soft rock in here pretty soon."

Mary snickered at that, knowing that Adam could sleep almost anywhere when he was tired enough.

"Sarah, where is your Bible?"

"It's over there on the ledge near the bed."

"If you will get it, I'll make the beds up." Everyone looked surprised at his remark until he started to line sacks of corn and wild grain, dried apples, and other supplies against the wall of the cave.

David adjusted his saddle and leaned against it.

"I've got my bed. Mary you should slide in there with Sarah tonight. The boys can sleep with our saddle blankets. I think we will do just fine."

Ben smiled, leaning against a firm burlap bag full of corn kernels and opened the Bible to Psalm 23. NIV

"The Lord is my shepherd; I shall not be in want. He makes me lie down in green pastures. He leads me beside quiet waters, He restores my soul."

Ben looked over at Adam. He had curled up with his arm inside the crate. He was cuddling a pup and was sound asleep. Ben continued to read by the light of the lantern as the rain came down cascading past the entrance to the Lion's Den.

In the morning, the skies were covered with a layer of solid heavy gray. It wasn't raining, but it looked like it would again at any moment. Ben and David stood just outside the mouth of the cave wondering what they should do.

"David, we can't cross the river to head home when it's high like this. We may as well try to get something done. Now that you know that you have the materials to make a bigger cabin, do you want to go stake out the corners or something?"

"Yes, thanks Ben, I'll take any help I can get. The trees and grass are drenched. We will be soaked, too, after a few minutes."

"That's fine, I have been wet before," said Ben shaking a branch just as David stepped under it.

"Oh, you got me! I thought for a second that it had started raining again." They laughed and decided to make some more stakes to mark the outline of the house. "Ben do you still have the triangle shaped thing that Jed made for leveraging the logs up into place for the barn? I could borrow it and that would save me the time and effort of making one, unless you will be using it. You must have been planning a project of your own or you wouldn't have had two wagons of logs ready."

"You're welcome to use it. It's behind the milk barn. The last time I looked at it, it was fine, but you are right, I want to get a cabin built on Mary's place in the trees by the spring. Our deadline for improvements is next spring, but I had planned on using the contraption that Slim built. It is down there in the edge of the woods and won't take much to make it usable again. We could both use that team of Father Bob's. He has been coming by with some nice animals. They would not hesitate to walk those logs up the ramp."

"We should talk to Matt Morgan. He will know where we can get a team to use. We might even be able to get a team at the fort."

"That's a good idea. I was also thinking that I would stop and ask Jake if he knew of some work horses that we could use for as long as we need them. It is going to be hard to get anyone to part with a team during the summer. If they are a good team, they will be using them."

"That's true, said David. "I will be going in to order a pump and some windows for the front. Do you want to ride in with me as soon as the weather makes it possible?"

""Sure, but if you want me to; I could order them for you, so you could work on your place and not have to use the time in town."

"That's a better idea. When you go home, I'll come borrow the big wagon and move the log rack down here. I could use Josh if it's alright. He could come with me and then take the wagon back to the ranch. He is growing up Ben." Ben nodded in agreement.

"The lines you made in the dirt have washed away, but you probably aren't going to use them now anyway. Where do you want the front corners of the house?" David walked a few paces closer to the first ancient pine and studied it. "What are you looking at?"

"I like the idea of this huge tree shading the house in the morning, but I was just looking to make sure it is strong and safe. I don't like the thought of it dropping on our roof in a bad storm."

"Some of the worst storms come out of the northeast. I guess it is good to be cautious. You could run the front of the house parallel to the river and that way the tree would still shade part of the end and would more than likely fall behind the house if it ever fell."

"Yes at first I was thinking that I needed to put it in line with the bluff, but on our land, lining up with the river feels comfortable.

Anyway I want to move up river a little farther from the church property, too. There is a place here that the river splits for just a little bit and has made a tiny island with one tree on the end of it. That would be nice to look out the front window and see. I was thinking that maybe I could make a two piece footbridge to span the water the way the men of the settlement made the four sections for the fingers of the Silver. I think Sarah would like that. She would probably transplant wildflowers and pretty things to that spot. I don't think she has even noticed the island yet. I'm saving it as a surprise."

"Yes, that is a nice view. How far from the river do you think you want the front of the house to set?"

"I think right where we are standing is a good distance." David drove the stake into the soil with a rock and found that it went only a couple inches before hitting a rock. He paced back toward the bluff and drove in another stake hitting rock again. "Well the Bible says to build your house on a firm foundation; I think we can forget about dugout rooms and tunnels here. We are on rock!"

"It will make digging a well difficult," said Ben.

"I mentioned it to Tim because his rock is right at the surface, but he didn't seem concerned. He said God has everything under control."

"He does, and there has to be a place here for a well somewhere that is dirt or the big trees couldn't grow."

"How far did you go on that back corner?"

"I just guessed, but whatever the length that Tom has cut these logs, is good for the width of the house. The length will be double the width, and then we can have a bedroom on the east end now and add one on the west end later on."

"The whole place looks good to me, but I have got to warn you. Women never think that what we have drawn out is big enough. Beth and Mary both like big rooms and Sarah probably does too." David stood in the middle of the area he had paced off.

"Here's what we will do. We will start smaller, and show them and when they get done moving the stakes out farther, they will put them where we have them now. What do you think Ben?"

Ben was laughing and watched as David moved the stakes marking the end nearest the church property. He took a big step and pushed the stakes down in the ground, shrinking the house by three feet or more.

"I am going to go get Sarah and show her before it starts raining." David hurried to the cave and brought both women back with him.

"Where is Kitten," asked Ben looking concerned.

"Josh is holding her for the first time. She is smiling at him and the boys all think she is phenomenal. I told Adam that he had to watch his brothers so we can't stay but a minute. Eli will be out in the puddles if we don't prevent it."

"Ladies here is the plan. Ben and I staked out a modest sized house that faces the river and runs parallel. Sarah you will be able to sit in a chair in the main room right here and look out at the pretty little island. How's that for a view?" David was so excited that he didn't see the look on Mary's face. She didn't say it, but Ben knew that she had figured out the ruse already.

Sarah looked at the Island and said it was nice, but that she was more interested with the house right now. She started at the front corner and walked the distance to the far stake.

"David, when you put the stakes back where they were, it will be perfect!" Mary had been looking out of the cave and saw what he was doing. She called Sarah over and they both watched giggling.

"Ben says that women have only one opinion when things are being built and that is that it needs to be bigger. I know he put you up to this," said Mary looking serious, but she couldn't keep her face straight any longer. They all started laughing and Ben had to confess that he had said that women like big rooms.

David put the stakes back and then added another foot just to show that he really did intend to make it that size. Sarah walked down to the river and studied the little island and the single tree, trying to survive surrounded by fiercely rushing water on both sides.

"That poor tree looks like it landed in a bad place for survival. Do you think we could do something for it?"

"Like what?"

"Like make a bridge over to it and add some big rocks to hold some more dirt and gravel and maybe some bushes or wildflowers."

"Sarah, that's a wonderful idea. We can plan it this winter and do it after the house is completed." David winked at Ben.

"I knew she would like that tiny island. She will be able to cross the footbridge and go to the vegetable garden on the other side of the river. We haven't discussed the size for that yet, but I know I have a lot of work ahead of me!"

"Breakfast is ready," said Mary, as she hurried back to the cave. Adam was feeding the pups and that was holding Natty's attention, but Eli was out front playing in the largest puddle he could find. He was soaked.

CHAPTER THREE
CONFRONTING THE PAST

Josh was gently putting Pili back in her cradle, and said that as long as it wasn't pouring rain that he wanted to start on a chicken pen for Aunt Sarah's chickens.

"We can't bring them here until you have a pen."

"Have you had a chance to think about where you would like it to be?"

"Actually, I haven't Josh. Do you want to wander around our land and see if you can find a couple of good locations and then I will come out and we can talk about it?"

"Sure Aunt Sarah. I would like to do that."

He wandered over and examined the area that David and Ben had marked for the house and took note of the location of the fire pit. He spotted the stick with a rag tied to it and figured that it marked the back of their land. He walked to the river and watched the swiftly flowing water and studied the little island and the land beyond it, on the other side.

That will be their garden over there and beyond that huge pine is room for a barn and a chicken pen. It is hard to make sense of this place with the river cutting it into two pieces. They will be crossing the river every time they have a chore to do. If it was my place, I would make my own crossing here and I'd make it strong enough for a loaded wagon. I would make it arch up and over, not nearly flat like the little sections near the settlement.

I won't have to worry about that on my land, because the river runs along the back of it. I am going to build a really nice place there someday just the way Dad intended.

Sometimes I get so angry inside when I hear Aunt Sarah and Uncle David talking about the Indians in the village. They killed my Dad and burned our house and everything! I know that was before; and everyone says they are changed and Christians now, but what about it? They stole our cattle didn't they? That wasn't that long ago, and what about me and Adam? They sure never did anything to show me that they were sorry or changed! I think Mom forgets how it was going to be because we are with Ben and Jed at the S and J, and she is safe there, but that's not what we talked about on the wagon trail. That's not what we planned! It's not the way my dad wanted it at all!

It had started raining again, but Josh hadn't noticed because he was swiftly walking up river, making his way between and around harsh growth and very deep in thought. The work and the surroundings of a new place and the planning had brought back memories that he hadn't examined for a long time. He was shocked at his own thoughts and reactions to them. He wasn't sure that he should have allowed himself to dig them up. That was a bad time for me! It was a bad time for all of us, he thought.

He stopped and sat down on a big flat rock near the surging river. Why are they so careful of the Indians feelings? They don't worry about us. It's wrong! It's all wrong! Ben just does anything he can to make them happy. They steal our cattle and he says it's alright, "I'll pay for more," he said. "Don't worry about it." What about us? Father Bob led the Indians and they freed the slaves, and everyone thinks they are heroes. The Indians took Aunt Sarah and killed her parents.

Now she pretends they are her family and goes to visit them. They could come on the prairie and meet us and say they are sorry, but no one even thinks to suggest that it's necessary or the right thing to do. I guess I expect too much.

When he reached up and swiped at his face, he knew instantly that some of the water on his face wasn't rain. Why am I worrying about this old stuff now? I know why because I don't have to be a full grown man to figure out that the logs he brought down to Sarah and David were ordered to build on my land. Why does he think that everything is his to do with as he pleases? Why didn't he ask me what I wanted to do or where I wanted to build?

It was at that very moment that he heard Ben shouting his name. Ben, David and Mary were all out in the rain searching for him. They feared the worst!

"Joshua, where are you? Josh can you hear me?" He could hear his mother. She sounded frantic!

"I'm here Mom. I'm alright. I'm coming."

"Josh, Oh Josh, where have you been? Why didn't you come in when it started raining? I was so frightened that you had gotten hurt or fallen in the river."

"Josh, Joshua," shouted Ben and then David. Josh could hear the voices in the distance.

"I'm sorry I worried you Mom. I was just sitting over there on that rock, watching the water and doing some thinking."

"Josh, it is pouring rain! Why didn't you come in?"

"I am sorry Mom. I just had to finish my thoughts."

"Josh! Are you alright?" Ben and David had spotted Josh and Mary standing there. "Son, I was so worried. I thought something terrible had happened to you!" He wrapped his arms around the young man and held him tightly. Ben was crying and not ashamed to show it. Josh stood stiffly and didn't respond.

"Come on, let's all get inside before we float away," said David. Sarah had built up the fire inside and had some tea brewing. Like everyone else she was prepared to ask several questions but decided not to. She could see that Josh was unharmed but upset and so were the people that had been searching for him. Joshua is usually so level headed and responsible, she thought. I wonder what caused him to act like that.

The rain stopped soon after and by noon the clouds finally started to lighten and the river subsided slowly. Finally the next day, it had lowered enough for them to control the raft and cross. They needed to head back to the ranch. David followed along the next morning to fetch the log rack. He didn't want to have to spend a night away from Sarah and leave her and Pili alone yet. He made sure that he was back before dark. Jed suggested that David take Johnny with him as well as Josh, so the boys could bring the wagon back together.

After they finally got the wagon rafted across and managed to move the log rack from it, David was very glad that he had listened to Jed's suggestion. Johnny had been a good helper. Josh was exhibiting a set jaw and a chip on his shoulder so big that it was in the way of him being able to work effectively.

The next morning, after the wagon was empty and back on the prairie side, Josh seemed strangely distracted and Johnny ended up taking the reins and headed Sundown toward home.

"Bye Aunt Sarah, Bye Uncle David. Thanks for the lunch," shouted Johnny as he pulled away. Josh made a small wave and turned his face forward.

"I am glad that young man has gone home," said David. "I had all I could do to hold my tongue. I don't know what is eating at him but I hope he figures it out before I have to deal with him again!"

"David, what are you talking about?"

"I'm talking about Josh. He has an attitude so bad that he was no help at all."

"Really David, that doesn't sound like Joshua. I hope he isn't ill."

"He didn't seem sick when he was in here last night," said David.

"He did seem very quiet, now that you mention it. I wonder if he is upset with us, because we left the ranch."

"No, Sarah. I think it started when he was out walking in the pouring rain. When we found him he just stood there like a fence post. His dad was upset and crying and he just looked angry. He has had that set jaw ever since. He needs to talk to someone but I can't imagine what is on his mind!"

"Let's include him especially tonight when we pray. It's never easy being his age. He works hard with the men but gets treated like a youngster."

"Yes, that could be part of it. Maybe I should say something to Ben, but I'm not sure if it would help or make it worse."

"David, I just thought of something. Josh could be feeling the way I was before we left. Ben makes all the decisions and charges forward without asking for opinions. If Josh figured out that Ben was preparing to build on Mary's land, he could be feeling that Ben is invading his territory!"

"Sarah, do you think that could be it?"

"I don't know but I hope that Ben can sense the problem and work it out."

David said he was going to go out and do what he could with the rest of the day and Sarah said she had something to do too. The day was almost over before David appeared at the entrance of the cave and asked Sarah to come see what he and Thunder had been doing.

"David, this is amazing. I can see the bottom row of logs for the cabin. How did you get Thunder to move them? He isn't a work horse."

"He is now. He is intelligent and strong and I think that if I take it slow, he will learn to help me with the log ramp and be able to do it without a problem. He pulled the logs for me and listened when I directed him."

"That's amazing David. Thunder deserves a treat!"

"What about me. I deserve a treat, too, he said with a grin. "I have been working hard all afternoon!"

Yes you have," she said as they entered the cave. "I'll get you both some sugar," she said laughing. "Can you believe it David? You are on our own land and building our cabin."

"It is a good time in our lives, Sarah, a time we will always remember." She had scooped a small amount of sugar from the tin and poured it into his palm. "Here, give this to Thunder. He earned it."

David knew that he was kidding himself. Thunder had struggled to pull the logs on the wet grass. He wasn't strong enough to pull the heavy logs up the ramp and hold them there until they were pegged into place.

"Thunder, you worked so hard today. You did everything that I asked you to do. You are a special horse." He gave him the sugar and saw that Thunder was holding his weight on three legs. The muscles of his back leg were bunched and David knew instantly that they were strained and hurting.

"Sarah," he yelled. "Can you make some liniment? I think Thunder has hurt his leg. You were right. I shouldn't have asked him to do that kind of work. He isn't strong enough!"

"David, he will be better if we can get the spasm to relax. Let's rub him with this. I will go get some hot water and we can wrap a warm, wet towel around it, too." David rubbed the solution on all of Thunder's legs, thinking that the horse had done too much. He was trying to please me. David felt terrible. He realized what the solution was when his own hands began to become numb. It was made from the purple flowers. It would deaden anything including the muscles that Thunder needed to stand. Thunder began to look unsteady and David encouraged him to lie down in the grass. He stroked the horse's neck and talked soothingly to him.

"David you shouldn't have put that medicine all over him!"

"I know it now. My hands feel dull, like they are frozen!"

"Quick, go scrub your hands in the river. Be careful!" She sponged Thunder's good legs with the warm wet towel and dipped it again in the warm water and wrapped it around his sore one.

"My poor Thunder." She said. "I am going to make a strong willow bark tea for him. Stay by him and I will bring more hot water when I come back out."

Pili was starting to stir in her crib. Sarah knew that she would be crying soon.

"Lord, I am beginning to feel frazzled. I need to help David with Thunder, but Pili wants me, too." She carried the pan of tea out and put it down near David. Next she brought more hot water.

"They are both too hot yet, but if you can get him to swallow some of the tea when it cools, it will help to stop the swelling in that muscle." She removed the towel and firmly massaged the knotted leg muscle. "I am glad that he can't feel this. It would be very painful without that solution on it." She dipped the towel in the hot water and spread it out for a minute until it was cool enough to handle. "I have to go to the baby, but wrap his leg again and when that starts to cool, you can rub the muscle again."

David looked up at her as she walked toward the cave. He didn't say anything, but he was grating his teeth and condemning himself for asking more than his horse had to give.

"Thunder, I am so sorry. I made a mistake. I didn't know that you would try so hard that you would hurt yourself. You are my friend boy. I didn't know you would get hurt." He stroked his horse over and over and then worked on the leg again, coating it carefully so that only the knotted leg muscle was wet. Sarah exchanged the pan of water for a hot one and checked the leg.

"David, look, the knot is loosening! Keep doing whatever you have been. It is working. He is relaxing and that is helping. The tea is cool, and it has some sugar in it, maybe he will drink it now."

"He can't drink it while he is lying down."

"Let's see if we can get him up. Are your hands still numb?"

"No, I didn't get it on me this time and I only put that stuff on the knotted part of his leg."

"Good. Coax him to stand David."

"He is acting like he can't!"

"He must David. Make him get up! Get up Thunder, get up!"

"His legs probably still don't feel right to him. Stop yelling at him!" David was sounding upset and angry. "Now I am shouting at you. I am sorry Sarah. I am not sure what we should do."

"Put your hands on him."

She placed her hands on the sore leg and spread her fingers and then she lowered her forehead until it touched his coat.

"Father, please make Thunder well. Make the knot go away. Give him back health and strength. Please ease his pain, please Father."

She stayed there until suddenly Thunder started to move. At first he lurched up on his side but rolled back flat. His second try was successful. He stood, breathing heavily. David brought the pan up to his muzzle and Thunder drank most of the tea in the pan.

"Thank you Father," they said at the same time. David removed the sagging towel and saw that the knot was much smaller.

"Should I put more of the solution on it?"

"No, I think God is taking care of it. We have done all we can."

"If I put some grass down, would you mind if I brought all the horses up close to the entrance tonight?"

"I think that Thunder would enjoy being near you, David. He doesn't blame you. He just doesn't know his own limitations. We have to figure out a way to get a couple of work horses."

Once the horses were all brought up close, Sarah enjoyed spending time with Pretty Mother and her foal.

"I have been so busy that I haven't taken time to be with her. She is such a pretty girl."

"Is that what you are going to call her?"

"I haven't tried to think of a name. Is that a good name?"

"I think so," said David.

"I guess I'll sleep on it," she said with a yawn. "I made us some food but we were too busy. Let's eat and then go to bed. I am tired." Sarah checked Thunder's leg and spread some more of the solution on it. That will be sore for a couple days, but he is going to be fine.

When she got into bed, she realized that David had not heard her. He was sound asleep.

Pili was kicking her covers off and playing quietly when Sarah looked over at her. The sun streamed into the cave and a beautiful day was under way. David had moved the horses away from the cave, back to the edge of the river in the fresh grass. She could hear him hammering by the huge pile of logs on their land.

After feeding pili and giving her a sponge bath, she put her in a light weight dress she had made for her and a bonnet of the same soft pink cotton. Her pudgy legs stuck out showing her bare toes and dimpled knees.

"Let's go say good morning to Daddy and see if he is hungry." She carried the baby up against her chest so she could see over her mother's shoulder.

"Hi Daddy; we are all clean and fed and we came to see you and ask if you are hungry." Sarah turned Pili in her arms so that she could see her daddy.

"Hello, pretty kitten. Did you come to see me?" Pili made a happy chortle and smiled at her daddy.

"She is getting responsive. It's fun to watch her face. I would take her, but I am all dirty and you have her so clean and smelling nice."

Sarah smiled and was glad that he noticed the things that she did for the baby.

"Do you want me to fix you some food or do you want to work a bit longer?"

"Actually I was wondering if you would like to spend the night at the ranch. I need to go to the settlement to find us a pair of work horses and I don't want you to stay here alone."

"I appreciate the thought, but I think one of us should be here to guard our supplies until the cabin is built. It isn't like we have a door we can shut and lock. Animals are less likely to steal our food if one of us is here."

"I was just trying to protect you and I didn't think about that."

"David, I will be fine here. Very few people know that we have moved here and I do have a gun and I know how to use it. You should go as soon as you can clean up and have something to eat. I won't like sleeping alone, but that has nothing to do with where I am," she said with a smile, "Come on, bring your tools into the cave and get ready so you can go. The sooner you go, the sooner you will come back."

"If you are sure you will be safe, then I will go."

"David I used to go off alone when I lived with the people. I hunted alone, or I would just go to think and pray uninterrupted. You know I did."

"I guess you are right, but I don't like leaving you way out here so far from anyone." While they talked they had walked back to the cave. He put his tools that he had been using near the others stored there.

"Bath time," she said, tossing a towel to him. "I am not going to wash you and make you smell as nice as Pili. I think the river will do just fine."

"You are a heartless woman!" He was laughing as he walked to the clean gravel bank that had been created at the crossing. She tucked Pili in for her morning nap and scooped up his clean leather work clothes and took them to him.

"You may need these after you come out of the water. Is it as cold as I think it is?"

"Yes!" He said it with clenched teeth and splashed the water up in her direction laughing.

"I'll go pack you some food to take." On the way she stopped to check Thunder and untied him and walked him in a big circle watching how he stepped on his sore back leg. She patted him and tied him back where David had put him, making a mental note to put solution on his leg after she got David on his way.

"I have my saddle on Blackie and I will have to take some of our money with me. I didn't want to spend that right now, but I can't do any work without a strong pair of horses to help me."

"I know David; we will use them for a lot of things. I am hoping that we can break ground soon for the garden, or it will be too late to get a good harvest."

"I was thinking about that while I was working. Maybe you can stake the corners where you want it and when I get back, hopefully I will be able to plow it for you before I start back on the cabin. Be careful when you cross the river."

Sarah wrapped her arms around him and as she hugged him she prayed out loud.

""Lion of Judah, we know that you are our protection and our provision. We know that you have work horses ready for us. We thank you for them. We thank you that you have shown us your image as a sign of your love for us. We are happy here and accept gratefully what you provide. Thank you for watching over all of us while we are apart."

"Amen," said David as he swung up on Blackie. He bent down from the tall horse and kissed her tenderly. "I will not waste time but I think I should spend a night at the ranch on the way back so that I can talk to Ben about Josh, if that's alright with you."

"Of course it is. We already talked about it. Give them all my love."

He plowed through the water at the crossing and was on his way. Soon he was out of sight. She didn't like being there, responsible for the baby with no other adult nearby, but she wouldn't admit it to David. She knew that would just add to his feeling of concern. When she had journeyed alone, she had been younger and she had been only responsible for herself.

She shook her head, dismissing her thoughts and decided that she was going to spend the day making bricks for an oven. Beth brought me the forms, I saw them here somewhere. I would like to have that oven available now. I would make some fresh bread.

After checking on the sleeping baby she looked for the forms and found them neatly stacked against the wall of the cave. It took three trips to carry them all out into the bright sunshine. The big tub they had used for the stew for the men soon held the clay and grass mixture. She had made it near the river where the supplies were available but now she had to decide where she would work with the forms. I don't want to make them here. I would be away from Pili too long, she thought.

The area in front of the cave gets the sun most of the day. I want to fill the forms there.

The tub of mud is too heavy for me to carry back there. I don't think I can drag it that far either.

I am going to make my own version of a skid. She used the branches David had cut when he was selecting the spot for the house. He had a big pile near the back of their property and with the handsaw she was able to cut six of them the same length. With two more nailed across the top and one on the back she had something that looked like a small raft. With a rope strung from the cross braces, I can get Moon Boy to pull this for me. She had to work hard to get the big tub of mud up on the skid and with the weight on it; the skid was hard to slide. The ropes were fastened to the saddle horn, one from each side and she slowly walked Moon Boy from the river to the front of the cave. The sound of it dragging behind him made him sidestep and flick his head around trying to see what was happening. She praised him and patted his neck, moving slowly and his trust in her helped to get him to pull this strange thing.

Once the first batch of forms was filled, she covered the tub with an old hide to keep the rest of the mud moist enough to rework.

As she washed her hands in the river, she looked up and saw the big deer again on the other side of the river. I think I am going to put my rifle near the entrance, where I can get it easily. We just might have to make drying racks, Kitten. If he comes back, I will be ready.

When you nap this afternoon, I will get some smaller branches from Daddy's pile and make the racks. She was sure that the deer would return and that she would have meat drying when David came back with the work horses.

With arm loads of branches and thin ropes she had made long ago at the ranch, she set to work making the racks by the mouth of the cave. She had folded a soft blanket and Pili was lying on it beside her.

"I think I will finish these tomorrow," she said, standing and stretching. She talked to the baby about everything. I want her to learn all she can, she thought.

When she looked around outside, she was surprised that it was growing dark.

"My sweet Kitten, your mommy is hungry and tired." She picked her up and cuddled her close for a moment, realizing that the day was gone and with it the possibility of seeing the image. "The Lion of Judah was probably right there above me while I was working. I wish I had seen it again." She lit the lantern and pulled the last bit of stew away from the fire. I know that it is wasteful but I just don't think I can eat that. She cut a small piece of cheese from the block that Beth had put with her kitchen supplies and put the coffee pot on with half the normal amount of coffee and half the water. She nibbled a few dried vegetables and then some dried apples while she waited for the coffee. "Tomorrow I think I will make a pan of Beth's chili."

She read her Bible and drank coffee until she couldn't keep her eyes open. It felt cold near the wall when she slipped into bed. She got back up and added an extra little blanket over Pili in her crib, and then quietly pulled it a little closer to the fire, away from the walls.

I need to stop fussing and get some rest. She is fine.

CHAPTER FOUR
MOVING FORWARD

It was just past noon when David and Blackie entered Silverville. He made the blacksmith shop his first stop.

"Hello Matt."

"Hi David, What can I do for you?"

"I need some advice. Where should I look for a good pair of work horses? They don't need to be handsome, but smart and strong would help."

Matt chuckled.

"It does help if they have a good brain when you are trying to get them to do what you want. Most of the folks that are building houses here in town are from the first wagon train this spring. They all used teams to get here. Just ride through town and inquire. I think you will find more than one man willing to part with a pair, but I have to warn you. Look them over good. Some of the people have not cared for their stock very well and some haven't the wisdom to treat them correctly. Check their feet and their mouth. When you find a likely pair, bring them to me and I will be glad to look them over for you. I will make the time to do shoes today if they need it before you head back."

"Thanks Matt. I appreciate it."

"Ben was here yesterday. He was talking to Tom. He said you and Sarah have moved off the ranch. I didn't know that you had already built a cabin on your land."

"I haven't yet."

"So where are you staying with the baby?"

"We are fine Matt. Don't worry about it." For some reason he didn't want to say that they were living in a cave. He said he would be back when he found some horses. The settlement was quiet. He saw only a few people in town, but it was easy to spot the new places going up. A new street had been added between Rose's house and the property next to hers. David saw the shell of a small house standing there. Its proud owner was putting on a roof when David slid off Blackie and hollered up to him. "Hi there, this is a nice place. I like the location."

He looked down at David and started another nail.

"Are you selling stuff?"

"No, I am David Sharpe and I am looking for a sound team of work horses. The man came down the ladder and shook David's hand. I am Lucas Donner and my wife is there in the trees with our boy. She's Hope, and the boy's name is Mark."

"It's nice to meet you, Lucas. Where are you folks from?"

"East of hell and glad to be here," The man laughed showing several missing teeth.

As soon as I put a roof over my family I will be building my saloon. It's going to sit right there at the start of this street by the river. The land's all bought and paid for. All I need now is time to get it up and running. I got me the biggest tent you ever saw and all the barrels on that wagon are filled with Kentucky whiskey! I sleep under it every night, me and my shotgun. Can't have any of it disappearing," he said. "What did you say you were looking for?"

"I need a team of strong work horses."

"I thought that's what you said. I got four of the best dang brutes you ever saw."

"Are you going to sell them?"

"Why else would I be telling about them?"

"Where are they? I'd like to see them."

"I'll show you, but don't think they are going to be cheap. These here are big, strong brutes. They hauled us out here and wanted to go farther!" He led David around the back of the house and into the trees. The man had them tied up short with no grass and no water.

David was disgusted and felt like hitting the man in the face when he saw them. How long have they been tied here like this."

"Do you want to buy horses or rent a hotel for them? My wife and son take them to the river for a drink every morning and every night. It's not my fault they eat every blade of grass I own!" David checked the mouth of the closest horse and could see sores where they had been abused by rough handling. He lifted a foot and noted the loose shoe.

David shook his head and started to walk away, but his heart said the plight of these animals would continue if he didn't help them.

"How much you want?"

"You want them all?"

"No, I don't want any of them. They are in bad shape, but I don't want you around them anymore! Just tell me how much!" Lucas took a step back, thinking that David was getting angry and might hit him.

"I'll take a hundred a piece. What did you pay for them?"

"I paid a hundred for each one of them and I had to put at least that much more in the feed on the way!

"I came to the settlement looking for a pair not a team of four. I will give you twenty five dollars each and considering that they all need shoes and have torn mouths, that amount is reasonable! I am going to have to wait until they heal before I can use them, and they may not want to work the way you have treated them."

"If you have thirty each I won't haggle. I am sick of them. I can't afford to feed them." David turned his back to the man and separated one hundred and twenty dollars from his money and handed it to Lucas.

"Take them to the river for a long drink and then leave them at the blacksmith's. I will be there as soon as I can. First give me a paper that says I bought them and all four are mine and sign it."

"Yes sir, David, I will make you a paper right away. He hurried to his wife and David saw him hand her the money. She pulled out several papers from a satchel in the tent and wrote on one of them. He could see Lucas make a mark on the bottom of it and hand the pencil back to her. Lucas handed him the bill of sale, and began to untie the horses.

"Lucas, they belong to me now. Treat them gently!" His son and wife quickly came over and took the leads.

"We will do it for you," she said. The big horses dwarfed the people leading them, yet they followed along docilely. "Thank you," she said as she moved them away toward the river and a better existence.

"Do you own any other animals?" David asked Lucas in a gruff manner.

"No I don't and I have no desire to. I don't like horses. They eat and mess. That's what they do all day long." David had to work hard to hold his temper and his tongue. He patted Blackie and slid up into the saddle.

"Let's go boy," he said. He walked Blackie to the edge of the river and let him drink, beside Mark. He was standing there with his hand on the big horse's neck.

"Mister, I am glad you bought our horses. I can tell that you will be good to them. Your horse is shiny and well fed. You don't wear spurs either."

"No I never owned a pair in my life. Do these big guys have names?"

"I don't know. Dad only used bad names on them. Maybe they are on the paper." David looked at the paper he had stuck in his pocket. "Mark, say goodbye to Dickey, Joey, Brownie and Buck."

"I don't know which name goes with which horse, but it doesn't matter now. Does it?" Hope clacked her tongue and gave a hint of a smile as she led three of the horses down the street. Mark led the forth and told David over his shoulder that he thought this one was Dickey. David smiled and nodded.

At the saw mill, Tom was very busy with several men waiting to give him an order for lumber. David saw Cookie and walked over to his big cooking fire.

"Hi Cookie, How are you?"

"I am good. Are you good?"

"Yes I am. I am hoping that you can tell me if Ben Slater has been here in the past few days."

"Yes I saw him and he buy logs. I fed him beans and biscuits. You want to eat? I have food ready. Tom said feed men who buy lumber."

"Thank you Cookie, maybe next time. You are a good cook!" Cookie smiled as David rode slowly through the people and out the gate. He glanced back and saw Tom wave. He waved back and kept going, wanting to see Matt about the team he had purchased.

Matt had started by introducing himself to them by giving each one a sugar cookie and talking to them while he scratched their ears. He removed the bit from each mouth and replaced it with a simple soft head harness with no mouth piece at all.

He was upset by the marks and injuries that were the results of ignorance and mistreatment.

"David, I am just getting to your horses. I was busy when the woman and boy brought them. She said she didn't remember your name but that you had bought them today from her husband. The boy described you as the nice man on the beautiful black horse."

David smiled when he saw Matt brush cookie crumbs from one of the horse's mouths.

"I took their bits out right away. All four have sore mouths. If you leave them out, they will heal up on their own. You will probably have trouble putting them back in because they will remember."

"What do you think of them over all?"

"They are good horses. They aren't too old. I'd say they are five or six at the most. They have strong legs and are sound, but they will be quirky now and probably hard to work with until they learn that you aren't going to hurt them. I haven't checked them all but the ones I did, have bad shoes. He probably came out all the way without even checking them. Can I ask you what you paid for them?"

"Sure Matt, I was mad when I saw the shape they were in and he had them snubbed up to trees where they couldn't reach any grass and had no water. He knew I was boiling and I told him so. He is lucky I didn't beat him. He deserved it. I paid thirty dollars each, but I would have paid a lot more just to get them away from him."

"I understand. I probably would have done the same thing. They are worth a lot more than you paid and I know that you will treat them right. I can get a couple done before dark, but it will take me time in the morning to do the other two. How are Blackie's shoes?"

"They are good. I am going to camp on the other side of the bridge and I will be back tomorrow. Thanks Matt."

"David stopped at the Trading Post and looked around. He wasn't sure why he had gone in there. He really didn't have anything in mind that he needed. When he saw the pretty dresses hanging in a row, he couldn't resist buying the blue one for Sarah. It will match her eyes, he told Sam as it was wrapped and tied with string.

"Is that your team that Matt is working on?" Sam had asked with a frown on his face.

"Yes, I just bought them from Donner."

"He is going to open a saloon. We have a nice community here and have never had a bit of trouble. I don't like him or the kind of people that his place will bring. You mark my words, he is trouble!"

The curtain to the back rooms moved and Helen entered the store.

"Hello David, that man's wife is scared to death of him and so is his son. She had a big bruise on her arm when they first got here. I think he might have caused it."

"Helen, you don't know that," said Sam frowning.

"I know how she acted around him when they came in here!"

"Thanks Sam. I have to go." He nodded at Helen and left leading Blackie across the four sections of bridge that spanned the fingers of the Silver. He was studying their construction as he crossed.

As he made his camp he wondered if Ben had found anyone that wanted to work at the ranch. He hoped that they would find a person that knew how to treat horses properly. That subject was uppermost in his mind after his experiences with Lucas Donner.

David suddenly realized that he hadn't eaten since breakfast with Sarah. I have accomplished everything that I came for. As soon as Matt gets the horses ready I want to head out. Maybe I can stop and talk to Ben and make it home tomorrow while there is still light enough to travel. I know she won't expect me that soon but I want to surprise her.

With his bedroll near the small fire, he made himself comfortable and opened the lunch that Sarah had prepared.

"Father, thank you for taking care of our need for good horses, and sending me to the right place and thank you that I was here to take them away from Donner. Please watch over my girls until I get back. Help me to know what to say to Ben. I don't want to offend him. He does try hard to do what is right. Bless the ranch and all the folks that live there." Blackie stepped close to him and nudged his shoulder.

"You think I have a treat in here don't you?" He searched in the bottom of the sack and brought his hand out with two sad looking crackers. "That's all I have Blackie. There is one for you and one for me." Blackie nosed the cracker and took it gratefully. To him it represented the love and care that he always received from David. "I wonder how you would behave if you had been treated like those big fellows we will be taking home with us. I am going to have to be very patient with them." He didn't fasten Blackie to the trees. He knew that his horse would stay near him.

David was startled awake in the morning by the sound of a horse being ridden across the bridge. The man pulled up his horse and looked down at David.

"Are you David Sharpe?"

"Yes," said David sleepily.

"I was told that it is your job that I will be taking at the Slater place."

"Who told you that?"

"That woman in the store did. She seems to know something about everyone."

"Don't believe everything you hear," said David as he stood and rolled up his bedroll. He looked at the man's horse carefully. Hoping to gain knowledge of the way it had been treated. He didn't see any scars. "Do you like horses?"

"Yes, I guess so, as much as anybody. I have been working on one ranch or another most of my life."

"When did you meet Ben?"

"I haven't yet, but the woman told me he needed help and pointed out the sign."

"If you are riding out that way, I would like to ride with you."

"I won't be leaving until around noon."

"Why's that?"

"I am having Matt put shoes on my work horses. You didn't tell me your name."

"It's Orville, Orville Baker."

David shook his hand but didn't say anything further. He made sure his little fire was out and saddled Blackie.

"Well, Orville I hope you and Ben get along well. I have to talk to Matt. He walked Blackie across the bridge to find that Orville was right behind him. David was getting annoyed.

"Is there something else you need from me Orville?" David asked.

"I don't need nothing, I just thought I'd come along. I'm not in any hurry."

"I wonder if the café is open," said David.

"Where's it at?"

"Just down the street a little bit. It's on the same side as the blacksmith shop."

David thought that it was probably closed. He had talked to Cookie at the mill. I doubt if Tom would close with that much business, he thought. He was wrong. Orville came back in just a few minutes and said he had ordered steak and eggs for them and to hurry because Cookie was already making them. David rolled his eyes and Matt grinned knowingly. David had no reason to dislike this man, but he just couldn't appreciate his company. When Orville asked for a third cup of coffee, David stood and said he would be at the blacksmith shop until his horses were ready and then he was heading out. He paid for both breakfasts and left a generous tip, exiting hastily.

When Matt saw him coming he started laughing and they laughed together until their faces hurt.

"The horses are done but it won't do you any good to leave now."

"Why's that?"

"He's coming down the street."

"Lord, help me!" David paid Matt for the soft head harnesses and the new shoes.

"When you need to put the bit back in their mouth, you can try coating them with sugar syrup. It will give them something pleasant to think about."

"That's a good idea Matt. I will do that." He gathered up their long leads and slowly led them single file across the creaking bridge sections.

"You are heavy!"

"That's for sure," said Orville coming up behind him and crowding in between the work horses.

"Orville, do me a favor. Drop back so my horses can see who is leading them."

"Sure, no problem, I just thought that you might want to talk and it is hard from back there." When they reached the falls, David stopped and let his horses drink. He had brought crackers from the café and gave one to each of the horses including the one Orville was riding.

"That's nice of you. She a good horse, I got her about a year ago. Her name is Tinkle."

"That's an unusual name for a horse," said David.

"I used to have gear that had some spangles that hit together and made a sound but I got rid of it because she didn't like it. I kept the name though."

"That's interesting," said David. "How did you know she didn't like the fancy tack?"

"She told me! Every time I tried to put it on her she would buck and kick and move away from me. At first I thought she just didn't like me until I rode her bareback with no trouble. Yup, she's a good girl. He patted her neck as they prepared to move out."

"Where did you get such fancy tack?"

"I won it at a rodeo. I sold it for fifty dollars. All those dangling things that she didn't like were made of silver."

When Mary's land came into view, Orville exclaimed loudly.

"Look at all those steaks on the hoof! I wonder who owns those."

"Well some of them belong to the Blue Stone Indians and the rest are part of the S. and J. Ranch." David knew he had left a lot of questions in Orville's mind. He hoped he would be busy thinking about it and would stop talking.

"I guess I will ask Ben Slater how it is that he has Indian cattle mixed in with his." David wished he hadn't said that.

When they reached a point where he was sure that they could be seen, David raised his hand and waved. He could hear the bell ring three times.

"What was that?"

"I gave a signal to the lookout."

"You did? Where is he?"

"I don't know if I should tell you. That's something else you will have to ask Ben." David chuckled silently, having a little fun at Orville's expense.

As David drew near the crossing he could see movement on the other side of the river. The family was gathering. It gave him joy to know they cared enough to come for him. They could guess it was him. This is my family, he thought. I know they love Sarah, but they love me, too. He smiled broadly and whistled as he led his work horses into the shade and tied them near the water, surrounded by the new sweet grass that grew there. He patted and scratched the ears of each one before taking Blackie across to receive greetings and hugs from everyone. He tied Blackie there on the ranch side; wanting him to be readily available.

Orville had followed him through the water but now for the first time since David had met him he was actually hanging back a bit.

"Ben and Jed, this is Orville Baker. He followed me out from the settlement. He's been talking to Helen at the store. She pointed out the note you wrote about needing help. Jed do you think you could talk to him while I follow Ben up to his house? I need to talk to Ben for a few minutes."

"Sure David, hello Orville, I'm the "Jay" part of the S. and J. Ranch. I am guessing that you are here for a summer job."

"Yes sir I am looking for work, but maybe if we get along it could be something lasting. I am getting tired of moving around. This is quite a nice place you got here. Everything is tidy and set straight. I like that."

"Tell me about yourself." David could hear them chatting as they walked up the path to Jed's house with Beth holding Lily's hand and following along behind very slowly. Johnny and Adam had given him a hug and taken the raft across the river to check out the team on the other side. Mary had brought her two youngest halfway to the crossing where Ben and David met her on the path. Ben took Natty from her and she hugged David inquiring about Sarah and Kitten.

"They are both great and she is smiling more all the time." He grabbed Eli and growled in his tummy and swung him up on his shoulders laughing. "Where's Josh?" he asked casually.

"He has been acting funny lately and keeps going off by himself. He isn't himself," she answered.

"I don't want to talk about it in front of the children, but that is why I am here."

"Did something happen that we don't know about?" Ben looked concerned. David didn't answer. Mary took the message to heart and decided that it was nap time for Natty and that Eli should take a basket with six eggs in the bottom to Aunt Beth. She quickly scrawled a note and placed it inside with the eggs asking her to please keep Eli until she came for him.

"Eli, I have a very important job for you. Would you please take these eggs to Aunt Beth right away? She is waiting for them. Don't stop at the garden or the lake. You may stay there and play with Lily and I will be over in a little while. Can you do that for me?"

"Sure Mom, you can count on me. I'm not a baby anymore."

"Thanks son, hurry along and don't stop."

"I will!" He ran out the door, nearly spilling the eggs. Instantly she turned to David and asked.

"Now David, what is going on?"

"That was clever." He pointed at the door.

"That's something we arranged so that we can send the kids, or a message."

"David, what's going on?" Ben was getting upset just not knowing.

"I am going to be quick and blunt. I want to be home with Sarah before dark. We talked about it and we agree that Josh has a chip on his shoulder. We think he has a heavy heart. He changed after you brought the logs to me. I think he figured out that you had ordered them to build on the Parker place. He probably feels that he should have a say in what takes place down there."

"Did he say something to you?"

"No Ben, but I can see the change in him. He is a good kid and always has been helpful and responsible. Now I can feel him carrying around something that is eating at him. Ben he lost his real dad. That is his dad's land. He is big enough that he should sit down with you and Mary and maybe Adam too and you should all talk about it. I think that if you don't it is going to get a lot worse!" Ben stood up so fast that he knocked over the bench he was sitting on.

"First Sarah thinks I am controlling her! Now you both think that I am taking Josh's dad's land! Well it's not his. It is Mary's to do with what is best for all the boys and this ranch! Mary, make David some food. He is leaving, and I am going to find Josh."

Ben went out the door slamming it behind him. He swung up on Sundown and rode to the bottom of the bluff.

"Boys did either of you see which way Josh went?"

"No," they chorused. "We don't know where he is."

CHAPTER FIVE
THIS IS MY LAND

Ben didn't know which way to head. He knew that he had to talk to Josh and set him straight! What is the matter with everybody? Don't they know that I have their best interest in mind?

He splashed across the river and stopped to give a quick glance at the team tied there. When he cleared the trees he looked in both directions hoping to see Josh. He couldn't.

Josh had planned his escape carefully. He had Ben's small hunting tent, a satchel of food, enough for several days, a bedroll and his rifle. He had taken the lantern from the hut and then thought better about carrying it and put it back. Instead he took the small box of matches and tucked them in his saddle bag. He had stayed in the trees after crossing downriver past Jed's house. He didn't want to be seen. He had gotten the idea when he saw the cave that Sarah and David were in. His destination was much smaller, but it would serve him well, he thought. I can even go into the settlement if I want to and get something from the Trading Post. For the first time in his life, Joshua was on his own by his own choice and he was still feeling angry, but as the distance between him and the ranch grew he began to relax. I could go into town and get a job if I wanted to or I can just be a drifter. He laughed out loud at the thought. It felt good to laugh. It seemed that he hadn't laughed in a long time. All I do is work, he thought. He passed the field of cattle and automatically scanned the fence rows to be sure they were strong

When he reached the bluff in the trees that held the cave, he wasn't sure where it was. Ben had pointed it out to him when they had ridden to the settlement with Father

Bob. He continued to ride Little Mouse slowly until he spotted it.

"It's up there higher than I thought, Mouse. Are you going to be able to climb up there? No, I don't think you can get up there. You will have to stay down here." I can't leave her down here. She could get hurt by a wolf or something.

He turned and started back the way he had come. Movement on the bluff caught his eye. He watched as a large cougar made its way there and greeted her cubs at the mouth of the cave. I'm glad I didn't go in there.

"Little Mouse, we are going to stay on my land at the spring tonight." He walked her slowly through the trees and slid off her back as soon he reached the clearing. His eyes went to the carving on the pine tree where Slim Parker had been buried. "Dad, I wish I could talk to you. I feel like things that were right a year ago, aren't good anymore. Nothing much has changed, maybe that's the problem. Ben still thinks I'm a little boy and gives me chores to do. I want him to see that I am almost a man. I want him to see that I have a plan and ideas of my own. Dad he is a good man and he does try really hard to take care of Mom and us. Why do I feel this way now?" He sat there under the tree thinking about Ben. He suddenly realized that Ben had lost his parents at about the age he was now. I wonder if I could build a big ranch like he did. He didn't have anything and no help at all until Uncle Jed came along. He has survived so much. Even a big cat attack! He built the hut and a storm made a mudslide that buried it with him in it. He has been through a lot! Josh realized that his own heart was pounding. For the first time he was beginning to appreciate all the things that had shaped Ben into the man he was. Josh looked at the undeveloped land around the spring and thought how hard it would be to live there unprotected. The clearing here is nice though and if I had two loads of logs and men to help, this is where I would like to build a log house. Maybe Adam would be willing to share it. I wonder if we should sell this piece and buy a piece that is next to the ranch. That way someday, Eli and Natty could benefit from it, too. They would be his sons too, if he had lived. I wonder how Mom would feel about it.

Josh was growing up in many ways. He headed Little Mouse back to the ranch after checking the cattle fence again. It was in good shape. The water hole held plenty of fresh water. Dad had a good idea putting cattle down here, there is no use leaving the land stand empty. He headed back to the ranch.

Ben saw Josh riding toward him and waved. Josh waved back, knowing he would have some explaining to do.

"Josh, I have been looking for you."

"I was coming to find you, Dad. We need to talk!" They both said it at the same time and then slid from their horses.

"Let's sit down here in the trees. It's as good a place as any and we won't be disturbed. I know you have been chewing on something; so let's have it!" Josh wasn't sure just how to approach it, but he finally got enough of it out in the open so that Ben could understand how he was feeling.

Ben was surprised when Josh said that he had been thinking about the way that Ben had been left for dead by the river, with his parents nearby in the grass and his sister gone.

"Dad I don't think I could have recovered as well as you did. I figure that everybody has a reason for being the way they are and you have had to be a take charge type person in the past because there wasn't a family there to talk things over. But now there is a family, Dad, and we have ideas and plans that should be discussed and worked out so they fit with every other idea or dream. It shouldn't be one person's job or responsibility to always make all the decisions."

"Josh, you are right. You are nearly grown and I think it is time that I leaned heavily on you to do some things and I know that we should start having family meetings, starting with a discussion about your mother's land."

"When should we have the first meeting?"

"Is tomorrow night alright? I need to talk to that man that rode in with David tonight."

"Sure, we can do it right after supper. I checked the fence and the pond and they are all fine."

"That's good son. Is there anything else you wanted to say before we head back?"

"Well, I was thinking that if I do a man's work, I should get some pay. Not as much as a ranch hand, because I am family, but I would like to be able to feel that I actually do a job."

"You can bring that up at the meeting," said Ben. He was smiling as they got on their horses and headed for the crossing. "What do you think of the team David bought?"

"I didn't see it. I crossed down river. I was checking out the cave you showed me on the way to the settlement. It is being used by a big cat and her cubs."

"It looks like David is getting ready to leave." Ben waved and David waited.

"Josh was down checking the cattle fence and the pond. We want to see your team." David knew there was more to it, but didn't want to get into it.

"These poor guys were being mistreated. All four have sore mouths from having the bit jerked. I bought them to rescue them. Matt says they are five or six years old which I think is good. They are mature but not old. He put shoes on them for me. Josh slid his hand down the neck of the one closest to him.

"All work horses seem huge to me. These guys look like they have big muscles and no fat at all. They must have been working hard!"

"I bought them from a man that brought out his family and things to start a saloon in Silverville. He is a little rough on the edges. I don't know how folks in the settlement will respond to him. He is building a small house on a new street that has been cut through the trees near Rose's place. He bought a piece at the start of it for his saloon. It will be right on the main street, on the Hickory. Rose won't like that when his business gets going. She will look out her front window right at that saloon!"

"What's his name?" Ben asked.

"It's Lucas Donner. He has a wife named Hope and a boy about ten, named Mark. I met them. They were nice."

"I am glad that you bought his team. They will serve you well once they figure out that you aren't going to hurt them."

"That's what Matt said. I won't be putting a bit in their mouths until they are totally healed, then I plan on starting slow. It will be hard for me to be patient with so much work waiting, but the investment of time now will pay off later."

"You have got four good animals. Just give them time to build trust in you. Are you sure you don't want to stay the night and leave in the morning?"

"No, I really want to get back. I have accomplished what I came for and I won't be comfortable until I get back to the Den. I will be well fed along the way. Mary fixed me a nice sandwich and two boiled eggs. I haven't had those in a long time. Come down when you can. I will put you to work." He laughed as he said it. He swung up on Blackie and gathered the four leads in his left hand again.

"Alright, here we go Brownie, Joey, Dickey and Buck. Let's go home guys."

"I wonder how he can tell which is which. They look alike to me," said Josh. "Dad do you think one of that breed was Big Boy's father?"

"I don't know Josh, but I guess it's possible, or maybe his grandfather." Ben and Josh crossed the river riding side by side and Ben headed for Jed's. Josh went to the hut and returned Ben's hunting tent and let Little Mouse into the corral. He walked up the path intending to go to Jed's but Mary spotted him and asked if he had come to help pull weeds from the garden.

"I'll help Mom. All the rows are up already! Sarah and David are late getting their garden planted. Do you think they have time to get things going?"

"It's always hard in the beginning," said Mary. "Did you and Dad have a nice talk? I know you were troubled. I hope you two worked it out. I don't like it when the men in the family are stewing."

"How did you know? Ha, that was a silly question. You always seem to know what I am thinking. Dad said we are going to have a family meeting tomorrow night after we eat. We may have to do it every week if we have things that need working out. The first problem I want to talk about is my land!"

"What do you mean your land Josh? It's my land and all your brothers, too. Actually, that's not right either; legally the land belongs to Ben now. As soon as I married him it became his land as well as ours."

"I didn't know that. I thought someday I could develop it and make a place like Dad planned."

"That's a nice thought, but you are wanted and needed here on the S. and J. son. You can see how much work there is here."

"Mom when you say that I feel like a ranch hand. I want to make something that is mine. Maybe we should sell the

Parker place and buy the land next to Sarah's cabin by the long pen and make the ranch bigger. What do you think of that idea Mom?"

"Honestly, I think it stinks! Your father is buried on that land. He gave his life for it. Would you really trade it for a different piece?"

"No, not when you put it like that! What about Johnny and Lily? Does the ranch belong to them, too?"

"Some of it does. Aunt Beth owns the piece of prairie straight across the river from their house. That gives each of their young ones a nice piece of land. Jed will need to put a well down and build on it before much longer."

"This is all getting confusing."

"We should draw it all up on a map like the one at the land office. That would be fun. Let's do it Mom."

"Right now I have enough to do."

"Mom, look. Dad and Jed are taking the new guy to the lake cabin. Does that mean they hired him?"

"I don't know, but I will need to get some clean bedding and food and coffee in there if they did."

"Mom where are the boys?"

"Aunt Beth picked Natty out of the wagon and took him and Eli up to her house. She said she would rather watch them than pull weeds any day. I don't blame her. I get a backache bending down so long. We each have one more row to go!"

"I'll be glad when it is done. It always looks so nice after we finish." They worked quietly and Josh grinned when he finished first.

"That's not fair. I did two rows before you came down the path!"

"Mom do you think I could take old Big Boy down to Sarah and David's place so they can get the garden started? They can't use the workhorses he bought until their mouths heal and even then Dad said that David will have to use them patiently."

"Oh my Josh, I didn't know that David bought sick horses."

"They aren't sick; they just have sores in their mouths. The man that owned them didn't treat them the way he should have."

"I don't think Dad would mind if you took Big Boy down to plow the garden for Sarah, but you should ask Dad first and don't forget you have a meeting tomorrow night."

"How could I forget that?" They laughed together as they stood admiring their work.

After finishing the garden, they washed their hands in the lake and Mary pulled the little wagon up near Beth's front door.

"We finished! It looks so nice with all the plants stretching up with no weeds for competition."

"Nothing is as pretty as a clean growing garden," said Beth. "I let the boys play but then I put them down for a nap. They should be waking up soon. Ben and Jed have taken Orville to the lake house. I have a pile of things to take over there. They agreed that they would let him stay and work at gentling the mustangs in the back field. Both of them told him no rough handling. I hope he is a good help. We need someone, with David gone."

"I was hoping they would find a couple of men. We have so much to do this summer. Maybe we will still get a family in Sarah's cabin, but first we have to put furniture in there; like I said, so much to do. Do you want me to take that stuff over to the lake house and make up the bed? By the time I come back the boys should be waking up."

"If you don't mind, that would help a lot. I am making a big deer stew if you want to come back to eat. You can meet Orville. They invited him for sundown. I am making cornbread and I'll open a jar of applesauce for desert. You don't need to fix anything."

"Thanks Beth, I'll head over there and come right back."

When Mary arrived at the lake house, the men were sitting at the oil cloth covered table drinking coffee and talking.

"It sounds like you have had plenty of experience Orville. I just want to make one thing very clear. We won't tolerate whips or spurs and we don't break animals, we gentle them. We have a program we have worked out that takes a long time, but when a horse leaves here, they are ready and willing to be ridden without using brutality."

When Mary and Josh opened the door and stepped in with their arms loaded with supplies, Ben and Jed both got up and offered help. Orville nodded at her but sat still holding his coffee cup. It wasn't like her at all, but for some reason that she could never have explained she plopped the bedding on the bed, the satchel of food on the counter and said she would see them all at Beth's at sundown. She left as quickly as she had come.

"I guess you have to make your own bed, Orville," said Jed. He stood and walked out and so did Ben.

"I wonder why she acted like that. Mary always tries to do more than enough." Ben looked at Josh and he shrugged his shoulders as he jumped in the back of the wagon. She had already started to move it. Mary stopped just long enough to lift her boys in the back and headed home. Ben followed shortly after.

"Ben, I know what you are going to say. Please don't ask! You and Jed need him and I will adjust, but don't expect me to like him."

"Mary, you didn't even talk to him."

"I hope that I don't have to very often."

Ben was still puzzled when he came out of the bedroom with a clean shaven face and clean shirt on. Josh took the hint and did the best he could to quickly get presentable.

"Josh, I washed clothes this morning. You have several clean shirts out on the line."

"Thanks Mom, I wondered where they all were." She handed him a basket and followed him out to bring in the rest of the washing.

"Look Mom, the new guy is out in the field with the mustangs."

"What is he doing?"

"I can't tell. It's too far. It is strange that he would go way out there now. Maybe he is just taking a look at them. He knows we are all supposed to go eat. Mom he just opened the gate and is going in with Star and Blaze. Dad will be furious if he sees him in there!"

"What is he doing? He seems to just be talking to them and scratching their ears. They aren't moving away from him so he didn't scare them. Dad said he has been expecting their foals soon. He said that he and Uncle Jed are going to put them in the back stalls of the barn but they haven't yet." Natty and Eli were placed in the front corners of the wagon and their shiny faces spoke of the fun they had in the tub earlier. Adam jogged up saying they had an all clear.

"Mom, will you wait for me while I change my shirt and wash? It was hot up there today. I want to ride in the wagon."

"Yes, I will wait, but hurry up. I don't like to keep Beth waiting."

Orville rode up to the front porch of Jed's house, riding bareback on one of the horses from the field. He tied her to the railing and knocked on the door. When Jed opened it, he could see that the horse was making a meal on Beth's flower bed.

"Orville, the horse rail is over there near the lake. Beth is going to be furious about those flowers. She grows them from seeds!"

"Sorry, Jed, but I wanted you to see that this one is friendly and calm."

"Yes, I know. My wife rides her often. That's her favorite horse. Why are you using her?"

"I just thought I would get acquainted with the stock here. I didn't know that you mixed your regular horses in with the mustangs." He led the tan mare to the railing and tied her there.

"Come on in Orville. The family is all here." Jed slipped out and managed to find a container and poured water from the lake on what was left of Beth's flowers and pushed the soil around them. She is going to be upset with him when she sees these, he thought.

"Jed what were you doing? We are waiting to say grace."

"Sorry," he said, standing still and lowering his head.

The evening went well and Orville proved to be entertaining with his many stories.

When they all started to leave, Jed told Orville to put the tan mare in his corral.

"I don't like the horses ridden off trail in the dark. The gate to the mustang field is back off the path."

"You have a lot of rules around here. It is going to take some time to learn them all." He chuckled, but Jed didn't laugh with him. Jed was thinking that maybe this man wouldn't be here long enough to learn them. Ben had walked over from his corral and now he drove the little wagon with his family in it.

"Mary, do you have any extra flower plants that you can spare?"

"Beth and I shared them when we replanted the seedlings. We put a few in front of Sarah's cabin, too."

"Jed said that Orville tied a horse to the porch rail and it ate most of Beth's flower garden before he got him to move it."

"For some reason you took a dislike to Orville right away. This isn't going to help. Is it?"

"He is annoying that's for sure, but if he is good with the horses we will have to live with it. We need the help."

"I will move my plants farther apart and see what I can do. I think we have extra marigolds in between the tomato plants, too. She and I will do it together. What a shame. They were growing so well."

Jed rode to the mustang field with Orville the next morning. He pointed out the few animals that did not need attention.

CHAPTER SIX
THE FIRST MEETING

"Orville, you can use your own gear or our extra stuff there by the gate. I want you to use our soft bridle and no bit yet. When you have one that is calm enough to ride the fence a couple times around without incident go out the gate and put it in the field beside Sarah's cabin. The gate to that field is beside her house. You can keep Tinkle in here for the day and use her to come to Ben's for supper."

"Do you mean I get no meal until then?"

"The food brought to the lake cabin yesterday, should be ample to keep you satisfied. We get together for one meal a day usually. If you aren't told to come, you should make a meal in the cabin. Sometimes the women can't provide a big meal so appreciate it when it is available."

"I'm no cook. A man's got to eat if he's working."

"Orville, if you want a hot meal tonight, come down to Ben's at sundown. Put the horses you have ridden successfully in the field by Sarah's cabin. Keep Tinkle in there and use her to come to supper. I will see you tonight." Jed rode back to his barn to find Ben gently leading Blaze in from the field. He put her in one of the big back stalls. Star was already there stirring the fresh hay and chewing it. The barn windows stood open so the breeze and sunshine could come in.

"I put Orville to work riding the mustangs. It looks like you are setting up a maternity area here. Ginger's daughter, Silk is due, too. Do you want me to bring her down here?"

"No she is fine. I put her in a stall in my barn for a while with the door open. She has always liked going out to the corral under the trees. I just wanted her to know that it was available for her if she wanted to use it. Ginger is in that corral with her and so is Little Mouse. Sandy, Adam's favorite is still in the field with her twin yearlings. I want to make sure she isn't in with any stallions until next year, said Ben."

"Both the white mares are getting heavy, maybe we should bring them in near the barn in a few days. I put Cloud out by the bluff with Big Boy. Buddy is strutting around out there, too. They can see the mustang mares from there," laughed Jed. So far they have tolerated each other.

"Hi Dad I was looking for you. Hi Uncle Jed, I just thought I would go give David a little help in the morning. Is it alright if I take Big Boy so we can plow the garden for them? Big Boy has done that and is good at it. I doubt if David is using his team yet."

"It's alright with me. Don't forget our meeting tonight."

"I won't."

"What meeting," asked Jed?

"Tonight after we eat, we are going to have our first S. and J. meeting. I didn't tell you, because you will already be there to eat."

"How are you going to get rid of Orville?"

"I will be blunt if I have to." They chuckled and then Jed said that he was going to put Sandy in with the mustang mares so that Orville can work with her. I will show him the weighted packs that we use so he can go slowly with her. I need to go talk to Beth, and then I am going to start cutting willow for furniture this afternoon." He found Beth and Lily in the cheese shed.

"The soldiers come today. I thought I should get some of this wrapped so that it is ready." Jed saw that the blocks of cheese were heavy for her and carried the wrapped ones out and placed them on the table outside where they would be ready to ferry across when the wagon arrived.

"Do you need help with anything else? I will be able to hear you if you holler. I am going to start cutting willow branches to make chairs for Sarah's cabin."

"That's good. As soon as we get the basics back in there we can look for a small family."

"Has Orville got everything he needs?"

"Yes, I took a loaf of fresh bread down this morning and a chunk of this cheese. He has butter and strawberry jam and dried beef and all the usual things. The coffee is fresh and he has extra lamp oil in a tin and a box of matches."

"Thanks Beth, you and Mary do very well at keeping track of all the houses. Did you figure out what you can do about the flower bed?"

"Mary sent down a note saying she will help me fix it tomorrow. She is making a roast and cake for supper."

*****

"Josh where is Johnny?"

"I think he is up on the bluff Dad."

"Would you send him and Adam to me and maybe after that you can give Jed a hand with getting the willow ready."

"Sure Dad." Josh was pleased that Ben intended to keep his promise about the meeting. He was also smiling because he knew that if he wanted both the boys it was because he was going to give them some real work to do.

Mary was making a huge roast with the last of the soft potatoes and a lot of carrots and onions. Once that is done, I will pull it out and put an applesauce cake with raisins in the oven. Natty was talking to a ratty looking stuffed bear and sucking his middle two fingers. He was standing on his tiptoes watching out the window as Jed piled the willow branches in the water at the back edge of the lake. He had also submerged many long strips of raw hide preparing to make chairs for Sarah's cabin.

"Ja, Ja, Ja," said Natty.

"Josh," said Mary. "Josh is helping Uncle Jed."

"Umble Ded," said Natty.

"Yes, Josh is helping Uncle Jed." She said the words slowly, enunciating clearly so he could learn.

Adam and Johnny had been assigned cleaning duties. Johnny was to clean the stalls in Ben's barn and the rest of them that Ben hadn't already done, in Jed's. Adam was to do all the chicken coops and put new hay in every laying box. Johnny was glad that he didn't have to do the chickens. He decided to finish Jed's first.

"Uncle Ben, do you and Dad intend to sell both their foals this fall? They are so beautiful. It is a shame we can't keep them. Dash Away is growing into a beautiful horse."

"We haven't talked about it yet Johnny, but I wish I didn't have to sell any of the horses. I get attached to them and I would keep all of them if I could. Keep working Johnny. I hear the wagon from the fort." Ben walked to the crossing in time to greet the soldier stepping off the raft. "I thought to bring you out a newspaper again. You might be interested in the stories. The top one is unbelievable!"

"INDIANS FREE THE SLAVES!" The headline shouted.

"I am surprised that they put that in the paper!"

"The Major is furious because the soldiers didn't know a thing about it until it was all over."

"Times are changing Private Webb. I haven't met the fellow that prints this yet, but I want to shake his hand." They had automatically loaded the heavy cans of milk from the cold cellar and taken the cheese on the raft to the wagon. "I'll get the can of butter. Have you signed the paper as always?"

"Yes, that should do it. The empties are as clean as a whistle. I scrubbed them myself."

"Thanks, that helps a lot. We will look for you again Thursday." The soldier pulled slowly away and waved. Ben held the newspaper and started to read the account of the rescue. It had lost a lot in the secular retelling.

Ben handed the paper to Jed as he walked by the growing pile of willow branches and said he had read enough.

"Johnny, are you still in here?"

"Yes, but I am almost done. I am just spreading some clean hay in this last stall."

"I thought it would be nice to introduce Chaco to Dart Away. She doesn't have papers, but I am sure she is a thoroughbred."

"Uncle Ben, I think she is beautiful. I don't know how anyone could lose a horse like her and not be telling everyone, everywhere about it."

"I am sure they want to find her Johnny, but she could have traveled a long way." Ben walked Chaco from the field she had been in, down the path to the field where Dart Away was king. Usually he was standing in the middle grazing. Ben had placed two young colts in with him for company. They could see the colts, but not Dart Away. "Johnny can you see him?"

"Yes, he is under the trees back by the bluff." Ben could see the shape of Dart Away in the grass. He knew right away that Dart Away was gone. "Jed, Jed," he hollered. "Dart away is lying under the trees by the bluff.

Ben, Josh, and Jed entered the gate and quietly closed it. Chaco wandered over to the two colts and blew at them, giving them the cold shoulder. The three men walked to the back of the field together. Ben knelt and stroked the beautiful horse's neck for the last time; he looked at Jed with tears streaming down his eyes.

"I will take good care of him, Ben. Adam can make him a sign. I will start digging right away."

Everyone on the ranch felt bad, even Orville. He understood what it felt like to lose a special animal. The conversation was subdued at the table and Orville excused himself as soon as he finished eating, saying that he was tired. He shook Ben's hand as he left.

"Sorry about your friend," he said.

Mary washed Eli, and Natty, and helped them put on their pajamas as soon as the table was cleared and wiped clean. Beth did the same with Lily.

"As long as you play nice you can be up for another fifteen minutes," Mary announced firmly. From the cupboard she pulled out a sheet of paper and a pencil. She carefully printed across the top.

"This is our first meeting."

Beth got up and filled coffee cups and quietly sat back down.

"Alright, I guess we are ready. This meeting is started," said Ben. "We need to talk about a lot of things so I think Josh should start." Josh looked at Ben and could see that Ben had a heavy heart.

"Dad if you don't want to do this tonight, I'll understand. We can wait a couple days."

"No, Josh. We need to do this, but I appreciate your thought." Josh took a deep breath and grinned, feeling a little self-conscious with everyone looking at him, but he began.

"I wanted to have meetings because of all the projects we have and I thought we should discuss what we want to have happen and about the things that have to get done by law and how we all want to do them." Mary wrote a condensed version of what he had said.

"What projects are you referring to Josh?" Jed asked to get Josh to continue and to help him relax.

"I know that we have to build on the Parker place by next spring and put down a well or we will lose it for not making improvements. I think we should build a log cabin on the clearing by the spring." He had deliberately said Parker place instead of my land or Mom's land.

"That is a good spot for one," said Ben. "I have asked Tom for two more loads of logs and he said it will be two weeks before he can get them ready for us. The well shouldn't be hard to dig with the water table as high as it is. If we put it near the spring it should be easy."

"Dad, if we dig a well near the spring, will it change the spring?"

"It could, I have no way to know for sure."

"Then I vote we dig the well on the other side of the cabin and leave the spring as it is."

Beth decided to speak up and remind them that the land across the river from their house would need the same things and they only had a year to go on that.

"If we want to keep the piece of prairie on the other side of the Hickory, we need to make improvements on it, too. It's been sitting there ignored. We will need it to run horses on it before long. I don't think we can spare the time to preserve the spring if it is a better place to put down a well."

"Aunt Beth, my dad is buried there and I don't want any ugly old pipes sticking up. My mom moved jonquils and wild violets there when we all lived there. I helped her do it. It is a beautiful spot. Can't we do what needs to be done without wrecking something else that's special?"

"Sure we can and if we have to I will camp down there and dig that well on the river side of the cabin myself," said Mary.

"All those in favor of a cabin on the clearing and a well on the far side say yes." Everyone said yes.

"What's next on the agenda?" Beth tapped her pencil.

"We will be building, small and near the river, said Jed, looking at Beth to acknowledge what she had brought up. I want to make it look like a house, but with a barn door so I can use it for horses. We need a corral there and a well, too. In time I want to extend it so that it can shelter a couple dozen."

"That's ambitious," said Ben. "What else?"

"We need to help Aunt Sarah and Uncle David get their place built," said Josh. "That has to be done this summer, too."

"Yes and the furniture needs to be made so we can get some help living in Sarah's cabin," said Beth. She made more notes, trying to keep track of what was said and who said it.

"I'm taking Big Boy up to Aunt Sarah's tomorrow so the garden can get plowed. I will stay to help David make a fence around it."

"That's good, Josh," said Mary. "Do we all agree that all these things need to get done?" everyone nodded. "We have basic chores that have to be taken care of every day. The milking, the chickens, the garden, the stalls, food cooked, clothes washed, not to mention horses saddle readied and taken to the fort when they are ready to be sold. After all, that's what keeps this place humming."

"It is Mom, but we should make time for fun, too. We don't seem to have time for crafts anymore. I haven't done any carving in weeks. Neither has anyone else. Sam pays us money for our crafts and if we can make time to do them, they would pay for the cut logs for the cabins. We set aside time for this meeting and we should set aside one night a week to work on stuff that we can take to Sam to sell." Beth wrote some more and smiled at Josh.

"He is right you know. We have let that slide. I am going to pick the wild strawberries with that thought in mind. I will make an extra batch of jam, for the Trading Post," said Beth.

"The next person that goes to the settlement should buy us a lot of canning jars. The apple trees gave us a wonderful crop last year and we can make apple butter and pie filling for the store." Beth jotted that down, too.

"If we don't get help we won't be able to do all this extra work we are planning. So what did we accomplish tonight?" asked Ben.

"I think we sorted out our projects very nicely," said Jed. "We decided that the cabin has to be first and that it is going in the clearing. We agreed that the spring should be left the way it is, and the well is going on the other side of the cabin."

"That's a lot for just one meeting," said Beth. "When is the next meeting?"

"Let's make it two weeks from now. Maybe we will have the logs by then," said Ben. "I think we should close with prayer. Who wants to pray this time?"

"I do," said Josh. Ben was surprised and pleased. "Father God, thank you for all our projects and that we are healthy and able to do them. Thank you for this ranch and the way it is growing. Thank you for helping us have this meeting and be able to say what we think without anyone getting angry. Thank you for blessing us and thank you that Blaze and Star are going to have Dart Away's foals. Thank you for all our animals and please bless Aunt Sarah and Uncle David and Kitten and help them to get their place built before winter."

"Amen." They all said together.

"This was a good meeting," said Ben. "I am looking forward to the next one." Beth made a note to figure out when two weeks would be.

"Ben, I was thinking that we have let our Sunday Bible reading slide. Nothing is that important. Let's do that this Sunday, right after the milking, at my house. We don't need a meeting to decide that. Did everyone hear that?"

"What Beth?"

"Ben will read the Bible Sunday morning at our house, right after the milking."

"Sure," "Yes," "good." They each agreed. They hadn't done it deliberately. It just seemed that things got in the way and it slid by unnoticed.

Josh helped Ben carry the sleeping boys into their beds and Jed took Lily in his arms when they left. Johnny said that he would do Ben's barn in the morning. He had forgotten after the news about Dart Away.

Adam had been quiet all evening. He was definitely feeling the loss of Dart Away.

It was early when Josh rode Little Mouse and led Big Boy to the crossing. Mary had given him extra food and extra hugs. She fastened a bundle on Big Boy containing fresh bread and another brick of cheese to add to Sarah's food supply.

"I am sorry that you have to be the one to tell her about Dart Away. It won't be easy. She loved that horse just like your dad did, maybe more."

"I know Mom." He crossed the river and waved from the start of his journey. He was happy that he could help David. He would make sure that they did not see his heavy heart. He was feeling the loss of his father more than usual. It helped that his mom had supported his wish to keep the spring natural, but it was more the knowledge that the place his parents had planned with him would never exist.

*****

"David, hello, I brought Big Boy to plow the garden!" He had hollered loudly and his voice carried into the cave where Sarah was. She and David met him at the church crossing with smiles and spared Big Boy the effort of wading across.

"I'm so glad you brought him to do the garden. Thank you Josh, this is exciting!" Sarah was like a child with a new toy. "I want to have it here in the opening where it will get enough sun. We have measured it and since it is late getting done we thought it should be conservative in size."

Josh could see the stakes marking the corners. He looked at David grinning.

"Aunt Sarah this is almost as big as ours!" David laughed but he decided to stay out of the discussion. Together they managed to get the sod broken and some of the grass and root clumps thrown out before it grew too dark to work. Sarah slipped Big Boy a lump of sugar and gave his sweaty neck and ears good scratches when he had finished.

"This horse is worth his weight in gold. He is strong and gentle. David rubbed him down with a burlap bag until he was comfortable and tied him on a long lead in sight of the other horses where he could reach the sweet grass and water. Sarah had a meal ready for them. Pili smiled at Josh and kicked her feet and waved her arms with delight when he leaned over her crib to say hello to her.

"She is growing! He commented with enthusiasm. He had brought in his bedroll and sat on it ready to rest when he found three young wolves walking on him and chewing his fingers and clothes.

"These guys are getting used to humans. They came in without being invited!" He laughed and tickled tummies and played tug with a strip of cloth that Sarah had given them as a toy. Uncle David, do you want me to take them out to their den?"

"It won't do much good. They would probably beat you back in here."

"I guess it is my fault they come in here," said Josh apologetically. I made the crate bigger and brought them in here because of the thunder and rainstorm. I thought it would just be that one day and it was keeping my brothers entertained. I'm sorry Uncle David; I know you don't like them in here."

"I have gotten used to them. Did you notice that they were under the bushes on this side of the river, watching us work on the garden all afternoon?"

"No, I didn't notice them. That's amazing." Sarah clapped her hands and the pups looked at her.

"Time for bed," she said pointing and all three responded by heading into the open crate and lying down. She gave them praise and pets, with a very small piece of dried meat for each before shutting and latching the crate. "They have been very good about being quiet. They only woke us once and we figured out that it was because there was wolf song in the distance."

Josh was still asleep when Sarah opened the crate door. He was instantly accosted by cold noses and wet tongues. He was giggling as he came fully awake.

"Good morning Josh. Are you hungry?"

"I'm starving!"

"Good, I made a lot of cooked grain with raisins in it and we have toast with butter and jam, thanks to your mom."

"That sounds good. Is David working?"

"He went out to get some more of the grass from the garden area at first light. He said to let you sleep until the pups got restless." Josh stood up and stretched.

"Come on guys; let's go down to the river. I will splash my face and you can get a drink." David saw them and came back to the cave to have breakfast. "Did you make good headway?"

"I guess I did. It is slow going."

"I always think that when I am weeding, too. Mom and I did the ranch garden a couple of days ago and it looked so nice when we got done. I know when I go back it is going to need to be done again!"

"This first year it will be really hard. After that it should be better," said Sarah. The pups came near Josh teasing for a bite of his toast. Sarah growled and pointed and the three pups bounded out of the cave. "I never give them their food in here. They know that I will feed them when I am ready. They are still learning the rules."

"You are a tough mother," said Josh.

"I have to be. Can you imagine Woof wanting your toast when he is grown? He would probably take it from you, if I didn't teach him now." Josh realized that she was right and looked at the young wolves with a different point of view.

"I won't feed them at all, I promise." She smiled. She knew he wouldn't be able to resist slipping those pretty little faces some treats, but she hoped he wouldn't do it in the cave when they were all eating.

They worked hard on the garden and by dark the ground was still a little rough but they decided it was ready to be planted.

"Sarah, if you want to work at getting the seeds in the ground, I think Josh and I can put up a fence and gate tomorrow."

"David that would be fine with me, I love to plant and the sooner I get the seeds in the ground, the better."

She used a light weight rope to draw the rows so that they would be straight. Sarah planted her garden with the same pattern that she had seen at the ranch.

"Now, while you finish the gate, I am going to get something to carry water. Every seed is going to get water from the river every day until God takes over the job."

"Thank you so much for coming and helping us. Josh, the planted garden makes it feel like home here now."

David hesitated and then he nodded to Josh.

"I think you should tell her now, Josh."

"Tell me what," asked Sarah.

"I told David while we were working but I have put off telling you. Aunt Sarah, Dart Away went over under the trees by the bluff and went to sleep. He is gone Sarah."

"I knew this news would come one day, but I hoped it wouldn't. He was my friend at the camp of the people when the only other faces I knew were those of father's work horses. Dart Away would come to me whenever I went to the herd." Her chin quivered and tears wet her cheeks. "Where did they bury him?"

"He is in the row with Father Pete's horse and the gold caches. Adam is making him a sign. We all loved him Aunt Sarah. He was very special. Did you know that Star and Blaze are both in Jed's barn ready to have his foals? Last year Dad and Jed had to sell Star's foal but Blaze's Dash Away is getting big. He looks like his father. He is a yearling now and someday there will be many horses with Dart Away's blood line."

"Don't cry Sarah, when we go to the ranch next time we will be able to see two of his offspring," said David wrapping his arms around her. "Josh, when they are born, do you think you could come get Sarah, and I will stay here to take care of things. I would like her to see them when they are new foals."

"I would like to do that. Aunt Sarah, I will come the very first day that I can. Please don't cry any more. I just thought of something else. You never told me the name of Pretty Mother's foal."

"It's Sugar Baby." I looked in the tin and the way the sun was in the cave, the sugar looked the same color that she is."

"Aunt Sarah, that's a nice name. I don't want to leave but I know I should get going." He hugged her tight and then hugged David, too. "I want you both to know that it means a lot to me to be here and to be able to see the start of your place. Thanks for letting me help." He got on Little Mouse and crossed the river. With Big Boy's lead in his hand he waved and headed away.

"Sugar Baby?" When did you decide that?"

"Just a minute ago, it was the first thing that came in my head. I felt guilty for not having decided by now and I have been playing with different names for too long." David chuckled.

"I like it. It's a sweet name," he said teasing. "Sarah, I have never seen such a change in someone. Whatever Ben said to him it was the right thing."

"Yes, he is back to his regular caring self. I wonder if we will ever find out what the problem was."

"Hey, lady doctor, I want you to come with me and check Thunder's leg and then the mouths of our work horses. I hope they are well enough to work soon. I am eager to start putting up the walls of our cabin." Sarah handed Pili to her daddy and led Thunder in a big circle, watching how he used his back leg. "He is fine now. He is walking normally."

"That's a relief."

"David, Pili is asleep. You should put her in her crib so we can check the team."

"Yes, I don't trust them yet. Don't get near them until I come back."

"Bring some treats for them," she suggested. "It will be easier to check their mouths if they are anticipating more of something good." They approached the big horses straight on and talked to them. David held the paper and read the notes on the back.

"This says that Buck was added to the team just before they headed west, that the fourth horse had pulled up lame. I want to see if we can figure out their names. "Buck," David said loudly. The end horse brought its head up and turned toward him. "So you are Buck. Hello big guy. I am so glad to meet you. We are going to work together and make this the greatest place you have ever lived. You will have a barn so you can get out of bad weather. You will have all the feed and water you want. You are a good boy, Buck." David had been scratching ears all the time that he was talking to him.

"Buck has scars but the current damage is healed over. Give him a couple more days and he should be fine for a gentle hand." Sarah smiled at the big horse and handed him a salty cracker before David moved him to a new spot with a lot of fresh growing grass.

"David, let's mark them somehow so we will always use the same name. I will be right back."

She hurried to the cave and came back with four wide strips of white cloth. She laid the first one on a rock and marked it with a big "B" on both ends written in wild grape jelly.

"That stuff stains everything it touches," she said laughing. After several dunks in the river, the cloth was clean but the letters were still brightly visible. She braided it into his mane, letting the marked ends hang free. "Who is next?"

"Joey, where is Joey?" David called loudly and a big horse's head shot up with its mouth full of grass. "I see you Joey. That's my good big boy, Joey," and so it went until all four had been checked and a name agreed upon. Only Brownie had a small sore that looked infected.

"I'll be right back with something to put on that," Sarah said. She smeared it with salve and patted him. "There is your cracker Brownie. We can't forget that."

"They are a good looking team. I hope that I can convince them that I won't deliberately ever hurt them."

"David, these horses are a blessing. God wouldn't send you to rescue animals that you couldn't use. I know they will work for you soon. Give them a couple more days, just to be sure and then start out working with Joey. His mouth shows the least damage, and I think he is a smart boy. Aren't you Joey?" She scratched and patted. When Sarah walked back to the crossing, Joey tried to follow her.

"Sarah, I think he likes you."

"Good, but honestly, I think he wants more crackers" I'll make a big batch when I go inside, so that you have them to use as treats."

CHAPTER SEVEN
NOT VERY EASY

Two Feathers sat leaning against one of the many large rocks at the bottom of the bluff and tried hard to sort out his thoughts. Father Bob had said some provoking things. He wondered if it could be true, that Clover was pushing Willow away. He said she was shutting Willow out. Why would she? She would be all alone if Willow left. No not all alone, I would be around and so would Water Bug. She can't think that I would choose her over Willow. She is too old, for me. She needs to find a man at the summer council. If she did, she could have the best of both worlds. Why is everything always so hard? I was hoping that she would be happy with us and that she and Willow would get along. Now I find out that Willow has been telling her problems to Father Bob. Why didn't she think she could tell them to me? I have always tried to be there for her. She knows that, doesn't she?

Clover had noticed his hasty exit from the camp. She wondered where he was going. Cricket had been left with the story mothers again. Dancing Willow and Blue Stone were sitting there, too. Happy Song, Blue Stone's little girl could talk nonstop and that is just what she was doing. Cricket was quickly learning many of the Blue Stone words without her mother's help. The two little girls babbled and laughed as they sat there in the shade. Smiling Moon the adopted grandmother from the Choyinaw camp laughed with them, but didn't talk. She sweetly patted the children and played with them.

Willow had taken her gathering basket and Water Bug and headed to the far woods with only a few corn cakes and a half filled water bag.

"These will seem heavy after we carry them. They are enough," she said to the boy. She lifted him on Grandmother and pulled Lady from the herd, using her own blankets and soft bridles. They rode outside the meadow fence. She pointed out a pretty black and white paint that had not been there before the campaign.

"Look how pretty that horse is. Someday you will have one like that. You ride very well. Maybe before long, Two Feathers will give you a younger horse to ride."

"I don't need a different horse Mama Willow. I like Grandmother. She is a good horse."

"That's good. I like her, too."

The old trees in the far woods spread their big branches and nearly covered the bright blue sky overhead.

"Water Bug, I want to find a nut tree so that we can fill this empty bag with nuts. Do you know what a nut tree looks like?"

"Yes, it looks like that tree, with all the brown stuff on the ground under it."

"Well aren't you the smart boy? That's just what I am looking for! The brown stuff is the husks that covered the nuts when they fell off the tree last fall. I am hoping that the nuts are down in the grass. Here's one, see! I found another. Can you find some?"

"Sure I can," he said confidently pushing his hands under the long grass feeling for the nuts in their shells. "See, I got some." She held the bag open and let him toss the nuts in. "Why did Two go away? He should come find nuts with me."

"I don't know, but I hope he comes back soon. I want to talk to him," said Willow.

"Me, too!" He was smiling when he said it. She laughed and dropped a handful of nuts in the sack. We need a lot more to make a good treat. I think the squirrels have taken a lot of these."

"The story mothers gave us nuts and raisins when we were hungry. Mama Willow, we should bring Cricket to the woods. She could find nuts, too."

"Water Bug, why do you call me Mama Willow?"

"Mama Two said that was your real name. She said Tiny's real name is Freedom."

"Yes, it is. Look, Water Bug, while we have been talking we have filled the bag nearly to the top. Come help me tie it shut. You hold it on both sides so it can't tip over and I will wrap the top with this rope and tie it tightly. That is a good job. We will have fun cracking these."

"I need a drink of water. It is hot here."

"Yes it is hot and we have been working hard."

"I think I want to swim. I want to go back now. Do you want to swim, too?"

"No, but we should catch some fish for our meal. Do you feel like fishing?"

"Sure, I like to catch fish."

With Grandmother back in the meadow where she could reach the water, Willow rode back to their tent just long enough to put down the big sack of nuts. She followed Water Bug to the side of the lake near the story mothers. She put Lady in the meadow, and sat on the grass to watch as he caught the fish by hand, one by one and brought them up to her basket. Each time he was met with praise and applause. He loved the attention.

"I think we need two more. Then we will have enough for all of us." He ducked under again, but was gone longer than usual. A look of concern swept over Willow's face. She walked to the edge of the water searching the surface with her eyes.

Finally he sprang up in front of her with a fish in each hand. "That's unbelievable! I don't know how you do that. I can't even catch one with my hands. Thank you, Water Bug. We will have a good meal." The women cheered him as he followed her back to the tent. Clover sat holding the baby and watching them.

"You should be in the water with him when you let him do that! He nearly drowned!"

'Don't be cross Mama Two. I like to swim and Mama Willow was with me. I could see her all the time." He bent carefully and placed a kiss on Tiny without getting her wet, but was not as careful with Clover. He kissed her cheek and asked if Cricket could come home now.

"Yes, of course. Tell her to come, but she may not want to until that other little girl leaves."

"That's Happy Song and she has two Grandmothers, but she doesn't have two Mamas." Willow and Clover laughed at that comment. Two Feathers walked his horse slowly to the lake for a drink and then through the back of camp to their tent.

"That smells good Willow. I see that Water Bug has caught us some fish again. That is very good that you can bring fish for the family," he said smiling at first Water Bug and then the family gathered in front of his tent. He sat close to the boy and talked to him about his unusual skill. I can't fish the way you do. I have to use a line and hook, or a net. How did you learn to do that?"

"I don't know. I just tickle their belly and they let me catch them."

"That's amazing. I wish I could do it." He looked at Clover and asked. "What did you do today?"

"My days are rather the same. I took care of Freedom and we rested."

"Willow, what did you do?"

"Well, Water Bug and I rode to the far woods and gathered that big bag full of nuts and then we came back and he went fishing."

"That sounds like fun. I wish I had been with you."

"Now that we have finished eating, I want to talk with you. Let's take a walk, Willow. Clover do you mind clearing up the meal mess this time?" She didn't answer him.

"Willow, I had a talk with Father Bob this morning and he opened my eyes to a few things. I am sorry that I didn't see it until he pointed it out. Clover is confused about her position in our tent. I think it would be good if we announced our intention to marry as soon as possible. Once we are married, she will no longer feel that she has a chance to replace you. She couldn't do that in a million years anyway, but I think she has that in mind. I feel something for her, but I don't love her. She has been through so much that I guess I feel sorry for her and want to make it easy on her now."

"Yes, I know. I feel the same way. Let's walk over and see if we can talk to Father Bob." She smiled a big smile up at him and he slipped his arm around her small waist. Clover watched from the front of their tent frowning.

"I told you that I love you, Willow. That will never change."

Father Bob and Tim were sitting on the grass by the lake with fishing poles in their hands and two small fish in a basket beside them.

"We could smell someone frying fish and it gave us the idea to try our hand at catching our supper. So far we haven't been very lucky. We need at least one more." Willow looked at Two Feathers and they started to laugh.

"That was our fish you smelled. Tomorrow I will have Water Bug show you his way of catching fish. He caught six for us in just a few minutes."

"That's marvelous!"

"It's good to see the two of you together. Have you decided to announce your intention?"

"Yes, we have. We want to do it as soon as possible."

"I am glad that you have talked and worked things out."

Just then Tim's line jerked hard and he got so excited that he nearly slipped into the water.

"This fish is large enough to fill our needs for a meal," said Tim.

"Since the earthquake, the people of the village have not taken the time to use the small lake as a food source. The fish have not replaced their numbers enough to be as plentiful as they were," said Father Bob.

"This is a good one. I'll clean them and get them in a pan," offered Tim, making a mental note to ask about the quake later. There are so many things about this place and these people that I don't know, he thought.

"Father Bob, we don't want to keep you from your meal. We just wanted to ask you if you would ask Chief Dark Wolf to have a communal fire, some night soon."

"I will do that in the morning and let you know what he says when you bring your little fisherman to visit me. I am glad for both of you." He made the sign of the cross in their direction as they walked back down the path around the lake. He was asking God to bless them. He knew that it was not an easy road they had chosen, taking Clover and her family into their tent was a challenge created by their love of her little son they had cared for. They didn't want to be separated from him.

*****

"Moonflower, I am so excited that I think I am going to be sick!"

"No you won't. Not in here! Breathe deeply, and calm down," she said laughing. "Three weeks isn't much time to plan a wedding and sew a dress for you and a shirt for Two Feathers. Do you know how to sew?"

"I have made basic clothing for us, but nothing that is fancy. Oh Moonflower, what am I going to do?"

"I'm thinking. Give me a minute. Does Clover sew?"

"I don't know. I haven't asked her. We haven't done any sewing since she came. People gave her some nice things to wear so it hasn't been needed. They gave her clothes for Cricket and Freedom too."

"Let's go ask her. Maybe she would like to help." Moonflower knew that it was best to include Clover in the plans. She walked slowly. Her leg bothered her a little but Sarah had said that she should walk the length of the camp every day. "Hello Clover, are you here?"

"Yes, I am here. Who comes?" Willow spoke up and suggested that Clover come out.

"Moonflower, the wife of our Chief, has walked the length of the camp to visit you." Clover could be heard scrambling to be presentable.

"I just put the baby down for her nap," she said apologetically. "Please sit down and I will make us some tea."

"Thank you Clover. How are you feeling?"

"I am well. It is nice of you to ask." Moonflower could feel the woman's discomfort.

"Clover, please relax. We have come to give you some very special news. There will be a communal fire tomorrow night and Chief Dark Wolf will announce that Freedom has been accepted to the camp of the people." Clover smiled but looked puzzled.

"Why would he do that? She already has a name and I live in the part of the camp that is for The People of The Lion?"

"He wants to make it official that your dear baby girl is loved and accepted by all of us. We know that you intend to one day be a member of The People of the Lion. We feel like we all are in some small way after the Lion led our men in the campaign that rescued you."

"Well, that is nice. There are many people in camp that have not seen Freedom."

"Clover, do you know how to sew?"

"I did when I was young. My mother taught me and we made many beautiful things."

"Willow and Two Feathers plan to announce their intention to marry at the meeting. I would appreciate it, if you would help us to make her a very special wedding dress." Moonflower watched as emotions played across her face.

"I will do whatever I can to help. Willow, why didn't you tell me?"

"Two Feathers and I just made our decision last night. We told Father Bob and he is arranging it with the Chief. Thank you for helping us. I want Two Feathers to look the very best that he has ever looked."

"He always looks handsome," said Clover.

We want to be married at the church, before the summer meeting. We said in three weeks, and Father Bob said it will be alright. We want you and Brother Tim, to be our standing witnesses. Will you do it Clover?"

"Yes, I will. It will be fun!" The three women sat by Willow's outside fire pit and drank the tea that Clover had made and talked of plans.

"Moonflower, I would like to wear a long white dress. I can remember a picture of my mother in her wedding dress. It was so beautiful. She had decorated the neck of it with pearls. It had long sleeves and the back of the skirt went out long and dragged behind her. I don't think I would need that part, but I have always wanted to wear white. Do you think there is a way that we can make it white?"

"If you want white, then I think we can find some white cloth somewhere in camp. Do you want Two Feathers to wear a white shirt, too?

"That would be wonderful if we could do it. Give me a day to talk to some of the women that sew and I'll see what we can come up with." Impulsively, Willow jumped up and hugged Moonflower, almost spilling her tea. "Oh, My, do be calm, girl. Cricket came close and patted Willow's arm.

"Mama Willow, where is Water Bug?"

"I don't know Cricket. I thought he was still with you by the story mothers."

"No, she said hunching her shoulders, "I can't find him. All day he did not play with me." Willow's face changed from a look of joy to fear in an instant.

"Cricket, stay with your Mama!" Willow ran from the area calling his name and asking everyone if they had seen him. The answer was always the same.

"No not today." She was starting to panic. She saw the men gathered in front of the church, talking to Father Bob.

"Two Feathers, where is Water Bug? Have you seen him?"

"No, I haven't, not since breakfast. Where have you been? Why aren't you watching him?"

"I was with Clover and Moonflower, planning our wedding. I thought he was with the story mothers with Cricket, but she says he hasn't played with her all day. Oh Two Feathers, Where can he be?"

"I'll go check the herd and see if Grandmother is there." Two Feathers hurried away. Willow continued to call his name and she could now hear others doing the same. Clover and Moonflower were also concerned. Willow ran to the edge of the lake and called his name over and over, but he wasn't there.

"His horse is gone. He has gone riding," said Two Feathers. "I will take patches and go through the big rocks to the prairie. You take Lady and go where you gathered the nuts. He said he liked that. He may have decided to go back there."

Willow was crying as she headed toward the far woods. Why didn't I keep my eyes on him? She was blaming herself. Clover had put Tiny in Smiling Moon's generous lap and had headed into the trees behind camp. She walked along the bluff, calling his name. When he answered, she was glad and relieved. Somehow she feared she would not see him again.

"Water Bug, why are you here in the trees? Everyone is looking for you."

"I just was riding Grandmother and she wanted to go here so I let her. It is cool here and I think she likes it here."

"Why didn't you tell me you were going riding?"

"I told you but you were talking to Tiny and didn't listen to me. Nobody listens when I talk, not you or Mama Willow or Two either. Everyone is too busy. Now I have two Mamas but I don't have much Mama, because she is working, working all the time busy."

Clover felt sad, and guilty. She knew what the boy said was true.

"I am sorry Water Bug. I guess I didn't hear you. Let's hurry back to camp. Willow and Two Feathers are looking everywhere for you."

"Don't cry Mama, I am not lost. I will find Willow and Two Feathers and tell them I am here."

"No, you stay here with me," she said sternly.

Clover spotted Pine Berry and asked him to please pass the word that the boy was found unharmed. Willow rode to the tent causing a stir of dust. She jumped down and caught Water Bug in a tremendous squeeze.

"Oh my darling boy, what happened to you?"

"Nothing happened. I am fine. Grandmother wanted to go in the shade by the bluff, so I let her walk where she wanted. I told Mama Clover that I was going riding, but she didn't answer me. She was busy with Tiny." Clover picked Tiny from Smiling Moon's arms and thanked her for her care. Two Feathers joined them and said that he wanted to talk to all of them.

"Cricket, are you able to understand my words?"

"Yes," I am learning words from the story mothers and my friend, Happy Song."

"Good. Sit down on the blanket. Water Bug sat down beside her. Clover and Willow sit down here please. I need to talk to all of you."

"Clover, I am sure by now that you know that Willow has agreed to be my wife. We will announce it at the next communal fire and we will be married soon, before the journey to the summer meeting. This is what I would like to see happen. I would like another tent made to sit close beside ours." Willow started to object. She thought she would be busy sewing a wedding dress and Clover had promised Moonflower that she would help, too.

"We can't do that now Two Feathers. We have many things to do before the wedding and Clover will be helping me with them."

"There are a lot of women and spare hides in this camp. Are you trying to tell me that they wouldn't be willing to help you if you asked them?"

"No I am just saying that it takes a lot of planning and work to make a wedding and I can't sew a tent and a wedding dress at the same time."

"Ask others to help you, or I will! This family needs room to grow I thought that two mothers under the same roof should be fine, but it doesn't seem to be working!

Clover, it is not the story mother's job to teach a child of a Sentu mother how to talk. Do not use the language of the Abalinah with Cricket anymore. They were your captors. Do not honor them! Teach her to use our language! I also want you to take more responsibility for the chores and the care of Water Bug. He is your son. Willow and I love Water Bug but we do not want to keep him from the care of his natural mother.

Clover, you have a lot to learn and a lot to forget. God has given you a new life and a new family. I am sure that you had to work hard just to survive before you came here.

Now all I am asking you to do is start preparing your heart to be a real mother to three children. You and Willow will live here side by side, as sisters. Willow, I think Clover has had someone telling her what to do for so long that she has gotten in the habit of waiting to be told. I want you to talk with her and decide how you will share the work. Once it is decided I expect that the meals will be prepared, shared and cleaned up after we eat. That the tents will be kept in good order and if I ask either of you, you will be able to tell me where our children are playing."

"Yes, my Chief," they said together.

"Thank you for that, but I am not your Chief yet. I too have much to learn." Two Feathers was smiling inside as he walked away. He went straight to Chief Dark Wolf. He found him standing with the group of men near the church.

"Chief Dark Wolf, I would speak with you."

"What is it Two Feathers."

"I have declared to Willow and Clover that they are to make a second tent. They are willing but they need the hides. Will you help me to barter for hides? It just isn't working out very well having Clover and her family in with us. She should have her own tent where she is in charge. She needs to be responsible so she will get her self-confidence back. I don't think she has a problem with doing work, but she waits for someone to tell her what to do."

"I sympathize with you but I don't think I can help you. There just aren't that many unused hides in this camp. The cow hides were used to increase the size of the big tent. We won't need to dry more meat until summer is nearly over. You are going to have to solve this one yourself. Clover may find someone at the summer meeting and then she won't need a tent."

"That would mean that she would move away and take Water Bug with her. I can't accept that." The Chief shook his head and lifted his hands to indicate that he had no solution to Two Feathers problem as he walked back to hear what Father Bob was saying.

Carpentry skills were at a premium as the work on the church addition began. Tim had been given the responsibility of getting the bridal party informed and ready.

As soon as Clover and Willow told Moonflower what Two Feathers had said, she in turn passed the word to the women in camp. They worked together each contributing their unique skills and spare pieces of hides, some of them rather small, to prepare an addition to Willow's tent that could be closed off for privacy. They decided that if they inset a section the size of several hides, it would provide a separate sleeping chamber and more room and it could be covered with cow hides in the fall before the insulation would be needed to keep out the cold.

While they worked on that under the trees, another project was underway. Several women had joined Moonflower to help with the wedding. Sheltah had heard their conversation near Willow's tent and knew that Willow wanted to wear a white dress. Sheltah brought out a beautiful wedding dress that she had acquired in Silverville, from the Trading Post. She carried it carefully to the big tent where the women were.

"How did you get this Sheltah? When and how could you go in the settlement and buy this?" Moonflower was very puzzled and concerned.

"We went there many months before we came to the Blue Stone Village. They gave us the information we needed to find this camp. We took several travois loaded with trade goods. I took six of my finest pots and Kier had bundles of furs. When I saw that dress hanging in the back, I had to have it. Debon said I was crazy. That it was a white woman's dress, but I refused to leave the settlement without it. The woman at the store told us about the woman that nearly died. Her name was Elizabeth and that some men found her and that she married one of them soon after. She said the women in the settlement made that dress especially for her. She gave it to the store to sell so they could use the money to help anyone that needed it. She said it had been there a long time." The Blue Stone Women had never seen anything like the dress that Sheltah displayed. "I think Willow should wear it. I want her to try it on."

"It is small enough to fit you Willow. The women stood in awe at the hairpin lace on the sleeves and neck. The embroidery was all in white on white cotton. The dress had aged gracefully and had turned a soft cream color.

"Sheltah, this is so beautiful. Why would you want me to wear your dress?"

"Willow, you offered me friendship when I first met you. You have been kind to me. Please, I would like you to wear it. We are both People of the Lion, that makes us sisters doesn't it?"

"Yes, I think it does. If I wear this beautiful dress, we will only have to figure out a dress for Clover and something special for Two Feathers."

Tim scratched at the door to the big tent.

"Is this meeting just for women? May I come in? Oh, that is a lovely dress. If you are not wearing the traditional Blue Stone dress, then all Two Feathers will need is dress pants and a white shirt. I think Father Bob will be able to lend him some. They are nearly the same size."

"Clover what will you wear?" Willow looked at her trying to remember what clothes she had been given.

"You are a woman of the Blue Stone People now. You can wear something traditional if you want. You can wear something very colorful." Moonflower was excited to see how quickly this was all being decided. Rippling Water, wife of Sky Fire, stood and said that she had something that might work for Clover. She hurried to her tent and returned with a dress made of leather. It appeared sky blue and was beaded entirely in waves of moving water.

"Clover you are thin. I think this will fit you. It is mine. I was much younger when I wore it. It is a ceremonial dress. Don't ask about the ceremony. I don't think your religion's Priest would approve."

"It is very heavy," remarked Clover as she slipped it over her head. You can turn back around now Brother Tim, I am covered."

"That is the color that your wedding needs, Willow," said Tim. "Clover you look beautiful."

"That's something I haven't heard in years! Thank you." Sylvia Warren was there in the big tent, but she stayed back observing. Finally she couldn't resist offering a thought.

"You should both have wild chicory in your hair. It is the same color blue."

"That would be perfect, I hope we can find some," said Rippling Water. Meadow Lark, Rippling Water's daughter-in-law said she was sure that some grew on the prairie just outside the big rocks.

"Yes, it does," said Tim. "I noticed because I like to collect and grind the seeds to add to my coffee."

"We shouldn't pick them then, if you want them."

"Nonsense, it is a big prairie and God is generous. I am sure there is enough for both uses. I will make some chicory coffee to share so you can all taste it this fall. I believe my work is done here. I declare this wedding completely planned!" He stepped out and smiled back at Clover. "Blue is my favorite color," he said to her.

She has a sad look in her eyes, he thought. He didn't realize that Clover was one of the rescued. Tim was pleased to see the church addition's frame of the front wall finally going up. I guess it took them some time to figure out how to start.

"Father Bob, I need to work with Jack, if you can spare me for a little while longer."

"Yes that is fine. How did your meeting about the wedding go?"

"It went very well. I hope all the women are not forgetting that we are having a communal fire and feast tonight. I didn't see very much cooking going on." Tim searched and found some hard pieces of sugar in the tin and decided to use those as a treat for Jack.

"Jack, come here Jack." Tim located his horse quickly and was surprised at the friendly response he received from him. He spent enough time with him that he was able to get on and off several times. Tim was glad when he looked up to see that women had prepared platters of food and were taking them to the feasting area near the communal fire. Father Bob had borrowed several cooking pots and lids so that he could provide popcorn again. Smoke was rising from the pit. The rich scent was making his mouth water.

CHAPTER EIGHT
JOYFUL NEWS

"The People of the Lion are beautiful tonight," said Willow. "Cricket looks nice with the blue beads in her little braid, and thank you, Clover, for braiding my hair back with the white beads. It feels nice. I hope it stays in for a few days. Willow had made a special effort to prepare a tan leather dress that she had not yet worn. She had painted white flowers around the bottom and across the front. I hope that dries well so that it doesn't smudge." Clover touched it lightly.

"The paint feels dry. It will stay on, I think," said Clover. "I hope the people do not think that I am trying to be fancy. I wanted to wear something special for Freedom's presentation."

"The dress you have on is perfect. Blue is always a happy color, don't you think? That is almost the color of the one you will wear at my wedding."

"Yes, it is my favorite color," said Clover, repeating and remembering Tim's comment with a little smile. It is strange how a simple little thing like having a favorite color can be erased by circumstances, she thought.

As they started to walk toward the communal fire, Willow picked up the heavy kettle containing the huge batch of maple nut pudding she had made. She carried it out away from her, so that she would not mark her dress with it.

"Clover, remind me tomorrow to tell you a little story about Water Bug's first braid. It will make you laugh." Clover and Willow walked side by side until Willow was able to set her contribution to the feast on the table with the rest of the foods.

"You both look very pretty tonight," said Father Bob. "Allow me to hold this precious little girl," he said, taking Freedom in his arms and showing her to the people seated near him. "Look at her long hair! She has a little braid with blue beads in it. She is lucky to have any hair. I was bald until I was a year old," he said. "Sadly, I suspect that I will have that condition again as I grow older. I seem to be getting a little thin back there." The people that heard his remark laughed.

Two Feathers came looking freshly scrubbed. After working hard on the church, the men had bathed in the lake scrubbing their hair and clothes while they cooled off. He was wearing a new shirt that Willow had made for him during the long months of winter. He had worn it once after they returned from the campaign. He sat down between Willow and Clover and immediately picked up Cricket.

"Hello ladies, you both look beautiful tonight. Cricket has pretty beads in her hair. You look pretty, Cricket," he said to her smiling. She patted his hand that wrapped around her waist and laid her head coyly on his chest. "Clover, where is Water Bug?"

"I sent him back to our tent to get a blanket for the baby. The evening air is getting cool. I have been watching him. He is coming."

"That's good. Where is Freedom?"

"Father Bob took her from me as soon as I sat down. He is carrying her around with him."

As Chief Dark Wolf stood to speak, Father Bob brought Freedom back to Clover and Sylvia approached timidly. Willow motioned for her to sit on the blanket with them. She smiled broadly and gracefully sat down in one smooth motion. Willow Whispered to her.

"I was looking forward to seeing you tonight." Sylvia smiled but didn't reply out of respect for the standing Chief.

Conversations ceased and the people looked at him with anticipation.

"My people, this is a happy time in the camp of The Blue Stone People. We have many reasons to rejoice! Many of our young, strong men are very tired tonight, because they have worked hard today starting the expansion of the church of the People." Applause interrupted him. "Father Bob tells me that he thinks that we will be able to have it enclosed and ready to use long before the first snow comes. Applause and cheers filled the air as Father Bob stood and moved beside the Chief.

"Anyone that is willing to help in the work is more than welcome. We need a lot of men. I am eager to see the windows go in the front wall when it is ready. It will be nice to stand inside in the warmth and look out at snow falling. We will be able to all fit in there for morning Mass and maybe sometimes we will be able to have breakfast in there, too. I know you like the sound of that. Most of you are hungry from your hard work. That's all I wanted to say, except thank you to the men that got us started today and I am looking forward to seeing you at the church early tomorrow."

He sat back down beside Tim and noticed that Tim was looking in the direction of three young women. Clover, Willow and Sylvia all smiled back at him.

We have an announcement to make. He extended his hands toward Two Feathers and Willow and motioned for them to stand beside him.

"These Two young people are certainly the pride of our camp. We have many fine young people here and we are proud of all of them, but you all know that there is a special blessing and favor that has settled on Two Feathers and Willow. They have accomplished much in their young lives. So much has been required of them and they have responded with success. Now they come to us tonight to announce that God has given them a new blessing. They no longer wish to live as brother and sister. They announce their desire to be married!" The people stood and cheered and applauded. Whistles and flutes, drums and Tim on the guitar all made a joyful sound. Two Feathers leaned near Willow's ear and quietly spoke.

"Willow, you have never looked more beautiful than you do right now." She blushed and smiled broadly up at him.

"Thank you," she mouthed, knowing that he would not be able to hear her response, over the sounds. They returned to their seats and Chief Dark Wolf motioned for Clover to bring the baby to him. She approached hesitantly. Suddenly she felt shy and a little overwhelmed.

"Clover is one of the wonderful people that God has rescued. When she arrived here in camp she was weak and thin. She was also very pregnant." The people laughed at that. "Now she has delivered this little, marvelous girl, born into freedom. She has chosen a name for her daughter unlike any we have here in camp. He moved slowly, removing the blanket that Water Bug had retrieved. Chief Dark Wolf lifted her up for all to see.

"Everyone, please meet Freedom Joy!" He had not asked if he could add to her name, but felt that it was appropriate. Clover was happy but felt tears escape her eyes as she took her baby back and wrapped her comfortably.

"I am not done. Next I want you all to see this sweet little one. He carefully picked up Cricket, taking care to be gentle and move slowly so that he wouldn't frighten her. Her mother has called her Cricket, but I name her Singing Cricket!" She makes us happy to see or hear her!" Again the sound of rejoicing filled the air. He waited patiently placing

Cricket back in her place with Two Feathers. "Clover has a third child, a son. I do not wish to change his name, but to let you all see him and know that if he is near, please help her keep him safe. He is very active." He took the boy's hand and led him all the way around the fire. "This is Water Bug. He already rides a horse and can catch fish with his bare hands. He is an excellent swimmer." Water Bug smiled his brightest smile. He liked being the center of attention. Chief Dark Wolf led him back to his mother.

"All of the people sitting here are very special. You are my people and I love all of you."

He nodded to Father Bob and he came to bless the people and the food. First he gave a blessing to Clover's children, asking God to watch over them and protect them and give them the gift of faith. Next he asked a blessing on all the people and the food.

"Let the feast begin," he said loudly after his prayer. Growling Bear and Big Flower proudly carried their twins around. Little Cub had been warned to stay close to his mother. Chief Dark Wolf and Moonflower were expected to start the feast. They opened kettles and stirred the contents making appreciative sounds. The Chief had filled a plate but it wasn't for him. He carried it to Clover and honored her by serving her first. Father Bob watched with approval. He and Tim decided that they would also serve one of the rescued. Father Bob brought his plate to Sylvia and Tim piled food on two plates and took them to Quiet Dawn and Son of Fire. Father Bob had pointed out the twins to Brother Tim and told him some of the story of the victimized Choyinaw. Sky Fire and Growling Bear each decided to copy this little kindness. Soon everyone that had been rescued had been given a plate, prepared by one of the men in camp. Two Feathers, prepared two plates, and brought them to Willow.

"Here are one for you and one to feed the children," he said.

Moonflower was proud of the way Chief Dark Wolf had started this action of service, by simply taking his plate to a woman that had been subjugated.

"You did well," she said to him. "Others have done the same and each time we are kind to them, they feel a little more accepted. This has been a good day." She was enjoying the gathering, and as she sat there she was thinking about the dress that Sheltah had shared with Willow, and the blue beaded one that Rippling Water had brought out for Clover to wear for the wedding. It is strange and amazing, how God used so many hands and a very long time, to provide the exceptional dress that Willow wanted. Thank you God, for all that you do for your people, she silently prayed.

After morning Mass, Father Bob allowed Tim time to work with Jack while he prepared breakfast for both of them. By the time they had eaten and cleaned up their area, the men of the camp were drifting over ready to work.

The days in the village were busy ones. Everyone was happy with the tasks at hand.

Chief Dark Wolf had not sat on his little knoll for weeks. He had been as busy as everyone else. Now it was a pleasure to settle on the little hill and survey the camp. The larger shape of the church was easily visible. The walls were up and the roof was ready for the wood shingles. Father Bob planned to get those from Tom soon. He glanced toward the meadow where he could see Tim riding Jack outside the fence. That young man has a fine horse. He has been faithful to work with him every morning. Anyone can see the progress he has made. I think that horse has developed a bond with him. It's nice to see.

He shifted his gaze in the direction of the row of tents that held the night guard. I wonder how many of them will actually be willing to leave the security of our village to follow Two Feathers when the time comes.

He saw Willow step out of her tent, put something down and then go back in. Tomorrow is their big day. Moonflower said that the women have figured out a way to add on to the tent for them and to give the new couple privacy. Clover and Willow both came out of the tent. They were dragging all the sleeping furs outside. Then he saw a group of women carrying a heavy bundle in their direction. They should have had some men take that over there for them. That looks very heavy. He could see they were struggling. Together they managed to maneuver it to the side of Willow's tent. She had completely cleared the inside of the tent where the addition would be added. The women worked steadily until late in the afternoon fitting the new piece into the seams of the existing tent. They had made a curtain of dark brown cotton and it was hung in place.

The Chief had given up watching earlier, but now he walked the length of the camp to see the finished product. The women had giggled and made the usual comments about the young couple needing a marriage bed, but all such talk was suppressed when they realized that he was approaching.

"This is a fine job, ladies. You have come up with a good solution." He walked around the back where he could see the exterior. The seams were tightly stitched and the whole addition had been greased to keep rain out. "It is nice and they will be comfortable in there. Tomorrow is your big day Willow. Are you ready?"

"Yes of course. We have to be. The people leave for the summer meeting soon."

The day of the wedding dawned bright and clear. The usual preening was taking place and Two Feathers had been instructed to not come to the big tent. Sylvia had been sent to collect as much blooming wild chicory as she could find. Tim had taken Water Bug for the day and so the three of them went through the big rocks and onto the prairie where they found an abundance of bright blue daisy like blooms and Queen Anne's lace.

"These are beautiful together," exclaimed Sylvia. "Willow is so small that it was a miracle to find something to mix in with the chicory that will keep her bouquet delicate."

"From what I have heard, she and Two Feathers have been surrounded by miracles. They are a good couple. They deserve to have a beautiful wedding."

"Tim, it will be fun to watch the faces of the people that haven't seen that dress. They will be stunned."

"Yes, it is a change from the usual colorful clothes that I thought I would see. I need to get back soon so that I can draw the lines on the grass with the crushed chalk stone.

"Do you think we have enough flowers?"

"Yes and I sat last night and wrapped coffee tins in tent canvas so they would look pretty setting on the grass holding the wildflowers," said Tim.

"That was a great idea. All we need to do is put water in them and plop most of these in them. I will take about a third to the tent and leave the rest of these with you and Water Bug. Thank you, Tim, for coming with me. I still don't like to go off by myself. I get scared easy."

"That's understandable, after what you have been through, but try to accept that you are under God's protection now. Not one person in this camp would ever harm you. John 14:27 NIV Says; "Peace I leave with you; my peace I give you. I do not give to you as the world gives. Do not let your hearts be troubled and do not be afraid."

"Thank you Tim. I will think about that, and thank you for the help, too."

Sylvia hurried back to the big tent.

"Look what we have. Tim and Water Bug helped me. We have some flowers for each of you to carry and enough for your hair, Willow and Clover's too. Also Tim is putting bouquets by the church where you will stand. He is there marking the white lines on the grass now."

"Willow, aren't these beautiful?" Clover was nearly as excited as Willow. "The white lacy stuff is pretty mixed in with the blue flowers," she said.

Moonflower returned with some white ribbon and quickly fastened the bouquets together.

Clover watched and then tucked several blue blooms in each side of Willow's hair where it was pulled back and worked into one smooth braid. The braid was decorated with white beads and small white feathers. Sheltah came to see how she looked and handed Willow three long willow branches. Let them trail from your bouquet to honor the tree that sheltered you during the raid on the Sentu.

Moonflower looked at the waiting wedding party.

"It is good," she declared. The last blue flower was added to Clover's hair and they stood waiting. "All is ready. The women have prepared the feast. Tim is signaling that they are ready at the church. We should go now."

Willow was hidden from view by a bed sheet of blue cloth with white flowers from the trading spot. It was carried stretched out in front of her by Sylvia and Sheltah. Tim strummed the guitar and strolled back and forth in front of the cross to catch the people's attention. Father Bob walked out of the church and took his spot and Tim signaled for Two Feathers. Tim started the Alleluia, Holy, Holy and the familiar sound washed a relaxing peace over the gathering. The last few women that had helped Willow found their places as the singing continued. Finally Tim looked at Father Bob and motioned for everyone to stand.

At the bottom of the hill, waiting between the two white lines of chalk, stood Clover, in the sparkling blue dress. Tim started the hymn again and she advanced up the hill to her position. He hesitated and started it again. Now, it was Willow's turn. She moved slowly across the grass and up the hill to stand beside Two Feathers. The people were silent. Willow was stunning. A bride all in sacred white was entirely new to them. Tim leaned the guitar against the cross and took his position beside Two Feathers.

Father Bob, read the prayers and the promises and helped them with their nervous responses. He looked at the two young people standing before him, and then glanced at the people seated on the grass and decided to say what he was thinking.

"Today we have seen the joining of two people blessed by God. We have also seen something else. We have seen the birth of a new people. Meet Chief Two Feathers and his wife Willow. They are Leaders of The People of The Lion.

Two Feathers smiled and bent down kissing Willow in the new tradition. The People cheered and whistled, clapping loudly.

Chief Dark Wolf was not ready for Father Bob's announcement and neither was Two Feathers. Chief Dark Wolf had a big surprise planned of his own, not for today, but soon.

A surge of happy faces and hands touching them surrounded them with hugs and open expressions of love. Willow was complemented and hugged. They praised her dress and Clover's. Two Feathers was amazed that this vision in sacred white was actually his wife, his bride.

Two Feathers was immediately ready to get out of his borrowed shirt and trousers. The sides of the pants had been stitched to make the waist small enough. He thanked Father Bob profusely, knowing that something prophetically meaningful had just happened. His future had been set in motion by Father Bob's words.

Quickly he slipped into the church to change his clothes. He was surprised to find a new leather shirt there with strips of mountain lion fur trailing across the shoulders and down the sleeves. His comfortable leather pants and moccasins were still there, where he had put them. He slipped on the new shirt. It fit perfectly. Willow must have made this for me, he thought. It is beautiful.

When he stepped out, she was not on the grass of the church. Many people stood there waiting for him. They applauded. These were his people. He knew it instantly. What has Father Bob done? I am not ready to lead a band. I must tell them now before they are disappointed.

They hugged him and slapped his back.

"Listen, all of you, Father Bob got a little ahead of me. I am not ready to be a Chief yet. I have much to learn. We are getting closer, but we are not there yet."

"We understand," said Debon.

"It's alright," said Spotted Feather. We are not quite ready either. But when you are, we will be. We just wanted you to know that."

"Thank you, all of you, for your confidence, loyalty and good wishes. Come with me. I want to find my wife." He walked quickly grinning broadly. I like the sound of that, he thought. Willow is now my beautiful wife.

"The celebration feast is ready. She is probably over there," said Spotted Feather.

As his entourage moved in that direction, Two Feathers saw Willow coming out of the big tent. She no longer wore the white wedding dress, but a simple tan dress that nearly touched the top of her feet. The shoulders of her dress were decorated with lion fur and the front with swirls of white bone beads. Resting on her neck was her mother's silver cross. Her hair was pulled up on both sides and a single blossom of the wild carrot had been tucked into her long, white-feather decorated braid that trailed down her back.

"You are lovely. How did you find time to make my shirt and your dress without me seeing them?"

"I didn't, Two Feathers. They are a gift from Sheltah and Debon. He hunted and she sewed. They are truly good friends. It was her white gown that I wore."

"We must be sure to thank them properly, when we can, but right now we must go to the communal fire. Chief Dark Wolf is motioning for us to come." They walked to the fire and sat down in a place of honor, beside Father Bob and Brother Tim. Chief Dark Wolf stood looking around at the many happy faces of his people. Today for a few minutes, he was able to see the clear division of young people that would one day leave his village. His heart was saddened by the prospect.

"Tonight we have a new married couple at our communal fire," he said loudly. The people cheered. "We hope they will always be happy and live with us, but I feel it is their destiny to become a new people. Two Feathers and Willow please stand." The new bride and groom stood smiling as the people applauded and cheered. "I would ask a promise from you. I would ask that you not leave us until you have a secure destination and a good hunting ground. Our hearts are bound with yours. We need this pledge Two Feathers."

"Yes, my Chief. I give you my word. We will not leave the Blue Stone People until we have a secure place of our own." Some had worried that all the young people might be leaving very soon, perhaps even before the summer meeting.

"Will you come with us to the summer meeting?"

"Yes, we will come." Once again the people cheered and dancing broke out with drums and flutes being played.

As soon as Chief Dark Wolf sat down, Father Bob leaned over and spoke to him.

"When will you tell the people about the blue stones?"

"I don't want them to know until we come back from the meeting. That will give us a full year to start collecting them and to secure the area before the next summer council. We need time to get started without others knowing about it."

"It is a good plan. When will you all leave for the summer meeting?"

"We leave in six days. I told the women ten but I am going to change that."

"That should be a good time for me to head to the settlement for more lumber. The men have done such a good job at putting the addition on the church, that by then we will need more wood so we can start the school. I still feel amazed when I stand inside the church and look out the front windows. It is wonderful how God blessed us with many hands and the common sense to put it together so it is strong and won't leak. They did such a good job. I wish I could reward them all somehow."

The next day, Father Bob and the Chief were both smiling as they watched two men generously applying the white wash to the bare boards. The gray wood of a shingled roof would stand in stark relief. The roof hole for the inside fire had been closed. Father Bob had already marked the place for the stone fireplace and would inquire in town about a grate and chimney flue. The pump for the well he planned would also be something he wanted to get this trip. He had given one to David and Sarah and the second one was on the church land next to them. This will be the third pump I have purchased from Tom and I still haven't a well. He had allowed his mind to wander. He focused on what the Chief was saying.

"It should be simpler to build a new structure. The part you had the most trouble with on the church was when you had to attach the boards to the log walls," observed the Chief.

"You can travel with us part of the way when we leave, if you want to. I know the settlement is west of here and the summer meeting is east, but you could go with us as far as the Hickory."

"I think that would be pleasant. Yes, thank you for suggesting it. That's what we will do. I know Tim will enjoy the experience of doing that. He has never seen the village move out in a column. I am sure that he will be impressed by their efficiency and organization."

Father Bob watched as the last few strokes of white wash were carefully painted on the base of the big cross. He was pleased that the men had worked even the smallest jobs with full respect. They said they were working for the Great Spirit and they knew that he was watching them.

"You have so many horses now, and sheep and two kinds of cattle and chickens. How many will you have to leave to take care of all of them?"

"I'm not sure. I will have a meeting tonight with just the men and we will decide who should stay. I intend to put everyone on a horse and the women always take a few packhorses too, so that will reduce the number of horses left in the meadow. Father Bob, are there any jobs that you need done while we are all away?"

"No, I can't think of anything. I hope that Night Hawk will help Tim hitch up the younger team again, when we leave. We will be taking Jack and Macho, too. I want to stop and visit my friends again."

"One day I would like to meet your friend that sends the cattle. I would like to thank him," said Chief Dark Wolf. Father Bob nodded, wondering how that could be arranged. He thought that it was something that should happen.

The next few days were hectic. Father Bob continued to add items to his list so that he wouldn't forget them. If I think of much more, there won't be room for any lumber, he thought smiling.

Tim had spread the word and everyone had heard that Father Bob wanted everyone to stop what they were doing and to come to the center of camp. The women clacked their tongues in annoyance. They were all extremely busy with last minute chores. The people would be leaving for the summer council as soon as everyone was ready. One by one they set down their task at hand and came.

"Good morning everyone, I will be brief. Please raise your hands for prayer to the Great Spirit and His Son, Jesus. Father God, we thank you that we are here, well, happy and joyous that you are with us. We thank you for all the blessings and favor that you pour upon the Blue Stone People. We are leaving this morning on a journey and we ask that you be with us and keep us well and free from harm. Protect us Lord and watch over those who remain in camp to care for the animals and corn. We feel sad as we place our beautiful jewelry on, knowing that our workmen find no more of the blue stones in the bluff. We know that you gave us the blue stones to provide prosperity for the people. We trust in your provision. We know that you always have a way. We thank you for that as we live in your favor. Amen."

"Amen" they repeated as they hurried away, returning to the last minute tasks they had been doing. The women checked and rechecked their bundles making sure that nothing needed would be left behind.

Chief Dark Wolf and Father Bob smiled at each other knowingly. They had agreed that the well for the church would be started as soon as they all returned, and Chief Dark Wolf would also have men start digging on the little knoll for the blue stones that had been revealed to him during the earthquake.

CHAPTER NINE
THE ENEMY STRIKES AGAIN

Adam and Johnny argued about how the bell should be rung.

"We can see Father Bob and Brother Tim coming on the big wagon. You ought to be able to recognize Macho and Jack walking along with them!"

"Sure I can, but I can see a whole bunch of Indians and they are not family!"

"Adam if you ring the bell at all, the Indians will hear it and they will know right where we are. We should go tell everyone what we see, but be quiet about it."

"Johnny, I hope Dad and Uncle Ben don't get mad at us!"

"Well they will, Adam, if you ring that bell! Come on we need to get down and spread the warning!"

*****

"This is strange weather. The women are covering their heads to avoid the blowing dirt. It is the first time that I have seen wind strong enough to bend the tall grass to the ground," observed Growling Bear.

"Yes, it is strange. The air feels like it is heavy. I just saw a streak of lightening. Maybe we should stop at the river and take shelter in the trees until this passes," suggested Chief Dark Wolf. "Father Bob we have been talking so much that I haven't paid attention. I should have headed the people up river earlier. They probably are wondering where I am taking them."

Father Bob laughed heartily and said that he had enjoyed their discussion and the entire journey with him.

"We will see you when we all get back to camp." Tim turned the team toward the huge oak he could see in the distance and then stopped. "What is it Tim? Why are you stopping?"

"Listen!" They could faintly hear the bell at the lookout ringing over and over.

"Those boys are going to get into big trouble," said Father Bob laughing.

"I don't think so. Look, I can see smoke, a lot of it and flames in the trees near the crossing!"

"Oh Dear God, you are right!" Father Bob jumped down releasing Macho's lead. "Go Tim, hurry! See if you can help."

Father Bob rode swiftly to the side of Chief Dark Wolf.

"Chief Dark Wolf, you expressed a wish to meet the man that provides the beef cattle. God has given you a chance to help him. His ranch may be on fire! Look!"

The smoke billowed above the trees. Growling Bear, Two Feathers, Falling Stones and others, rode swiftly up beside the Chief.

"What should we do?" Growling Bear spoke, sounding gravely affected. Chief Dark Wolf quickly gave directions.

"Flying Eagle, take the women back where the grass is sparse. Choose two men to help you watch over them."

"Yes, my Chief," he replied as he moved away, turning the column of tired people back the way they had come.

"Growling Bear bring all the rest of our men. We have a fire to fight."

"Yes, my Chief," he said as he rode the column spreading the word that all the men were to follow the Chief. Father Bob set a swift pace as the column divided. The men rode steadily toward the crossing at the oak, led by Father Bob and Chief Dark Wolf. The entire area was engulfed in smoke.

Tim arrived ahead of them and crossed the Hickory on Jack, not giving the half trained horse time to think about it.

He could see the flames in the short bushes along the river on both sides. The tall pine trees were feeding the moving fire as it was pushed down river. Ben and Jed had chosen a place down river and were trying desperately to cut trees to make a break.

"What do you want us to do?" Tim asked after he rode to the lake and tied Jack where he felt he would be safe, for now. "Chief Dark Wolf is coming with men to help you. They will be here very soon."

"What? The Indians are here?"

"Yes, they are coming to help." Ben couldn't quite comprehend all that was happening.

Suddenly he was surrounded by Indians in their traveling clothes. They had left their horses on the prairie and walked across the Hickory, deliberately allowing their beautifully decorated leather clothes to become soaked. Brightly colored blankets had been dunked until they were soggy. They were using them to beat down the flames. Others knelt in the grass using their hatchets to scrape the grass from the dirt to open a bare line of dirt to defend the side of Jed's house. Chief Dark Wolf had ridden across and he and Father Bob stood near Ben trying to get his attention.

"Ben, what can we do to help? Where should we start?"

"Thank you, Father Bob; my horses are still in my corral. If the wind shifts it could take the flames there and they won't have a chance. Would you open the gate so they can leave? Ginger is in there with Silk, her daughter. She is ready to foal any day now. Jed's barn has the thoroughbred mares and they can't get out without help. If you open the back door they can run into the back field. They aren't fastened in the stalls. They should be safe there in the field."

We will lead Ginger, Silk and the rest of the horses up river and put them in the field by Sarah's cabin. Don't worry about them. We will take care of them. I can see that Jed's barn is empty from here. The big doors are open and so is the back door. Someone already let them out.

Tim came with a pair of the work horses from their freight wagon. He hitched them to Jed's plow.

"I'm going to help them widen this break,' he said.

He worked furrows the length of the side yard, plowing back and forth until he could see that the horses were too tired.

He switched them for the other two after moving their big freight wagon away from the river and far from the burning trees. Two Feathers and the men of the night guard were at the crossing trying to keep the fire on the prairie side contained to the bushes and undergrowth. They were beating the flames with the wet blankets and challenging the fire for every inch.

The wind swirled and sent sparks flying down river. The lightening had hit the tallest pine in their area. It was only thirty yards from the big oak that marked the crossing.

"I have never seen lightening and heard thunder without rain." said Tim. Father Bob had just returned from riding up river to Ben's house where Beth, Mary and the children were huddled together on the bear rug praying. He was sure that this had to be in God's plan but it certainly didn't make sense at the moment.

"Tim, pray for rain. We need rain now, a lot of it!"

Orville Baker rode up beside Ben and shouted over the roar of the fire that he needed Jed.

"I can't see him in the smoke. Where is he?"

"He is over there somewhere." Ben pointed down river. A few minutes later, Orville and Jed rode by swiftly, riding double on Tinkle. Ben looked in the direction of his house, but he could see that it was safe and then he scanned his barn and corral and Jed's. It all seemed normal, except for the heavy smoke in the air coming from the fire at the river. The trees whipped wildly in the wind. The willow trees at the lake were bending back and forth but there was no fire in that direction. He couldn't see through the smoke which direction Orville had taken Jed.

Ben was coughing and could hear others doing the same as they had to back away from the vaulting flames. Both sides of the river were blazing. Father Bob and Brother Tim knelt on the path by the lake praying for God to intercept the fire and stop it.

A deafening bang overhead sent the men recoiling as the sky opened its windows and a dense wall of water poured down on the fire, and the ranch. The exhausted men cheered.

It washed the air clean of smoke and turned the burning trees into pillars of steaming black sculptures.

As the rain continued, the men of The Blue Stone people gathered on their knees beside Father Bob and Tim. Ben knelt with them, praising God for his mercy.

Chief Dark Wolf stood beside Ben with outstretched arms.

"We needed help from the Great Spirit and he gave it," said the Chief.

"It is a miracle. No one was hurt or killed. All the livestock are safe. Thank you God," said Ben. It was at that moment that he remembered Orville and Jed rushing past him. He stood and headed for Jed's barn at a run. Others followed.

"What is the matter? Where is he going?" Chief Dark Wolf was puzzled.

Father Bob saw the men in the field adjacent to Jed's barn. They all rushed through the gate.

"Jed, what has happened? What is the matter?"

"It is Star, Father Bob. She is trying to foal but something is very wrong!"

Josh came running from his mother's kitchen.

"Here is the pot of grease you asked for, Orville."

"Please everyone, back up a little and Jed, hold her head," Orville said. "This is going to hurt her a little. Jed knelt and cradled Star's head in his arms trying to comfort her.

"You are going to have Dart Away's foal," said Orville. "This isn't going to be easy girl, but this baby is very important to this ranch. We have a responsibility to bring this baby out alive and well." He felt her flinch. "Be calm pretty girl. You and this baby are very precious to us." She jerked again. "We all love you and we are here to help you."

Her eyes were wild with fear and pain. Orville had greased both his hands and arms all the way to his shoulders. His old work shirt lay beside him on the meadow grass, as he gently searched for the foals head and front hooves. Pulling and pushing he maneuvered the foal into the proper birth position. Suddenly, as he removed his arm; a wash of birth water accompanied the treasured baby into the world in one fast motion.

"There you go, pretty Mama. You have a beautiful baby girl!"

Jed held Star still for another moment and then he released her head and she rolled to her side.

"Is she alright? Jed, is she going to be alright?" Ben was shaking as he stood and wrapped Jed in a big hug.

"We owe all of you a debt of gratitude. Thank you for coming to help us." We are glad you are all here! Without your help, we may have had a very different outcome."

"Chief Dark Wolf, I am Ben Slater. Thank you for bringing your men to fight the fire. Please come to my house, all of you, thank you for fighting the fire."

"It is good, that we were here to be of help to you. I have wanted to meet the man that provides the beef cattle. We are glad that the Great Spirit has given us an opportunity to meet you, to say thank you."

Jed introduced himself and recognized Tim and shook his hand.

"Father Bob, how is it that you have brought the men of The Blue Stone People to our ranch, just when we needed them so much?"

"These valued warriors are with their families. They were traveling to their summer meeting. The women and children are waiting on the prairie for them to come back so they can continue their journey."

"I see," said Ben trying to absorb the fact that he had all the men from the Indian village right there on his ranch.

As they talked they had walked slowly to the gate and let themselves out of the field. Ben turned to Orville.

"That was a great job, you did, Orville. You saved that mare and her foal. I won't forget that when you get your pay." Jed was smiling and so was Orville.

"Thanks Ben, it's nice to be appreciated, but I did it because she needed me."

Two Feathers and the men that had remained on the other side of the river drew near.

"Ben and Jed, I want you to meet Chief Two Feathers. He is Chief of The People of the Lion. He and his people are also part of The Blue Stone People. One day they will form a camp of their own.

They shook hands and Ben and Jed each said how wonderful it was to finally meet all of them.

The rain had continued, until every blade of grass and pine bough was bent with the weight of the water. The wind had let up and changed to a warm soft breeze that would soon dry their clothes. The rain diminished and stopped.

"Chief Dark Wolf, all your people are wet, hungry and tired. Please bring the women and children here to the ranch where we can give them food and shelter tonight. Our barns are large and the horses can stay in the fields. We will put down clean, dry hay. Several can rest in the hut and we have space for some in each of our homes. Your people are welcome here."

"As you know, we are many, but it would be good to dry our clothes and rest here. We can leave early tomorrow."

Jed had sent Johnny to Mary and Beth, to tell them that their prayers had been answered. Josh explained about the arrival of Father Bob and Brother Tim and that they had brought all the Blue Stone Indians.

"They fought hard and kept the flames along the river. It is out now. God dropped a wall of water on it as soon as Father Bob and Tim knelt by the lake praying. The Indians got their beautiful leather clothes wet and stained. They used their blankets to beat the fire and those look ruined, too. Mom and Aunt Beth we need to help them as much as we can. They saved the ranch!"

"Let's go down there. We need to greet these people and thank them," said Mary.

"Thank you, Johnny, for telling us. We didn't know any of that. We couldn't see much from here because of the smoke. Now that the smoke is gone, we saw all the men walking around and had no idea where they came from."

"You didn't say. Is Star's baby alright?"

"Yes, they are both fine. The foal is a girl. She is pretty like her mother. Orville saved them both. He is really good with horses. He knows a lot of important doctoring stuff."

"It sounds like it!" Mary and Beth were starting to relax with the good news he had delivered. They smiled at his enthusiastic comment.

The children were helped into Mary's wagon and the women rode down the path, following Johnny to the area where they could see Ben and Jed standing and talking to Chief Dark Wolf and Father Bob.

After a brief conversation with their husbands, they continued on to the front of Beth's house and immediately began to uncover a stack of wood that was kept there near the big fire pit. Beth brought out a couple of live coals from the inside fire. It had died down with no one tending it. Josh brought the two biggest tubs they had and soon cut up beef, potatoes, carrots, peas, onions were all simmering. Another big tub was filled with water and put on to heat for tea. Three coffee pots were placed near the heat to brew and Beth went to the cold storage and brought out two big pitchers of milk, and then some cream and a large chunk of mild cheese.

Orville had returned to the field to check on Star and her new baby. He fed her sweet medicinal syrup that he always carried in his saddlebag. It would help calm her and prevent infection. She and all the horses were fine but a little nervous with all the strangers in sight and the scent of smoke still in the air.

Jed had gone to the crossing and was helping to bring the women and children across the Hickory on the big raft. It took three trips to bring them all. He was amused to notice that they didn't wait to be invited. They headed to the big fire and its warmth and food. They spread oiled hides and sat comfortably.

Each woman had brought what amounted to a satchel outfitted for a picnic. They carried basic essentials with them close at hand when they were traveling and since they didn't know what to expect, they had all decided to bring theirs. The women settled their blankets on oiled hides along the path to Jed's barn, away from the burned trees. Beth's lawn was covered with seated men, women and children. She had added two huge roasts to the fire and Mary was inside making the biggest batch of sweet apple and cherry pudding that she could concoct. With no notice or planning time the woman were doing the best they could to prepare food for an entire Indian village. Mary had baked bread late the day before, but three loaves were not much for so many.

"I have a loaf and a half here and I put a loaf in Orville's cabin this morning. If we get that and cut all of them into slices it will go a long ways," said Beth. Mary hopped up on her little wagon and retrieved the bread from the lake cabin and quickly brought the fresh bread from her own kitchen. She scanned her pantry and added two jars of raspberry jam to the wooden crate she was using. A stone jar full of butter and a wide knife pushed into it and she was back on the little wagon rattling toward Beth's home and the crowd of people there waiting to be fed.

Moonflower and Snow Star had hoped to see Sarah and David here when they learned that this was the home of Ben Slater. They recognized that name and knew that Ben Slater was Sarah's brother. Moonflower asked Father Bob right away.

"Where is Sarah? Why are they not here?"

"They are building a house farther up river, but don't look so disappointed. I am sure that you can stop on your way to the council meeting and see them. It is on your way. Moonflower isn't it wonderful to be here and see Sarah's family and see where they live? Now you can feel satisfied that she is well, safe and cared for."

Moonflower looked at him with puzzlement written on her face.

"Why does she not live here?"

"She wants to have a place of her own. They are fine. You will see." She shook her head not understanding. She only knew communal living. It offered love, security and friendship.

He smiled his best smile and offered her a cup of the mint and lemon grass tea that he had smelled brewing.

Most of the men from the camp had stripped their shirts off and he could see them being cleaned and turned inside out by the women. They were working them as any wet hide would be worked to preserve and soften it. The men had scrubbed the marks from their wet trousers and were still wearing them. Jed strolled over to the Chief and said that he needed to go to the cow barn to milk the cows.

"Would you like to come see what we do?"

"Yes, I would and Flying Eagle and Growling Bear, too, will come." Growling Bear had been sitting nearby on a blanket with Big Flower and their children. He got up immediately, glad to be included.

The men of the Blue Stone People were amazed at the number of cows lined up in the barn and watched as Josh milked the first one. The Chief pointed at the loft that held bundles of hay and said that it would make a good bed. The men laughed. Tim came in and Father Bob came ready to lend a hand. Jed flexed his scarred hand trying to regain the ease of movement he wanted and once had.

"Fire is good in the winter, but it can be a terrible enemy. I am glad that no one was burned today."

"Your hand and arm carries the mark of a fire. You know the pain it can cause," commented the Chief.

"Yes, I tried to pull a pan of burning grease away from the fire and it spilled on me. I work with it and some days I don't think about it at all. It could have been worse." They chatted as the milking progressed.

"That is the fastest that we have ever finished the milking. It takes quite a while with just Josh and me," said Jed. "Ben helps, too, sometimes, but he works with the horses more than I do."

When Josh returned from placing the full cans of milk in the cold storage, he went straight to Ben.

"Dad, the door of the cold storage room is burned. I think we will need to replace it as soon as we can. The leather hinges are gone and it was leaning sideways. I put an old hide in the doorway over the door and wedged it shut with a rock, but it isn't as insulated as it was. It didn't feel cold in there."

"Thanks Josh, Beth told me she saw that the fire damaged it when she went to get milk. I didn't know it was that bad though. I'll take care of it." Father Bob approached Ben as he ended his conversation with Josh.

"Ben, I want to make sure that you meet Chief Dark Wolf's wife. This is Moonflower. She is Sarah's Blue Stone mother, and this is Snow Star, her sister. This young man is Snow Star's boy, Watching Owl. Flying Eagle is her husband. You met him earlier. He is sub-chief of the people." Father Bob knew that Sarah would be sad that she had missed this very special introduction.

Moonflower rose gracefully from the place she had been sitting.

"We are very happy to meet you, Ben Slater. I think God allowed the fire, to bring us together. We are grateful to you for your generous supply of meat for our village. God has blessed our people through you. The Great Spirit and His Son, Jesus has come into our camp and into our hearts.

Our people have changed their ways as well as their name. We are all sorry for the past deeds of the people when we were the Winahatah. We cannot change it, but we pray that we continue to change and become more like Him. Thank you for having all of us here."

She had covered several very large issues in just a few sentences. Father Bob was amazed. Moonflower had never let on that she could speak fluently in the white men's language. He knew that she understood when he spoke, but she had always held back speaking English.

"It is good to meet you all," Ben replied with a tired smile. Adam and Josh stood just a few feet from Ben. They heard every word she had said.

"I guess they are sorry for the things they did," said Josh in a whisper.

"What did you say?" Adam looked up at his brother.

"I said it is time to eat. I am hungry."

"So am I." Beth covered the table with the plaid oil cloth and began carrying large quantities of food and placing them on it. They had sliced the bread and coated it with butter. It was piled high on two big platters. Mary put the two roasts on a cookie sheet and Ben sliced the meat for her. The fruit pudding was placed on the end on a pair of hot pads with a big spoon in it.

Both women were relieved when they saw the satchels being opened and plates and utensils and cups were readied. There was no way that they would have had enough for such a large number of people.

Mary added another blanket to the grass and sat Eli and Natty on it. She asked Adam and Josh to sit with them as babysitters. She handed the little ones a piece of bread and butter.

Father Bob took that as his cue, to stand and say a prayer.

"Father God, today we have seen another of your great miracles. Thank you for the many hands that were here just when they were needed to contain the fire. Thank you for the downpour that stopped it. Thank you that Ben has finally met Chief Dark Wolf and Moonflower. Thank you for the wonderful food you have provided. We praise you Great Spirit. We know that you are always with us. Amen."

"Amen," they repeated.

Beth saw that the people hesitated to come to the food. She boldly handed a plate to Chief Dark Wolf and one to Moonflower and asked them to start the feast. He smiled at her and appreciated being honored. Mary noticed the regal bearing of Sky Fire and Rippling Water, although she couldn't have known, she sensed that he was a person of importance. She handed them each a plate and asked them to please come get some food. Chief Dark Wolf picked up a handmade wooden plate from Moonflower's satchel and handed it to Ben.

"You must eat now, with us, so we can talk together." Ben was sure that he didn't have very much to say to this man that he would want to hear, but he took the carved plate from his hand and ladled a bit of the rich stew onto it. Beth handed him a spoon and slice of bread. Ben was struggling to push down the long years of pain over the death of his parents and the separation that he had endured, when he didn't know where Sarah was

Mary carried the pitcher of milk to each family offering it to the mother's for their children and telling them that she had coffee with cream and sugar and tea with honey if they wanted it. Growling Bear took his cup to the fire and filled it with coffee and added a generous amount of cream. He had found this fire an exciting diversion and now it was followed by a feast. How can a man ask more of life? He thought. The trip to the summer meeting was always tedious and tiring. This year's incident would be remembered and told for years to come. He wondered what the outcome of Ben meeting the Chief would be. He had carefully watched Ben's face as Moonflower spoke to him.

Beth had stirred up two applesauce cakes and now she went inside to see if they were cool enough to cut. She frosted them before stepping out the front door with one pan in each hand. Once on the table she cut small squares and took the first piece to Moonflower. Beth noticed that Moonflower had been talking to Morning Dove ever since she sat down near her. Beth took her a piece, too and introduced herself. Pointing out Lily and Johnny as her children and Jed as her husband. She sat on the grass nearby and ate a piece of cake while questioning if anything could be done to save the beautiful blankets that appeared to be ruined.

"I think we might be able to improve them if we wash them in the lake and rinse them with vinegar water. The colors have run but at least they will be cleaner and won't smell like the fire, suggested Morning Dove.

"I have plenty of vinegar. I will help you wash them as soon as you are finished eating. Maybe if we do it now, they will dry during the night and be useable tomorrow. I am so sorry that they were used like that, but even now they are beautiful."

"Many of the women in our village make the blankets. We have plenty of wool from the sheep that Sharp Knife and Singing Wind brought the people after their journey. It was hard to take the wool from the sheep until Father Bob brought several pairs of shearing scissors from the settlement. Now last spring the sheep were clipped and the big bundles of wool were there for the women to use. The shepherds are still learning and the sheep's coats were not smooth when they clipped them but I know they will do better next time. Flying Eagle traded for a weaving loom at the trading spot and once the wool is cleaned and spun into yarn, it is used white or dyed and then woven into the blankets. Our men made a second loom copying the first one. The wool keeps many of us busy during the cold months. We work together in the big tent," said Moonflower.

"I like to work with wool. I made a sweater for Jed and a shawl for myself." Beth got up from the grass and went in the house. She came back with her shawl and a ball of yarn and her knitting needles that held a nearly finished white blanket for Pili. "This is for Pili for winter. She will be in her own new room by then. I am eager to go see Sarah and her family again. Maybe when this is finished, I will take it and visit."

Morning Dove was interested and wanted to see how the knitting needles worked. Beth did a few stitches and then placed the work in Morning Dove's lap, helping her hold the needles and yarn properly. After a few false starts she was able to knit a few slow stitches. Moonflower laughed.

"Now that we have visited here, you and Mary should come to the village to visit and to teach the women how to knit. You can come with Sarah. You are all welcome. We too will make a feast and it will be good to know that you are our friends."

"Yes, I would like to do that." Beth stood and placed her shawl around Moonflower's shoulders. "I want you to have this as a gift. This is a thank you gift, for giving help when it was needed and offering friendship now to all of us." Moonflower was touched and very pleased. She smiled broadly and stood up giving Beth a hug and then suggesting they get the blankets washed so they would have time to dry.

Mary had been visiting with Sylvia Warren. She was seated on the grass beside Willow and Clover. Lily had found Singing Cricket and they were having fun together. Freedom Joy lay on her mother's lap sleeping.

Mary began to be able to recognize other rescued people by their extremely thin bodies and hesitant manner. She felt compassion for them all and wished that there was something she could do for them. She was glad that they had been rescued and were now gaining their strength and health back, but she felt that there should be something more that she could do. I can't help all of them, she thought, but maybe I can help one.

"Sylvia, after the summer meeting, would you like to come back here and stay with us? We have room for you, and we could certainly use an extra pair of hands. There is always more work than we can do and our men will be away much of the time the next two or three months to build two small cabins and dig two wells. We girls will have to take care of our families and the chores, too. Our garden is big. It is there on the other side of the lake. We will be preserving that. We dry a lot of it and save the seeds for the trading post. We hope to get some canning jars from the store so we can do some cold packing. If you are willing to help, we would like to have you."

"Thank You, Mary, that is very kind of you to offer but I don't think I would be a very useful person. I have never been on a farm. I was a city girl. I don't know what I am now. I know that I can work hard. The Abalinah taught me that. Let me think about it. You have made me a good offer. I guess I am still feeling lost."

"Yes, think about it," said Mary. "I am going to get a cup of tea, would you like some?"

"No thanks, I had some and a piece of the cake. It is delicious. Everything was," said Willow. Clover glanced around trying to see Two Feathers. She could see Water Bug. He was on the blanket with Mary's boys. They were laughing and having fun.

"Willow, where is Two Feathers?" Clover asked quietly.

"I saw him walking with Ben Slater. They had a lantern and a hammer. I think they were going to fix something."

"Yes, said Mary. The fire burned the door to our cold storage room. That's where we keep the milk cold. Ben said he was going to repair it. I guess Two Feathers has gone to help him." Clover smiled. She seemed to always be more comfortable if she knew where everyone in their little family was.

Although they sincerely tried to get people to come, sleep inside no one took them up on their repeated offers.

When it was time the Blue Stone People bedded down right where they had sat to eat. The night sky was clear and the stars sparkled above them. This was their way when they were traveling. It was nothing exceptional.

At daybreak the people were up preparing to leave.

Father Bob knocked on Ben and Mary's door to tell them that the people needed to be ferried across the river.

"Tim and I will be continuing on to the settlement, but Ben, I think you should go with them. It will settle a lot of questions for Sarah without them being asked."

"Yes, I am sure you are right."

Chief Dark Wolf was at the bank of the river waiting for a hand with the big raft, as Jed arrived at the same time Ben and Josh did.

"Good morning Chief, how are you?"

"I am fine. I do not allow myself to be otherwise," he said with a chuckle.

Jed steadied the raft as the first load of women climbed on, jockeying for the space in the center. No one wanted to take a chance on a fall in the moving water. They giggled and tucked themselves close together with their belongings in their laps.

"That's a good attitude to have," said Ben. I would like to ride with you to visit my sister. Do you mind if I join you?"

"Come, you can show us where she is." As Jed brought the raft back for the second load of women and children, Ben told him that he wanted to go with them as far as Sarah's.

"Do you mind keeping an eye on things here?"

"No, in fact if you hadn't mentioned it, I was going to suggest it."

"Thanks Jed. Don't try to do anything with the burned area while I am gone. I will help figure out what to do with it when I come back. I have to go tell Mary and I am going to ride Cloud. He needs the exercise."

Father Bob and Brother Tim were hitching the big team to the freight wagon when Sylvia Warren approached.

"Father Bob, would you allow me to ride to the settlement with you? I just want to see it. I will stay near and not delay you. I can ride back to the camp with you."

"Don't you want to go to the summer meeting?"

"No, I think that many Indians will be intimidating and overwhelming." She stood in the prairie grass, with her head down.

"You can come with us if it's alright with Chief Dark Wolf. I will ask him."

"Thank you so much. I won't be a problem, I promise."

Chief Dark Wolf and Ben walked their horses slowly across the Hickory and up onto the prairie grass. It wasn't until that moment that Ben noticed that Cloud and the Chief's horse were almost identical.

"Your horse is the symbol of a Chief. You selected your mount wisely. He is handsome and strong as is mine."

Ben smiled but felt that not answering was the best answer.

Father Bob spoke briefly to the Chief and then rode to the area that Moonflower and Morning Dove stood near each other fastening their satchels and bundles on the horses they would ride. Ben observed as Father Bob took the reins to a nice brown mare and received two satchels that the women hastily selected. A water stained blanket covered the mare's back and a soft saddle was put on, complete with a water pouch. Father Bob returned to the big wagon and handed the reins to Sylvia.

After Sylvia made three tries to get up on the horse, Tim tied it to the back of their wagon beside Jack and Macho and helped her up on the seat between them.

All three were waving and smiling as they headed the team toward Silverville.

Josh crossed on Missy. He wanted to remind Ben to tell Sarah that Star had her foal and that Blaze would very soon.

"I don't know if I would have remembered with all that has happened and having the whole Indian village with us."

"I almost forgot. Mom gave me this for you to eat on the way back. She said she didn't think she would see you until tomorrow, but it was alright. She said to take your time."

"Thank you son, help Jed and tell the boys to clean the chicken pens and anything else that needs it. See you tomorrow."

Josh nodded and headed back across the river to help Jed with the milking.

CHAPTER TEN
A SECURE LAIR

Chief Dark Wolf rode in the middle, with Ben on his right and Growling Bear on his left. Behind him rode Flying Eagle and Two Feathers. The caravan followed at a slow walk. Ben knew that the pace was to accommodate women that rode only once a year when they went to the summer meeting. He turned and looked at their clothes expecting to see remnants of stains caused from the fire, but he couldn't. Each rider looked fresh and sharp. He wondered how they had done it. He had taken soap and a towel to the river after the ranch was quiet and scrubbed his body and clothes. His work clothes were still on the line. Mary had laid out his leather clothes to wear this morning. He compared his to the Chief's.

"Our horses are similar but our clothes certainly are not. Moonflower dresses you in the finest. The beadwork on your shirt is beautiful."

Now it was the Chief's turn to hesitate before answering.

"Moonflower is known for her many skills. Sarah has learned to do such work. She also learned the art of healing from Singing Lark and Talking Mountain. Our people miss her. She is held in high esteem. How long will it be before we reach the place that she and Sharp Knife have chosen to live?"

"It is hard for me to say. Your people move very slowly. It usually takes half a day with one stop when the horse needs rest."

Without a word the Chief turned his horse back and rode along the column smiling and nodding until he came to Clover.

"Clover, would it be difficult for you if we move a little faster?"

"I don't think so. I certainly am willing to try."

"Big Flower, would it be more difficult for you if we move a little faster?"

"I am sure we would be fine. The children are all fastened in comfortably."

"Thank you ladies, you are both good mothers."

He had asked the two women that each had three little children they were caring for. As soon as he had directed his horse back in place at the front of the line he increased the speed they were moving.

"Can you show me the spot that you would normally stop to rest?"

"Yes, I'm sure I can."

"You have made this trip with wagons. I can see their marks in the grass."

"Yes, Sarah has many things."

The Chief laughed.

"What she doesn't have she will soon make." It was more difficult to converse at the faster pace. Ben pointed out the wild apple trees ahead.

"That is where I stopped last time." The Chief raised his hand and the column slowed to a stop. Horses were led to the water to drink and babies were given whatever attention they required. The women were glad for a chance to get off and walk around a bit while they ate a snack. Ben offered the Chief a piece of the roast that he found in the bundle that Josh had handed him. He reached up to pick an apple, intending to give it to Cloud, but the Chief stopped him.

"The apples are not ripe. They will make you or your horse sick. Our women pick them when the leaves turn color, but not now."

"I know they are sour, but I didn't know they would make me sick. I am glad that you told me."

"It is good to learn something new each day. That was your lesson. Did you know that Father Bob has gone to get lumber to build a school for the Blue Stone children?" He has many boxes of books with wonderful stories in them."

"He is a good man. He loves your people," replied Ben. "He will teach them to read."

The Chief got up on his horse and the rest of the people hurried to do the same.

Growling Bear rode along silently. He had not said much at the ranch either.

"What are you thinking about, my friend," asked Ben?

"You were in the wagon that left the wagon train. Your parents were killed and your sister, Sarah was taken by Chief Dark Wolf. Where were you when that was happening?"

Ben was caught off guard by his blunt statement and question.

"Well, I was on the back of the wagon and someone chased me down into the raspberry bushes. An arrow cut through my shoulder and I fell and hit my head. When I woke, it was all over and Sarah was gone."

"I came there with a scouting party, to that big oak to find the wagon and a sacred book that she spoke about, but we couldn't find the wagon or the book. Where did it go?"

"I took it apart down to the last board and carried it away."

"After all that, you have accepted our people and sent them food. Why?"

Ben smiled at the aging warrior.

"The words in the Holy Bible, tell me to forgive and to love. Growling Bear, do you believe in Jesus, the Son of God?"

"Yes, I am baptized. God loves me and he proved it by giving me two baby sons! I have three boys."

"That's wonderful. I am also a Christian. That makes us brothers. I and my family were praying for the chosen men during the campaign against the Abalinah. I know that you were one of them. If God chose you to do His work, how can I do less than choose you to be my friend?"

"You are a good man, Ben Slater," said Chief Dark Wolf. He appreciated that Ben had made an effort to befriend Growling Bear.

"Look ahead. There where the trees are down and brown. That marks the land that Father Bob has chosen for a church here on the river. Sarah's place is next to it. We are nearly there."

Ben led the way through the bushes and trees, wanting to be the first one that Sarah saw. He moved slowly across the river and rode up to the cave where Sarah came hurrying out with Pili in her arms.

"Hello, I brought you some company!" He slid down and wrapped her in a hug, taking Pili from her arms. Moonflower had broken tradition and hurried her horse along, out of position, eager to see her daughter. Soon Sarah was engulfed with people giving hugs and greetings.

David came through the trees as soon as he could secure the pair of horses he had been using. He went straight to Ben and greeted him and then the Chief and Moonflower. Snow Star and Flying Eagle were laughing with Sarah when Ben turned to her to see the joyous look on her face.

"Ben, how can this be? How is it that you have brought all the people to visit?"

"We are on our way to the summer meeting and stopped to see you and Sharp Knife and our grandchild.

Where is my beautiful Pili?" The Chief reached for the baby, but Moonflower intercepted.

"I want her," she said, gently removing her from Ben's arms.

"Ben, I can't believe what I am seeing. You have done the impossible! I couldn't figure out a way for you to meet even a few of the Blue Stone People without a problem. You have brought all of them. I wish Mary and Beth were here to meet them."

"They did. All these people stayed at the ranch last night! Father Bob was traveling with them and when the lightening caused a fire in the trees by the river, the boys rang the bell and they heard it and all came to help put out the fire."

"They stayed at the ranch? You had a fire? How bad was it? Is there a lot of damage?"

"God poured down an enormous lake of water and put out the flames before it could reach any of the buildings. I believe that God allowed that fire so that we could meet these wonderful people. Sarah you were right. They are good and blessed. They worked very hard at keeping the fire contained until the rain came to drench everything and put it out."

She looked up at Ben with a big smile on her face.

"Ben, I am so happy. Thank you for coming with them. This means so much to me." She linked her arm with his and headed him to the spot that she could see David and most of the men gathered around the start of their cabin.

"I wish I could stay and help, but I have an awful mess back at the ranch to deal with and Blaze hasn't had her foal yet and neither has Silk. The two white mares are close, too.

Star had her baby yesterday in all the confusion. Thank God for Orville. He was able to help her or I think she and that foal might have died. He sure knows a lot about horses."

"Who is Orville?"

"He is a ranch hand that followed David from the settlement when he bought your team. Didn't he mention him? I don't think so."

"Hello, everyone, have you all met Ben my brother? I am so glad that you all stopped here on your way to the summer meeting. Now that you know where we are I hope that you will plan to stop each time you are near here. You are all welcome here anytime," she said loudly.

"Yes, you are and if you want to stop on the way back through and help build this cabin, you are welcome to do that, too," said David laughing heartily.

"What if I told you that some of the men have suggested that they would prefer to stay here and help you rather than go to the summer meeting?" Chief Dark Wolf was not laughing. "I would like to stay and help too, but I feel I must go for the sake of the people we rescued. They need a chance to find their people if it is possible."

"I don't know what to say. I was joking. Of course we need the help but I know that the summer meeting is important to all the people."

Two Feathers joined the conversation.

"The People of the Lion wish to stay and help. Most of them were not chosen to go to the Abalinah camp. I think they would appreciate a chance to do something helpful."

"This is more than a man could hope for. I need the help and we will enjoy having you here for as long as you can stay."

"Then it is settled. My men of the night guard and their families may stay if they want to and the rest of us will continue on to the summer meeting. We will stop again on the way back," said Chief Dark Wolf.

He was looking very pleased with his young men. This would assure Sarah of a warm winter house. He didn't like the idea of her living in a cave. He was not aware that it was guarded by the Lion of Judah.

The young women were excited to stay. Willow asked Clover if she was sure that this was what she wanted.

"You know that I love you like a sister and Water Bug is like my own son, but you are passing up a chance to find a good husband. We will understand if you want to go, and if you don't see anyone there that you want, you will come back with the people."

"No, Willow, I want to stay here. I don't want to marry a stranger. I think God will send me a husband. I want to have a man that I can love and marry like you did Two Feathers. I hope that the Chief will let me stay here. He probably thinks that I should go."

"Just stay out of sight until they leave."

"How do I do that?"

"I don't know. Maybe you can go in the shade of the big rocks away from where the men are working, or ask Sarah if you can sit in the cave."

That's a good idea. When she goes to put Pili to sleep I will follow her and ask if I can put Freedom and Cricket down in there, too."

Growling Bear and Night Hawk had followed the base of the bluff until it diminished and the river turned gently to the right. They wanted to return with a large animal for the evening meal. They moved quietly knowing that as the trees gave way to grassland, they would have a better opportunity to see an animal.

They didn't expect to see a large herd of deer. The majestic animals ignored them as they grazed.

The two hunters each chose a target and counted down to fire at the same time, knowing that any loud sound would send the herd bounding away. Successfully, the hunters returned, each pulling a quickly made travois to transport the heavy animals.

The women would now be as busy as the men. One animal would be readied for a feast and the other sliced and dried to help with Sarah's winter supply.

Growling Bear made sure that all the men knew that he was still capable of leading a hunt, when there were animals.

White Grass and Cat Claw volunteered to dig a big pit to roast the large animal. Pine Berry and Spotted Feather gathered wood, breaking it in lengths that were manageable.

Soren and Debon gathered rocks for the bottom of the pit and searched the bottom of the bluff for pieces of thin slate that could be used for the top when the time came. They found one that was nearly round and brought it back, leaning it against a tree. It would make a good door for Sarah's oven. They had noticed the drying bricks in the forms.

Many women were willing to help. Cumae had shyly offered to help with the slicing of the meat for the drying racks. Willow and Sheltah began to peel the skin back and Meadow Lark took a large chunk of the haunch to slice. Moonflower and Morning Dove instructed the young men digging the pit. Then they sent Soren and Debon to cut four green branches of oak to support the meat and keep it clean when it was lowered to the coals.

Ben noticed the huge antlers and asked if anyone minded if he used them. No one did. After he cleaned them thoroughly he carried them into the cave and told Sarah that he had put them up high where the wolf pups couldn't reach them.

"I will work on them when I visit and when they are finished, you can hang them in the cabin on your fireplace."

"Ben that is wonderful. The ones you made for Jed are beautiful."

"Thanks but that just reminded me of another job some of these men can do that are standing around."

He left the cave quickly before she could ask him what he was talking about. Ben retrieved the stronger travois that had been used for hauling the deer. He added more branches to it and then lashed a hide to the bottom, coating it with a thick layer of grease.

"Who wants to go fishing for rocks?"

The men looked at him with a puzzled expression, but followed him to the river as he moved the heavy skid into position so that he could hook one of the big horses to it when it was loaded. He picked two rocks from the edge of the water, holding them up and explained that the smooth one was nice and that he didn't like the other one. He tossed it back in the water.

"We are going to collect enough good rocks so they can build a fireplace in the cabin."

Night Hawk and Growling Bear had seen a fireplace in the Major's office at the fort. He had also noticed the chimney on the back of Jed's house. His eyes recorded everything. They both nodded approval and understood what Ben wanted to do. Each rock was held up for Ben's approval. The skid was ready to be moved. Night Hawk brought Joey to the skid and gently attached the ropes to him. He still wore only the soft bridle that David had been using. Joey didn't object. Night Hawk had a way with animals and his easy manner assured the abused animal that this man wasn't going to hurt him.

"Come, big man, pull the rocks for us. We will go slowly and you can show them all how strong you are." Night Hawk pulled gently on the bridle and Joey felt the ropes tighten across his chest. He leaned into it and easily walked in the direction that Night Hawk led him.

"David, where do you want the fireplace rock unloaded?"

"The square drawn in the dirt is where I plan to build it, so somewhere near that. That's great that you are doing that. Thanks a lot." David was grinning.

Night Hawk led Joey a few more steps and stopped. Quickly the skid was emptied and Joey was taken back to the riverbank for another load.

The drying racks were standing behind the big fire pit and Sarah's campfire, which was heating a huge batch of tea and cooking two huge deer roasts. The hides were on the grass and each had been given an initial scraping.

Clover and Sarah had tucked the two baby girls in the crib and watched as they smiled and touched, examining this new small person so near them. Now they slept. Sarah wondered where the wolf pups were. With so many people here, they probably will stay hidden. She suggested that Clover bring Cricket and go with her and they took food and water to the den, but the pups were not there.

"Don't worry; they are just hiding because of all the strange people walking around. When it gets quiet tonight they will return and find the food. They can always get a drink from the river."

"I know that you are right, Clover. I guess I shouldn't worry about them, but they don't have a mother to teach them and I think sometimes that they might need protection and she won't be there to help."

"Look Sarah, the men have put up more of the wall of your cabin. They have added another row of logs."

As they walked back toward the cave Sarah could feel the heat radiating from the fire in the bottom of the big pit.

"They will soon be able to lower that deer in there and close the top. Let's go back and put on a tub filled with dried vegetables to cook. I like it best when the pan gets to the bottom. It is a wonderful rich vegetable soup."

"You are making me hungry," said Clover smiling.

The afternoon had slipped by swiftly. It was well after dark before the deer was fully cooked and tender. The outdoor campfire and nearby pit became the center around which the people gathered as the night came. The atmosphere was that of a communal fire in camp. Little Pili was handed from one set of arms to another. Freedom Joy was enjoying an equal amount of attention. Somehow she finally ended up in the Chief's lap where she slept contentedly. Clover fidgeted, not wanting to go get her from the Chief. Willow whispered to Two Feathers and he boldly collected the baby, saying it was time that she was back with her mother for a feeding. Big Flower sat near Clover with all her sons on the blanket. Little Cub had eaten well after playing in the trees with Water Bug. He was sucking his thumb and about to fall asleep. Growling Bear asked David if they could stay right where they were until morning.

"You could probably all sleep in the cave, but we haven't explored it. I don't think it is safe to go back any further until we do."

"No we don't want to sleep in the cave. We are fine here." He brought his saddle blanket and covered his wife and sleeping children before settling down in the grass beside them.

Chief Dark Wolf stood.

"I want to remind all of you that are coming to the summer meeting that we will be leaving at dawn. Now get a good rest and God bless this new home and everyone here."

"Amen."

Moonflower had stuffed pine boughs and grass beneath her blanket and had made a cozy nest for them under a pine tree. Snow Star had done something similar for Flying Eagle and Watching Owl. When they traveled, they did not expect to have the comfort and security of a tent, but oddly, the trees overhead and the close proximity of others offered a feeling of security.

The people woke to the sound of Chief Dark Wolf's voice.

"Hurry and get your things gathered. We need to head out. We are two days later than we should be. They will think we are not coming."

There was an urgency in his words that was not necessary. They all knew they had been delayed, first by the fire and then by stopping to visit with Sarah and Sharp Knife.

Moonflower clung to Sarah, urging her to come with them.

"We will bring you back here and you aren't leaving Sharp Knife alone. Many of the young people are staying to help him."

"I know Mother, but I need to be here to cook and do what I can to help. It is exciting to watch the house grow. I want to see every step of it made."

"Mother, now that you know where we are and that it is alright and safe, you can come here to visit me. Have you gathered all your things and fresh water in your water bag?"

"Yes, I am fine. Sarah it was good to meet your brother and his family and I am glad to know where you will be living."

She turned the gentle mare that she was on and crossed the river slowly, along with others. David stood beside her and squeezed her hand.

"I never thought that I would see it. It's still hard to believe that the people were here and that they met Ben and all of them were at the ranch. It is hard to wrap my mind around the fact that two different worlds have met without a war."

Ben eased Cloud close to them and said he would have to be going too.

"David, I will be going into Silverville. Do you want me to get Calvin Briggs to do your fireplace? He did both of ours and he did a great job."

"Ben, that's a good idea. If you can send him out, I would sure appreciate it."

"Sarah, if you want to ride to the ranch with a couple of the women you could see Star's baby and maybe Blaze will have hers by then too."

"Thanks Ben that would be fun. I'll think about it. Thank you for coming with the people. It means a lot to me to see you with them."

His big white horse crossed the river and headed home. When Ben looked in the opposite direction the column of Indians was well on its way. The Chief was setting a steady pace.

It was not yet noon when Johnny clanged the bell to announce family coming. Everyone that heard it breathed a sigh of relief. Now maybe the ranch would begin to return to normal. It didn't feel the same when Ben was gone. Mary tucked the boys in the wagon and met him at the crossing. Beth had been in the garden with Lily and they walked down. Jed and the boys left their chores too, eager to hear about the visit of the Indian village at Sarah and David's place.

After hugs all around Ben asked if they had any more new foals.

"Yes, we do. Dart Away's bloodline is guaranteed. Blaze had a miniature copy of him in the middle of the night. That was the easiest foal we have had around here for a while.

He looks just like her first foal, Dash Away. He is a beauty. I think we have the start of something special. The rest are waiting for you to come home I think."

Mary hugged him again and asked if he was hungry.

"I baked bread last night and have food ready if you need to eat."

"I am hungry, but not starving. We had deer meat last night. Growling Bear and Night Hawk went hunting and each got one. I think David is going to be successful hunting in that area."

"Well, that's good. Was Sarah excited when she saw the Blue Stone People coming with you?"

"You can't imagine how happy she was that we had all finally met. She was smiling and laughing."

"It was nice having them here although Beth and I really had to scramble to make food for so many without knowing about it ahead of time. Are they all still there? Sarah won't be able to feed so many for very long."

"The Chief took the caravan out to the meeting this morning. He has the older warriors and hunters and their families, along with the people they rescued, but the younger ones that call themselves "The People of The Lion," are there with the exception of two young unmarried men. I think they are going to the meeting to look for wives. The rest are helping David get the cabin built and it is going well. The work horses he bought are really nice animals. We used one of them to pull the skids of rocks for the fireplace and it was very cooperative and gentle."

"Jed, are you still happy with Orville being here?" Ben asked.

"I sure am. That man has done a lot of work while you were gone. He put Star and her foal in the barn and brought Blaze back in there. He has Ginger and Silk in your barn and the two white mares are in your corral again. Orville helped me get the cold storage totally repaired with a new door. We lost a lot of ice when the fire passed over and burned the door. We put in extra grass bundles for insulation. I sure hope the ice we have back in there will last until cold weather."

"It will. God is good that way. Remember the story of the little dab of flour and small amount of oil and how it lasted? When we count on Him for our supply He doesn't disappoint us."

"Yes, you are right."

"How many horses do we have that are saddle ready, to take to the fort?"

"Orville says we have fifteen but I am not sure about two of them. He has been working them every day, but I think the brown stallion and the paint are still both unpredictable."

"I am going in to Silverville to check on supplies for all our projects and I want to take a dozen horses with me. It won't hurt to have cash in hand when I tell Tom that we need the logs as soon as he can manage it."

"The fort will take any mounts that we can provide and that will give us more room in the field where we work with the mustangs."

"We should remove any of the horses that we aren't thinking of selling. We can put them in the far field beyond Sarah's cabin."

When Ben and Jed entered the back door of Mary's kitchen they could smell the big batch of blackberry jam that she was stirring.

"That smells wonderful. Where did you find the blackberries?"

"We took the children for a walk in the woods a couple weeks ago and found the bushes. They weren't ready then but they were this morning. I am going to have to use large jars though. I haven't any more of the jam jars. Next time you go to town, would you ask Sam and Helen if they have any?"

"Sure Honey and that reminds me that I need to find Calvin Briggs and tell him that David and Sarah need a good fireplace before cold weather sets in."

"You should make a list or you might forget something. Ben did you remember that we have a meeting here tomorrow night?" I will make chili and apple pie. We are going to eat at Beth's tonight. She is still trying to use up the leftover food from the campfire for the Indians."

Josh came in the door and stood there looking like he would explode if he didn't say something quickly.

"What is it Josh?"

"There is a large herd of horses on the prairie heading this way slowly. I tried to count them. I think there is about thirty and I saw that same big stallion with the dark mane, tail and legs leading them. Dad, he is so beautiful, but I don't think we can trap him again. He is wise to our ways now."

"I am glad that they are back in our area and that we know about it. Let's all work to bring the mares in from the far fields and transfer Orville and the mustangs to the double fenced area while he and his herd is in the area. Josh, tell Adam and Johnny that I want them to bring all our riding horses in near the buildings. They will like that job a lot better than cleaning the chicken pens." Ben chuckled.

"Jed, are you alright with having our ranch meeting tonight at your house?" I would like to leave in the morning and I probably should take Orville with me so that if that stallion comes along I will have some help keeping our string of horses."

"Sure, that's fine. We can make a list for you at the meeting, and Orville can help dicker with the Major on price. He claims to have experience in that area."

"Jed, he is rough on the edges but so far he has been able to do everything that he claimed."

"That's true. I am heading to the house for a minute and I will tell Beth about the meeting tonight instead of tomorrow."

Josh had gone out to tell the boys to bring in the riding horses and he came back, ready to help move the horses from the far fields. Jed had motioned to Orville and talked to him. He told him that he was needed to help move horses and why. Orville got quite excited hoping that Jed and Ben were planning on trapping some of the mustangs.

"No Orville, not at this time. Don't worry you can't work yourself out of a job here. Ben wants you to go to the settlement with him in the morning to escort a string of horses. With the wild herd in the vicinity, one man is not enough to keep our horses safe."

"Well that's fine. I won't mind doing that at all. How many are we taking?"

"Ben said a dozen would be enough for now."

CHAPTER ELEVEN
GOD PROVIDES

As the men worked steadily, the walls became taller.

Soon square frames appeared in the front wall for windows and a doorway was created using the first of the planks that David had purchased from Father Bob. Two men worked at making shutters for the window frames and Two Feathers shared with David that none of them would have been much help if they had not learned a bit of carpentry while helping to build the addition on the People's Church.

David watched as Night Hawk coaxed Brownie and Buck to pull a log up the ramp and hold it steady while it was pegged into place. They were making his cabin taller than he had envisioned. There would be plenty of room for a loft.

While their men worked, the women became more comfortable with Sarah and the surroundings.

"Sarah we should take a lantern and go back a ways to see where the cave goes and what is in it. Two Feathers and I thought we were going to live in a cave once. We put our things in there and investigated a bit. It had a sparkling room of crystals, like this one. That's where I got this." She touched her necklace and then continued her story. "The mountain had an opening that wrapped around a folded wall that revealed a beautiful meadow with marvelous old trees with feathery foliage. We thought we had found the Garden of Eden. It was just the opposite. Our cave was inside of a talking mountain.

Soon after we moved in, Two Feathers had to leave me and Water Bug so that he could find our Chief and send him to the spirit world.

As soon as he left, the mountain began to rumble and the cave became hot. Steam poured out of the walls and the mountain shook. Our horses had all been in that beautiful green meadow, enclosed by rock walls. I started to lead them out but they ran past me frightened by falling rocks and kept going. I put Water Bug in his harness on an old mare we called Grandmother, so that he would be safe while I carried all our stuff out of the cave. We had large sacks of wild grain, corn and dried meat for the winter. By the time I went back the third time the floor of the cave was so hot that it burned my feet.

When I got all our belongings carried out into the open, the mountain sent ash and dust into the air making it hard to see or breathe. I ran through the trees but I couldn't find our horses and I thought I had lost Water Bug. It was so awful. I was petrified.

Finally I prayed and cried and prayed some more and then I heard him making a happy sound on Grandmother's back. I found our horses and caught most of them and the mountain was pouring out fire. After I had all of the packs and sacks tied on, we hurried away as fast as we could with the fire burning the trees chasing us. The wind was pushing the fire until I asked God to help us. The horses were all tired from running and the fire was gaining on us. God reversed the direction of the wind and pushed it back the way it had come, away from us."

Clover was leaning forward with wide eyes of concern. She had not heard that story.

"It's alright Clover," said Sarah. This cave doesn't make a sound. We are all safe here and I will tell you how I know this is true."

Sarah spoke softly but with conviction.

"The day that we arrived here, Father Bob and Brother Tim were with us. Brother Tim owns this land with the cave on it. He said we could stay in it until our cabin was ready. They had been to the settlement and had a big load of lumber. David asked them to let us buy it and they did. So they brought the big wagon here for us.

Most of the people that you met at the ranch had come with us that first time. Only Mary had stayed at the ranch with the littlest children. The men had to work hard to bring the small wagons from the ranch across the river. They built the raft that day. When everyone and all the small wagons were on this side, Brother Tim led the way through the trees to the cave. When the rest of us came around the boulders and trees and saw the cave, we also saw Father Bob and Brother Tim kneeling. We all knelt!

Above us on the bluff was the image of the Lion of Judah. It looked like he had ripped open the bluff and revealed the cave for us. The sun was going down and as the rays fell behind the trees the image disappeared. I want to see it again but it seems that I am always busy somewhere else or the sky is cloudy or it is raining. Maybe I'm not supposed to see it again, I don't know. But it was very awesome and special. I feel we are blessed and protected here."

The women were silent. Nothing they could say would add to the two stories they had just heard. Finally Clover whispered.

"That explains why we can feel the peacefulness of the whole area."

"Yes, this is a special place. We all have commented about it," said Sheltah. "I would like to go explore with you."

Sarah shook her head no.

"I don't think that is for us to do. I know Brother Tim and David went back a little way, but they found the floor was wet and soft. David said he thought that it might be quite dangerous. I do have an idea though that I think you would all enjoy. Ben invited as many of you as would like to come back to the ranch, to see the new foals. One was born the night of the fire and several others are due."

Willow was enthusiastic.

"I would like to go, and we all have horses here. We should take our own food though. That was a lot to ask of the women at the ranch. They managed to make a meal that fed everyone," said Cumae.

Let's take a couple of big gathering baskets," said Sarah. "We can gather whatever we see along the way." David thought it was a fine idea and said that the men were quite capable of feeding themselves.

"Sarah, if you leave in the morning, it will give you time enough today to make a big tub of the chili that I like. The men will like it too and we can eat whenever we need to."

"Sure David, that sounds like a good plan." Sarah made the chili and Willow and Clover made two huge baskets of crackers.

Sheltah had noticed the forms that Sarah had baking in the sun and asked if she could tap out the bricks and refill them. She went to the river and came back with a big pan of clay mixed with wire grass clippings. She showed Sarah what she was doing.

"This will stay strong for many years," said Sheltah. "I love working with clay. This is good to make the oven but it has too much sand in it to make pots. It would crumble."

When the women wandered over to see the progress on the house, they saw that three huge logs were being stripped of their bark.

"Two Feathers, what are those going to be used for?" Willow asked.

"These will go across the ceiling to support the loft."

"They will be beautiful with all the bark removed."

"They will put three more upright. This cabin is going to last a very long time. I would like to build us a cabin like this one day." Willow was surprised to hear him say that. She thought that Two Feathers was not a person to change his traditions easily.

"Even better than a cabin, would be to live in that cave. Did anyone tell you what happened the day they arrived here?"

"Yes, Sarah told all of the women about seeing the image. I would like to explore this cave with you. When I suggested it earlier, Sarah was not in favor of it."

"She said that it should be done by men."

"She is right. David said that he and Tim found a soft sandstone floor where they went and that is as far as they got. They didn't take a lantern or rope, just a torch and it was really dark. Maybe I can get a chance to take a look before we leave."

"Oh, I hope so Two Feathers. It looks like it could be big enough for all the People of the Lion."

"What are you thinking? It belongs to Brother Tim. We can't just move in there."

"Who knows? Maybe we can someday," she said with a grin.

*****

"Thank you Beth, you work magic in the kitchen, said Ben. Orville agreed and happily carried a box of fresh supplies for the lake cabin that included a soft loaf of bread and a batch of sugar cookies made just for him.

"Easy Tinkle, while I get this balanced. There we go. Just go slow and then I won't drop it."

"He talks to that horse like she understands every word," said Jed. "He talks to all of them that way. When he is working on one of the mustangs he is jabbering the whole time."

"I think that's a good thing. I talk to Ginger a lot when I am near her. She seems to like it."

Beth had stacked the plates and submerged them in the sink of soap and water. The glasses and silverware were already rinsed and draining on a towel.

"Does anyone want more tea or coffee while I get Lily ready for bed?"

"I'll pour it right after I help myself to another piece of that apple pie," said Josh. "You and Mom are the best bakers in the whole world, Aunt Beth."

"I am glad to hear that Josh. I wouldn't want to think you are taking seconds just to make me feel good." Everyone laughed as she and Mary took the children in to get them washed and into their pajamas.

Suddenly Orville was banging on the front door.

"What's the matter Orville?"

"It's that wild stallion. He is down there trying hard to stomp his way into the field where we just put your mustangs. He is kicking the section that has the latches and I think he remembers that it went down last time he was here. You said you had him in the long pen for a while, well he seems to think that you owe him a batch of mares and he is aiming to collect!"

"Thanks Orville for being alert. Let's go see if we can talk him out of a few more wives." Big Boy had proven his ability to hold his own against this very stallion. Ben saddled him swiftly, knowing that Big Boy was no longer in his prime.

"Don't worry Big Boy; he is older, too."

Orville said for Ben to relax.

"Tinkle has done this before."

"Done What, Orville?"

"She and I will lead that big stallion toward the field when you drop the first fence. Josh if you will stand ready to let me through the gate in the second fence when I come, we will have him and all his new wives in the long pen again."

Ben, you and Jed need to bring that fence up and latch it as soon as the last mare crosses it. He will quickly figure out that he has made the same mistake again and he will be coming at you full speed. Josh, be sure that you are in the field when you close the gate. We don't want you in the long pen with that fierce monster. He would kill you for sure."

"Orville, you sound like you have trapped wild herds before."

"That's one of the things I have done many times. Its job security," he said causing the men to laugh. "I have been riding the saddle ready mustangs along your fences until I know this ranch as well as you do, and I knew when we put the mustangs here that he would come for them. It is just far enough from human activity that it makes him feel safe."

Orville's plan went like clockwork and their timing was perfect. Ben and Jed laughed at the way Tinkle lured that stallion into the long pen. She swished her tail, strutted her stuff, until he followed her. He was trapped before he could change his focus from Tinkle to the heavy section of fence closing behind his herd. Orville and Tinkle dashed through the gate in the second fence and it was all over. Josh closed the gate and latched it as the angry stallion barreled at it full speed. He raised his head and hit the gate with his chest as if he were a battering ram. The wood splintered sending a spear flying through the air. Josh dove into the mud behind the water trough as the horse ran victoriously passed into the field followed by his herd.

Ben yelled for Josh and Orville to get out of there.

"Josh climb out! Get out of there!"

Using the side of the water trough to boost himself up, Josh leapt over the top and was out of harm's way. Orville rode to the trough hoping that he could exit the field as Josh had. The Stallion wasn't ready to allow that. He thundered across the grass and reared as he approached Orville. Tinkle was not the object of his rage, but she interpreted his actions that way. She whirled and kicked at him with both her hind feet. As she did that she unseated Orville and he landed hard. The stallion spied his opportunity and that would have been the end of Orville had Ben not opened what was left of the shattered gate and allowed Big Boy to enter. Unfettered by saddle or bridle, Big Boy raced the short distance to challenge his adversary, while Orville and Tinkle made a hasty exit. Jed had retrieved hammer and nails and was quickly nailing the thickest supports they had to the gate. Ben brought a partial roll of box fencing from beside the long pen and they cut it the length of the gate and used that to further strengthen it.

"Let's wind some branches through it, too, just to make it look more solid," suggested Orville. The four of them stood behind the gate watching as the two huge stallions circled and reared, pawing and biting. Oddly enough, the wild stallion turned and ran to the far acres of the meadow and stood there pawing the ground like an angry bull, with his sides heaving. Ben unlatched the repaired gate and coaxed Big Boy to come out, but he was still very disturbed and not ready to call this confrontation over. The stallion remembered him and had given up before Big Boy was satisfied that he had really beaten him. Without notice Orville rode into the field beside Big Boy and talked to him. He patted his neck and literally crowded him sideways with Tinkle and slowly they came out together.

"Orville that was amazing!"

"I didn't do it, Tinkle did. She gets the boys to go where she wants them to, every time."

Jed looked at the field and shook his head.

"That big guy thinks he has what he came for. He has his herd and our mustangs in there with him. He hasn't figured out yet that he can't get out of there. The fence is too high to sail over and if he did he would find himself all alone in the long pen."

"I think I will take that string of horses to the fort in the morning," said Ben. "At least we know that he is not going to bother me along the way. Orville you can remain here at the ranch and help Jed to keep an eye on our new horses. They have plenty of fresh grass in that field, just keep the trough full of good water, and don't turn your back on him. I don't think you are one of his favorite people." Orville chuckled.

"I don't think that stallion likes anyone. That's not a horse I would want to work with. He has had too many years of experience running free."

Ben nodded agreement as he saddled Big Boy and scratched his ears and talked to him making sure that he had calmed enough to ride. Orville headed for the lake cabin and Jed and Ben stopped at Jed's corral long enough to check the twelve horses that Orville had put there for morning.

"We will be able to tell in the morning if they are as gentled as he thinks," said Ben. "They are a good looking lot. We should get enough money for them to pay for the logs we will need."

"Josh, would you go tell your Aunt Beth that we are back and that we will be in soon?"

"Sure Uncle Jed, but are we still going to have our meeting?" Ben looked at Jed for agreement and then said yes, but that it was getting late so they should probably keep it short.

While they were trapping the wild horses, the sounds had carried to the two barns and surrounding area. Star and

Blaze stood in their stalls with their new foals looking unsettled. Ben and Jed each stroked the mares and offered them grain and talked in a soothing manner until they seemed calmer.

"I need to take a quick look at the mares in my barn. I want to know they are alright, too," said Ben

"I'll come with you," said Jed. "I have been thinking of names for the foals and I was hoping you would like "Comet" for Star's baby."

"That is a good name for her. I like it. That will be quite impressive on the paperwork. I can see it now, "Flying Comet, out of Star Shining, sired by Dart Away of the S. and J. Ranch."

"We need to come up with something as suitable for Blaze's foal. Yes, and it looks like we will need one for Silk's too. Look at that beautiful golden baby girl! She is gorgeous and Silk did it all by herself. I think Ginger looks like a very proud grandmother."

"She sure does, but our white mares are still holding out on us. Well, maybe they will come tomorrow."

After giving them all some attention and grain, the men walked together around the lake to Beth and Jed's house.

Beth and Mary had gotten all the youngsters asleep and made a new pot of coffee. In the middle of the table sat a platter covered with jam filled cookies.

As soon as the men had washed their hands and taken a seat, Mary said, "This meeting is in session. Last time we talked about the two pieces of land that need improvements. Ben, here is a pencil and piece of paper so that you can write down all that you will need to do in town. Are you still planning on leaving tomorrow? Josh told us that you had actually trapped that big stallion and his entire herd in with the rest of our wild mustangs."

"Yes, I want to go and get things in motion. We have a lot to accomplish before snow flies. We did trap that stallion again but I really don't want to deal with him. Big Boy challenged him again, but the whole thing didn't take long. I am grateful that it gave Orville time to come out of the gate with Tinkle. The stallion backed down and went to the bluff at the far end of the field. Make sure that all the children stay away from that meadow. He is mean spirited and would hurt them. He broke through the gate like it was made of twigs."

Mary shuttered and continued.

"I'm just glad none of you were hurt. Ben you have to order logs for three cabins."

"Three? No Honey, just two."

"Remember when they surveyed our land; Sarah's cabin is on ours, so you need to build one on hers."

"Our house is half on her land. I think that counts," suggested Ben.

"No Ben it doesn't. I talked to the man at the land office, last time Beth and I went to the settlement, and the whole building must be on the land and twenty feet from the property line," said Jed.

"That's all bad news. Alright I will tell Tom we need logs for three cabins, one by the clearing, with a pump and well pipe for the Parker place, the second on Beth's prairie piece opposite the house and a pump and pipe for that and a third for Sarah's land, with a pump and pipe for that too. We can't do all that! It's impossible!"

Jed was frowning.

"Ben it does sound like things are getting to be more than we can handle. We need to get a crew of men that know how to build. David has two pair of big work horses that will be available after his cabin is done, but men cost money. We will have to get some more of the rough mustangs ready. We have at least six mustang foals out there. It is not in our best interest to sell our prime mares. We need to think about it."

"I will tell Tom the locations and that we need two loads of logs at each. I think I will tell him that we want just one window each for those cabins. Then I need to find Calvin and tell him David needs a fireplace before winter."

"We need you to stop at the Trading Post and get us a lot of canning jars and jelly jars," said Beth.

"How many is a lot?"

"Six dozen jelly jars, and six dozen quart size would do for this year and we will add to them next year. I will give you a list. We have been jotting things down that we will need, like sugar for the jam and boxes of pectin."

"What's that Mom?"

"It is a white powder that when mixed into the boiling jam, it helps it set up. Josh that reminds me, we will need paraffin wax, too, to seal them. Write that on my list son."

"That stuff is fun when it is soft. I like to chew on it."

"Ben have you got all that down on your list so far?"

"I think so. Order logs for three cabins and stuff for three wells, and three windows. Go to see Sam with your list and find Calvin. Is there anything else?"

"No, this is not for your list, but what are we going to do about that ugly black part of the river. Many of the trees are black on the sides or bottom but still green on one side when you look up higher."

"Josh, I think we will be able to tell by next spring which trees are dead and those we will need to cut down to make the area safe. Time will heal the area."

"I am glad that Tim plowed that area at the side of our house. I think I want to move some raspberry bushes and blackberry bushes there."

"That's a good idea Beth. That way you can get the berries before the birds and bears do," said Jed. "That's another job for this fall, after the first frost."

"Is there anything else? If not lets close this meeting with prayer," said Mary. "Jed, would you lead us in the Our Father?"

He stood with his hands folded for a moment before he spoke.

"Father this meeting was about activities and on-going work, but it is also about our stewardship of the things that you have given us as blessings. We all thank you that you brought the Blue Stone People here to fight the fire. We are glad to meet them and make friends of them. Thank you that the fire was put out swiftly and no one was injured. Thank you for protecting our growing ranch and all the beautiful animals on it. Help us to have wisdom as we care for them each day. Watch over us and help us to solve the problem of the wild stallion. Be with Ben as he goes tomorrow with the mustangs to the fort. Please keep him safe and bring him back successfully. "Our Father in heaven, hallowed be your name, your kingdom come, your will be done on earth as it is in heaven. Give us today our daily bread. Forgive us our debts, as we also have forgiven our debtors, and lead us not into temptation, but deliver us from the evil one. Matt 6: 9-13 NIV

"Amen."

Ben smiled at Mary and kissed her on the forehead as he slid up on the seat of their small wagon beside her. All their boys were in the back on a bed of hay. Josh yawned widely as they pulled up near the door of their house. He jumped down and took Natty in his arms and waited for Mary to open the door. He tucked him in his bed and then said a soft "goodnight" and went to his own bed. Ben carried Eli in and laughed as he saw Mary through the front window, trying to wake Adam enough to get him to walk in the house to his bed.

Ben and Jed were up at dawn and found that Orville was already bringing the horses out of Jed's corral and fastening them to a long line.

"Good morning Orville. I will be taking Jed's wagon and pulling it with Sundown. What do you think would be the best way to lead these guys with the wagon?"

"Let's make three lines. One on each back corner and the third in the middle of the back, but why are you taking a wagon? They won't like following that thing."

"I need to pick up a few things that won't fit on the back of my saddle horse. Let's just string them out so they aren't crowded. They will figure it out," said Ben. "Do you need anything from town?"

"No, as long as I have food and clothes on my back and my Tinkle, then I don't need much else."

"As soon as we get a bundle of hay in that wagon and my satchel that Mary packed for me, I can be on my way," said Ben.

"We will keep a sharp eye on the stallion, and the boys will do their chores with a little reminding. Don't worry about the ranch. Oh, I forgot last night at the meeting. You should see about getting a few essentials for Sarah's cabin, so when we get furniture in there, it will be useable. I cut a bunch of willow for chairs. Maybe I can still use it if it hasn't dried out," said Jed.

"I thought of that myself after I got in bed. I better add a note to the list right now. I don't know for sure how we stand with Sam on our account, but he knows that we will be there with a wagon load after the garden harvest."

Jed helped to ferry the little wagon across the river and the three strings of horses were led across one string at a time and fastened to the wagon. None of them objected to wading across the river. That was another sign that Orville had schooled them thoroughly. Ben waved as he pulled away slowly. He was eager to be underway. His head was whirling with the jobs they had planned in the meeting.

*****

"Have I got everything?"

"Sarah, if you take anything else that packhorse will get sway backed," said David. "Who would think that one tiny little girl would need that much stuff?"

"It is not all for Pili. We are taking gathering baskets, blankets, bedrolls, food packs and water bags, too." The women were amused by Sarah's efforts to be sure they would want for nothing. They headed out to the prairie and followed the trail down river. The path of the heavy wagons bringing the logs was visible and the many horses of the people had worn a path. Sheltah giggled as she handed out portions of sweet dried fruit mixed with nuts.

"The men do not need to know everything we do," said Sheltah.

"If that is your goal, we should have left Water Bug with the men," said Clover. He gives Two Feathers a full report of his day whether he wants it or not." They all heard the remark and laughed.

"Cumae, does Obona tell Soren everything that happens during your day?"

"No, she was taught the rules of the Abalinah. They do not say what they have done or where they have been. It is accepted that they simply are serving the people, but it is not talked about. It was Chief Gray Fox's law."

"Now that you say that, I have noticed that Singing Cricket is that way, too. It is difficult to get her to tell me what she did when she was with the story mothers. She must have learned that rule without me teaching it to her. I don't know if that is a good thing or not."

"Clover, I don't think it is good. A child should always answer their mother truthfully. That is something we can work on together with her when we get back to the camp of the people," said Willow.

Sarah slid off her horse, picked several plants dropping them in one of the baskets and got back up.

"What did you pick?"

"It is medicine. Good for a poultice when a person gets a burn or cut."

They spotted the wild raspberry bushes and got down, picking great handfuls for their baskets and eating many as they picked.

"If we pick some of the grain, we can cook it for breakfast and add the berries. They have milk and sugar at the ranch. Cooked grain is delicious with them on it."

"Considering all the stops we made, we have come a long way. I can see the big oak tree ahead," said Willow. Just then they heard three loud clangs of the bell.

"What is that sound?" Sheltah asked.

"The lookout is letting everyone at the ranch know that he sees family coming." Mary came to the crossing with her little boys in the wagon. Her first thought was that Ben had returned for some reason. Her face went from concern to an expression of delight when she saw Sarah riding Moon Boy and leading the packhorse across the river. Adam came down cautiously from the lookout post, but hit the ground running. He met Sarah with a tight squeeze as soon as she got down from Moon Boy. Water Bug slid down from Grandmother to greet Adam. The two headed for Jed's barn. Clover gave a shrill whistle and they both stopped.

"Where are you going?"

"Mama Two, Adam says they have new foals in the barn and he said I can see them."

"Alright, but stay away from the back legs of the mothers, and absolutely no playing in any water without permission."

They each gave her a big smile and were gone in a flash.

Beth had looked out her window and saw Sarah and the four women she had brought to visit. She had been kneading bread dough and hurried to wash her hands.

"Lily, come with me to the crossing, Aunt Sarah is here and she has brought some of the Indian ladies to visit."

Beth rode with Lily in front of her to the crossing. Jed lifted Lily down and she and Singing Cricket hugged like long lost friends and started jabbering together right away. Obona wanted to be included but was shy. Singing Cricket took her hand and the three girls moved toward Beth's house where Lily was taking them.

"Girls, stay away from the water and don't go in the barn to see the horses without a grown up with you."

Beth grinned at Clover.

"It sounds like you have got this mothering thing figured out."

"It is hard to keep track of them and to know they are safe."

Mary took Pili and tucked her into the hay in the little wagon. Beth did the same with Freedom.

"Let's all go up to my house for a cup of tea," said Mary.

"Please would you mind all coming to my house instead? I have dough in the pans rising for the oven and the girls ran in the front door and I am sure they are playing dolls in Lily's room."

"That's fine," they all agreed.

Sarah suddenly realized that she felt different being there as a guest or visitor.

"Have the men found the time to make furniture for my cabin yet?"

"No, they have been too busy to do it. We need to get the basics in there so that we can use it for a family to live in. We need help here more than you can imagine," answered Beth.

"I hope you will excuse me ladies," said Jed, "but I need to do some chores. I will see you later Sarah." Jed gave her a quick hug and headed toward the milk barn but Beth noticed that he detoured long enough to check on the boys in the horse barn.

Water Bug was sitting beside Blazes' sleeping foal in the hay stroking its neck gently. Adam was standing near Blaze talking to her and scratching her ears. All seemed calm, so he continued on his way to the cow barn.

Johnny had been given the job of cleaning the cow barn and had not left to greet the visitors.

"Dad, I looked out and saw that Aunt Sarah is here and she brought some of the Indian women with her. I thought that it would be best for me to finish in here before I went to say hello to her."

"Thanks son, it looks like you are almost finished. It is a good thing that the cows get plenty to eat in the fields because when I checked the loft this morning it is getting nearly empty. Just put down a little for them to chew on during the milking this evening."

"Dad, what are we going to do with all the manure? The pile behind the barn is getting really big?"

"When we go to the settlement next time you should go with me. Sam has a catalog at the Trading Post with all sorts of things in it that can be ordered. One of the sections is all farm equipment. There is a machine that our horses can pull that spreads that manure on the field and then it gets it away from here and serves the purpose of enriching the soil."

"Can we order one? When can we go?"

"Well, Johnny I think that you should attend our next ranch meeting and suggest it."

"Really, I can be at the meeting. Mom always makes me go to bed."

"I wish we had that machine right now, but we don't need any more jobs before the fall," said Jed. "I know that it would be good to get that pile away from here but maybe after the last snow, we can do that and by then I hope that we have our other projects done."

"What projects Dad?"

"Well we made a mistake when we built Sarah's cabin and it is sitting on the edge of Ben's land so the man at the land office said we have to have a cabin built and a well dug on Sarah's land by next spring, or we will lose that land."

"What land?"

"The land where the long pen is and the field along the bluff where the wild mustangs are right now, that's all technically hers."

"Gee Dad that is strange that some man can tell us to build another cabin just because it is not exactly where they want it. Josh said that we have to build a cabin on the Parker place, too. We do have a lot of projects!"

"That looks clean now Johnny. That's a good job Son. I will finish the work in here and you should check with Mom to see if she needs help with anything. Did Ben's barn get cleaned yesterday? Silk had her foal. Have you seen it? She is beautiful."

"I didn't know Dad. We were all busy. I know that Adam and I were supposed to do the chickens, but then Uncle Ben sent word for us to bring all the riding horses to the corrals. Is it alright if I go see the new foal now?"

"Sure Son. We need to start thinking of a name for her. Hi Josh. I was wondering where you were. Johnny is on his way to check the other barns and make sure that the chickens have been cared for today. Silk had her foal late yesterday. Have you seen her? She is solid golden tan. That's very unusual. I don't know if your mom or Aunt Beth has heard about her. You can pass the word if you want to."

"What about the white mares?"

"Still no babies, but I think we are really close. Do you think you can help me make some furniture today? I cut that pile of willow just before the fire and it is drying out."

"Sure, I will help with the chickens and peek at Silk's baby and then come back to the lake. You will probably be starting by then."

"Thanks Josh."

CHAPTER TWELVE
THE WATERWAY

Adam and Water Bug peered through the front window, standing on tiptoes so they wouldn't step on the few remaining flowers. Beth had not been able to replace the ones that the horse had eaten.

The boys came in the door quietly, seeing the sleeping babies on the bear rug.

"Mom we want to go fishing. Is it alright? We will use the platform that Dad made and be careful." Clover and Willow looked at each other and laughed.

"Mary can Adam swim well?"

"Yes, he has learned because the lake is here and the river. We felt it was safer if he knew how."

"Do you think he would like to go swimming?" Mary was puzzled but said it was up to him.

"Water Bug, did you want to show Adam your way of fishing?" He grinned and nodded.

"We will come down to the water for a little while so you boys can catch us our supper." Willow asked Beth for a big empty basket.

"With luck, they will get enough for all of us."

"I like your optimism," said Mary.

Beth glanced at the oven and sleeping babies and said she would stay there. Adam led the way to the platform with two poles in his hands. He laid them down intending to dig a few worms, but Water Bug didn't wait. He walked to the edge of the water and waded in. He circled the edge staying near the reeds and ducked down. "What is he doing? He looks like he is sitting under the water," said Mary. Cumae, Clover and Willow knew what he was doing.

When his head came to the surface he took a quiet breath and submerged again. They waited observing.

Finally he popped up with a large sunfish in his hands. Willow had the basket ready. The women applauded.

"How did you do that? Will you teach me?" Adam walked in slowly, knowing that disturbing the water would send the fish away. Water Bug explained.

"When I see a fish that I want to catch I move very slowly and just tickle their tummy and they act like they go to sleep, then I put my fingers in their gills and bring them out."

"That's amazing. I want to try."

"You have to move very slowly and be quiet."

Adam saw a big catfish enter the reeds. It sat there in the shade seeming to be resting. Its tail moved slightly, but the fish didn't go forward. When Adam brought his hand up under it the fish abruptly swam away.

"What happened?"

"You have to be gentle. He can't know that you are tickling until you have done it many times so he gets used to it." Water Bug was doing his best to explain how it was done to Adam. "Watch me under the water." After two tries Water Bug had another fish in the basket. Adam tried again. He had learned that the most important element was gentle patience. This time he was successful. The women applauded and cheered his achievement. They were having as much fun as the boys. Lily, Singing Cricket and Obona came out of the house when they heard the cheering.

"I want to swim-fish, too, Mama," said Obona. "You know I can do it." Beth had been watching out the window and hurried down the steps with a cotton shirt for her to put on in place of her leather tunic.

"If you let her in the water she can use this, but please don't allow Lily in. She doesn't swim very well." She could see that Clover was holding Cricket tightly on her lap and had no intention of letting her near the water. Cumae formed a visual shield between Obona and the boys and slipped the shirt on her.

"Be careful, Obona and just have fun," said Cumae. Water Bug moved farther down the edge of the lake, knowing that another person in the water would send the fish away from that area. He was surprised when she popped up beside him laughing.

"You swim very well; can you catch fish, too?"

"Yes, I learned at our old camp that got the bright light. It made us go away."

"Did you have a lake like this one?"

"No, our lake was very big and cold, but it had a lot of big fish in it. Many people caught fish with their hands." She ducked under and Water Bug waited for her to come back up near him, but she didn't. She had smoothly moved under the platform and when she came out near her mother she had the largest fish so far! Once again the women had cause to applaud and cheer.

Lily and Cricket were whining. They wanted to go in the water, too. Sarah volunteered to take the two little girls to visit the foals in Jed's barn. She was eager to see Dart Away's off spring. It was a hit with the girls and their mothers. Both mares were used to a lot of attention. They simply stood and watched as the girls smiled and stroked their new babies.

Tears came to Sarah's eyes when she looked up to see Dash Away standing in the back doorway. Although just a yearling, he was like his father in every way. Sarah wasn't sure how tame he was, but she should have known that he had received attention and love from everyone that entered the barn.

Just then Orville stuck his head in the back door.

"Howdy miss; you are Ben's sister, aren't you?"

"Yes, I am Sarah."

"I am Orville. I didn't mean to disturb your fun with the children; I just came to check on the mares and their new foals. Have you seen the ones in the other barn? There are two there and one expected any time now. I'm heading over there to stay till she has it. You're welcome to come on over if you want to."

"Thank you. We may be there in a little while."

He put his arm around the young horse's neck and led Dash Away to the side field that had been his father's domain and came back just long enough to explain and close the back door.

"That young fellow has a lot of energy. He needs to be out where he has space to run. Oh, and it might not be wise to take the children near the far field by the bluff. We just trapped a wild stallion and his herd and they are in there. I wouldn't want him to charge the fence and frighten anyone."

"Thank you, Orville.

When Sarah led the girls back to the group of women, she found that Pili was in Willow's lap and Freedom was awake too and being nursed by her mother. Cricket moved close to Clover and started talking about the baby horses. Clover smiled and responded that she would like to see them, too. Sarah took Pili and sat in the shade to nurse her.

The three clever children had done well. The basket was overflowing with fish. Water Bug hopped up on the platform beside Adam and Obona.

"Adam, why is the water back there all stirring and muddy?" Water Bug asked. "What makes it that way?"

"I don't know. I never paid any attention to it. We always fish and swim here by the platform."

Water Bug jumped in and headed toward the roiling water. He came to the surface and then disappeared. Willow was the first to show concern.

"Where is he? I can't see Water Bug! He has been down too long!" They waited still longer. Finally Cumae ran down the bank and dove in near the churning, muddy water.

"The children are tired. We should not have let him go back in." Clover was shaking and Willow was starting to cry. Sheltah stood and she too was ready to go in the water when Cumae bobbed to the surface with her hand holding the back of Water Bugs shirt and pushing him up, above the water. The boy was coughing and so was she.

"Water Bug, what happened to you?" Clover had pulled him out of the water and was holding him tightly.

"Put him down Clover. Lay him down on the platform."

Cumae spoke with authority and Clover responded. Instantly Cumae rolled him on his stomach and pushed on his back helping him to get more of the muddy water from his lungs. Beth brought a blanket and towels and eventually things calmed down.

"Tell us what happened to you, Water Bug." Sarah wanted to know what had caused this very good swimmer to lose control under the water.

"The muddy water is made by a strong push of water coming into the lake. I tried to swim into the hole to see where the water was coming from but I only got a little ways before it pushed me back and twisted me around. I couldn't find the hole to come back out! I couldn't breathe in there! I thought there would be a little air at the top, but there wasn't. It was awful. Mama Two, my chest hurts."

"Beth I'll come with you in the house. We need to make him some medicine. Cumae needs it, too, or they will get very sick." Sarah hurried along the path and all the women and children followed her. Sheltah had the presence of mind to bring the fish and stepped in the front door just long enough to get a knife from Beth. She took the fish to the edge of the river and cleaned them.

Later, with both Water Bug and Cumae asleep after taking the strong medicine that Sarah had made, the rest of the women sat at Beth's table enjoying tea and slices of the freshly baked bread, with her first batch of blackberry jam.

Beth started a large kettle of vegetable beef soup for the evening meal. Johnny came in long enough to give his Aunt Sarah a hug and said that he and Jed were going down to check on the stallion and his herd. Beth cut him two slices of the bread and coated it generously with the jam.

"Give one to your Dad, and remind him to be careful, Son."

"Thanks Mom, I will.

"Mary, when did Ben leave for the settlement?"

"Sarah, you missed him by just a few hours. He took Beth's wagon and twelve horses for the fort. I don't expect him back until late tomorrow. He had a lot of things to do."

"I'm sorry we missed him and certainly very sorry that Water Bug and Cumae have swallowed that churning water. I hope they will be alright."

Josh tapped on the door and stepped in to bring the happy news that Ben's barn now held Silk's baby and two brand new white foals.

"You ladies should come see them. They are so beautiful. Orville stayed in there with them, but they really didn't need him. Silk's baby came yesterday and the first white one was during the night. The second one was born a little bit ago. It isn't even standing up yet."

Beth handed him a thick slice of the bread and jam and said they would come to the barn to see it as soon as Water Bug and Cumae woke up.

Sheltah brought the basket of pan-ready fish into the kitchen and accepted praise from Beth.

"Sheltah, these will be delicious, thanks for cleaning them. We can have them with the soup I have cooking and we still have a lot of fresh bread. We seldom have fish. None of us know Water Bug and Obona's quick way of fishing"

"Thank you Beth, I am sorry that our visit is making you more work. We all enjoy being here. Your ranch is lovely."

Beth poured her a cup of tea and cut another slice of the bread, placing the jam and a knife near her plate.

After they wake up, we will all go see the new foals.

"I hope that they feel better after sleeping," she said.

The women chatted and Mary said she would have to see the foals later.

"I need to put these boys down for their naps. Beth I will bake a cake for supper. I'll see you all later."

She drove the sleepy boys back in her little wagon. Sarah placed Pili on the big bear rug to play, and stepped out on the front porch. She had a strange feeling that something wasn't quite right.

When she walked across the grass to the edge of the lake, her eyes were drawn to something tumbling in the water on the other side. Sarah ran to the spot that Cumae had entered and without thinking about it she dove in and grabbed the fur as it rolled past her. With two hard strokes of her free hand she was in the shallow water and was better able to support the poor baby wolf. She hollered for help. She couldn't get it to breathe. How could she get here? She wondered.

Jed came running and the women poured out of the house. He thought as soon as he knelt that the little wolf was not going to revive. He pressed on its chest and blew into its nostrils. Suddenly the little thing struggled to get air. He pressed again and water trickled out of its mouth and it gasp for air and began to pant making a harsh sound. Sarah picked up the little gray wolf and squealed with joy that he had saved her life.

"Jed, how could she get here? They didn't follow us. I would have seen them. We stopped several times." Cumae came out of the house with Water Bug.

"Sarah, I think that cave you are in has an opening to an underground river. It must surface in our lake," said Jed "I think if we search for it, we can find the place where it goes back under, maybe on the other side beneath the willows. That's why the water seems to always be stirring here. Ben and I thought that the lake was fed by a big spring or maybe two."

When Tim and David went in the cave they said that the ground got soft and sloped down. Your wolf pups wouldn't know to stay back. This one must have slipped in. That is a long distance to be carried underground. She must have been able to bob to the surface and get air some of the time."

"I just hope the other two didn't fall in, too," said Sarah. "There is so much work being done that no one has been watching them. David promised that he would put food and water by their den tonight. This poor little girl almost died."

Beth came out and stood beside Sarah with a towel. She wrapped the small wolf in it and took it in her arms.

"It's one of your wolf pups! How did it get here?"

"We suspect that she and her littermates found an opening to an underground river in the cave. We think that the hole that pours water into the lake over there is part of it. It has to travel out somewhere or the lake would overflow."

"Sarah, should we try to give this poor baby some of the medicine you made?"

"Yes, she has water in her lungs. Bring her near the house. She needs food, too. She must have been struggling for hours, trying to survive." Sarah took the wet wolf and put her on the grass by the steps. She sat down beside her and stroked her and talked soothingly. Beth brought out a cup and spoon with a small amount of the medicine in it. She also had a bowl with some of the soup and a fork. She sat next to Sarah mashing the meat and vegetables in the soup while Sarah dosed the pup with several teaspoons of the medicine.

"This is just warm now. She can have it. Beth set the bowl of soup down beside the pup, but she didn't want to eat. She crawled into Sarah's wet lap and cuddled there shivering. Not until then did Sarah notice that she was as wet as the little wolf. She rubbed her lap with the towel and placed the pup on the dry grass.

"Beth, do you have some clothes that I can borrow?"

"Of course we can find something that will work."

"We had two near drownings in that lake in one day and both because of that waterway. I am going to fence it off so that all the children stay away from it," said Jed. Josh and I have to do the milking and some other chores before supper, or I would do it now but right after the milking in the morning we will put a barrier in there." He whistled shrilly and Adam came down from the lookout post.

"Did you need me Uncle Jed?

"I need to know if you remembered to take care of all the chickens, today."

"I took them feed and water and brought in the eggs, but I didn't clean the pens because we have company."

"Promise that you will do it tomorrow without being reminded."

"I will, I won't forget, Uncle Jed."

"Good Boy!"

"Water Bug, how are you feeling?"

"I have a sore throat and my chest hurts and I am sleepy," he answered with a gravelly voice.

"Cumae, how are you?"

"I feel well, but I do feel sleepy."

"I think that the medicine makes you feel tired. Sarah will probably suggest that you both take more."

"Ladies, if you would like to, I think it is time that we all went to see the new foals in Ben's barn. Follow me."

Jed was smiling when he entered. Orville was a good choice when they hired him. The barn was immaculate. The new mothers all had hay and grain and fresh water. The women were impressed by the pure white foals and asked permission to touch them.

Ginger had freedom to come in the barn or walk out to the corral, but she had chosen to stay with Silk and her new baby. She stood beside Silk in the largest stall and accepted scratches and pets.

"Ladies, this horse is Ginger. She is the first horse that Ben owned. He got her by rescuing her from a mud bog when she was a foal. He hand fed her and took special care of her. She is still the favorite of all of us."

"Aw, that's nice. Have you named any of the foals yet?"

"Yes, we have had two thoroughbred foals in the other barn and I want to give the name Comet to the little female from Star."

"We haven't seen those yet. We need to go there next, said Clover."

They headed in that direction without hesitation. That barn also showed Orville's efforts. It was pristine. Jed was very pleased. The women and children crowded each other trying to see the two beautiful foals. Blaze proudly greeted her fans with a whinny that made them laugh. Jed glanced out the barn window to see Chaco getting acquainted with Dash Away.

"Are any of you interested in seeing the barn where we milk the cows? That's what I need to be doing." Josh had already put the cows in their stalls and had done a good job of tidying up a bit so it would be as clean as possible for the visitors.

"I want to learn how to milk a cow properly," said Willow. Father Bob milks the cows at the village, but when he is gone only one of the men knows how to do it and he doesn't get as much milk as Father Bob." Jed patiently showed Willow and let her try. The women giggled and watched, but no one else wanted to try.

"Willow you can milk this next one if you want to. Then you can be sure you know just how to start and will be able to tell when the cow has given all she can."

"I am a little afraid of this one. She is turning her head and looking at me."

"She just wants to know who is milking her. Pat her neck and say hello before you start. She is gentle. She won't hurt you."

Willow stood beside the big black and white Holstein and pretended that it was a horse. She liked horses. She scratched her ears and told her she was a beautiful woman.

When Willow finished, she had more milk in her bucket than Jed had ever gotten from that cow.

"You have the perfect touch, Willow. You should be proud of yourself. Not everyone can do such a good job."

Willow smiled at Jed's compliment and then asked if she could just walk around and peek at things.

"What's in that little building on the side of the path?"

"That is where Beth and Mary make the cheese. You can go in and look around, but be warned that some of the aging cheese has a strong odor."

"I think I will skip that. I saw a door on a hill of grass back by Ben's corral and Barn. What is in there?"

Jed continued to milk and answer her many questions. That is a small house that Ben built when he was here alone his first year. We have added on to it, and copied what the first room looked like. God covered the main cabin in dirt and rocks during a storm, and Ben was inside at the time. Ben had to reinforce the roof. Later on a buffalo stampede loosened a huge boulder and it went through the roof, so Ben built out in front of that thing. It is really cozy inside. You should look in there. You are all welcome to do whatever you want. We like having you here. I guess I should warn you and you can pass it on to the rest. The far field back by the bluff has a lot of horses in it. Stay away from that, because we just trapped that stallion and his herd and he is not happy with humans right now. He is quite dangerous."

"Thank you Jed. You have been so nice. We all appreciate you making us feel welcome. I want to go see the little grass house."

"We call it the hut," he said as he stood and poured his bucket of milk into a tall can and seated its top securely. "Is that the last one Josh?"

"Yes, I am finished too. I'll open the door to their field and let them out."

As he swung open the big door, the cows lined up and strolled out.

"They are strange creatures. They walk in that way, too, and go right to their stall. Each one knows where they are supposed to be and go right to it. When we put them in their back field to let the grass in this one grow, Josh goes over there and opens the gate and they follow him back just like that."

"They feel comfortable with you. The sheep that the people have follow the man that takes care of them. As long as he sings their song they will follow. He takes them out on the prairie to feed and all around and they just stay with him. It's amazing."

With three clangs of the bell, everyone looked toward the crossing. Adam and Johnny had both been up at the lookout post.

"It's Father Bob and Brother Tim, they said at the same time. The big freight wagon, loaded with lumber pulled up under the oak tree and Tim jumped down and unhitched the big horses walking them up river where the grass grew green and tall. The team tromped through the brush to drink from the river as Tim separated them and fastened them where they could each reach the water and grass.

"Hello again," said Father Bob as he crossed the river on Macho. "Hello, everyone well it is certainly good to see you ladies here visiting."

"The men are helping David to build our cabin so we came here this morning to see the new foals and visit," said Sarah. "I am surprised to see you back here and with a load of lumber, so soon."

"Yes, it was quite a job for Tim and I to unload the first wagon, but then we decided that the men of the village would be gone at least another week so we headed to the settlement and bought another load. When they get back, we will have all the supplies we need to build the school."

Tim had crossed on Jack and was happy to see Mary's wagon coming down the path from her house. Jed and Josh followed the ladies from the milk barn after cleaning up and getting the barn ready for morning. The milk was placed in the cold storage until the soldiers would pick up most of it the next day. Beth and Lily came out and greeted them.

"You are just in time for supper, Father Bob. Hello Brother Tim. Is Sylvia Warren with you?"

"No, she wanted to stay in camp when we got there with the first load."

"I think we should eat outside tonight," said Beth. Orville wandered over and shook their hands.

Jed decided to use the opportunity to praise Orville for the way he had cared for the new foals and the barns they were in.

"Everyone, if you haven't met him, this is Orville Baker. He is the best ranch hand I have ever had the pleasure of working with. Orville hand delivers our foals; gentles the wild mustangs and if that's not enough to keep him busy, he keeps their barns clean too."

"Gosh, Jed, no one ever said anything nice like that about me before. I really appreciate it." He shuffled his feet and looked down feeling a bit embarrassed.

"Orville, would you help me? I need to lift the table outside? It is a nice day and Beth thinks we should eat outdoors."

"That's a good suggestion. There isn't a cloud in the sky."

With two tables and several blankets on the grass, the campfire was lit and the soup set near it. Two big cast iron fry pans held the fish and Mary lifted the butter cake from the wagon and put it on the table. Eli and Natty sat near the steps on a blanket playing blocks with a set that Beth had brought out.

Father Bob said the grace and at the end he thanked God for the presence of so many lovely ladies to brighten the meal. It wasn't until then that Orville noticed the gray wolf pup that Adam was cuddling.

"Boy where did you get that stinking wolf. That thing will grow up and kill one of the foals. That's not a dog, boy!"

"I know that it's a wolf and don't call her stinking! She almost drowned today! Aunt Sarah had to jump in the water to save her!"

"Adam, mind your tongue! You should not speak to an adult like that. Apologize to Orville right now!" Beth was trying to be a good parent, but inside she agreed with her son.

"I'm sorry Orville," he said. "Mom, may I be excused. I am not hungry tonight."

"Yes, you may." Adam carried the little wolf and its bowl of food all the way to Sarah's empty cabin. He sat on the bottom porch step and put her down beside him. He coaxed her to eat and finally she did. After her meal, she crawled in his lap and went to sleep.

He could hear the voices across the lake and smell the food. He was hungry.

"Mama Two, is it alright if I go talk to Adam?"

"Well first I need to know how you are feeling."

"I feel better. My throat isn't scratchy anymore."

"Have you eaten all your soup? Would you like a piece of the lovely cake that Mary made?" Beth intervened.

"I have an idea. Would you like to take a plate with two pieces of cake and you and Adam can have some together? Water Bug I am glad you are feeling better." Beth stroked his forehead in a way that it seemed to be affection. She suspected that the boy had a fever and she was right. "I'll make you a deal. If you will take some more of the medicine I will give you the pieces with the most frosting." She stepped in the house and brought out the pan of medicine. "Sarah, I can't remember. Did you put willow bark in this?"

"Yes, I did."

Beth held a cup and ladled it half full of the concoction and then added a spoon of honey and a large spoon of something else, stirring it until it was cool.

"Water Bug, are you brave? This is going to be a little bitter, but I want you to drink all of it, and then you can take the cake to Adam." He took a sip and made a terrible face.

"Pinch your nose while you drink. Some people say you can't taste it that way."

"That was the worst stuff ever!" He downed a cup of water and then smiled at Beth, giving her a quick hug around the waist with one arm as he said thanks and took the edge of the plate carefully. Clover and Willow were both smiling. Clover watched as the boy walked away carrying the plate.

"Water Bug, please stay on the path. Don't go near the water anymore until you are well," said Clover.

He looked back and smiled nodding.

"He has a fever doesn't he? I thought so. His face looked a little too rosy. What did you add to the medicine you gave him?"

"Sarah, you added a little infection fighter but I have a strong brew from the same plants that I keep on hand in that bottle. That's what I added."

"That's good."

"Is he getting sick in his chest?" Willow and Clover were both looking concerned as their eyes followed the little boy down the path.

"I had planned on heading back in the morning but maybe we should stay another day so that he and Cumae can rest. Cumae you should take another cup of that medicine before you go to bed tonight."

"Thank you, but I feel fine."

"Cumae, are you going to be a difficult patient?"

"No of course not," she laughed and poured a cup of the bitter brew. I do want to use some of that honey in this stuff. Have you tasted it?"

"Yes, I know. It is awful."

Jed, Father Bob, Brother Tim, Josh and Orville, were all coming out of Ben's barn as Water Bug walked slowly by.

"That boy looks sick," said Jed. "I hope that he can fight off the bad lung sickness. People can get that when muddy water gets in."

The women smiled as the men returned.

"Sarah, I think we should make one of those chest poultices for Water Bug. He doesn't look well to me."

"I was just sitting here thinking the same thing. You are right, Jed. He has a fever. We will give the boys a few minutes to enjoy each other and their cake and then I think my cabin is the perfect place for all of us to bed down for the night. Mary, would you let Adam stay in there with Water Bug tonight? I think they would like that.

"He can stay if you want him, but they will probably giggle all night."

Sarah and Jed worked together applying their knowledge. This was a sickness that Jed feared more than any other. It had taken his grandfather and left him alone.

When they walked down the steps the women were gathering their blankets and had washed the utensils and bowls from their travel satchels. Jed asked them all to lay their things down for a moment and join hands. He didn't ask Father Bob to say a prayer. Instead, he opened his heart and voiced his concern and need for help from the Great Healer.

"Father God, maker of heaven and earth. You above all know how precious a son is. One of our boys is ill. He has a sickness that we cannot see. Our ability to help him is very limited. Please come close to him and stay with him tonight. Help his body to fight the infection that is building in his chest. Watch over him and bless him. Bless Cumae who bravely dove in when she was needed to rescue him. Please bless everyone gathered here, yes Lord, even the little wolf. Please make her well. We ask it because Sarah loves her. Thank you Father, we know that you always hear our prayer. Amen."

"Amen." The people gathered there whispered their response. They hadn't known how serious Water Bug's illness might be.

Jed lit a lantern and led the ladies to Sarah's cabin. The two boys still seated on the steps had eaten the cake and allowed the pup to lick the plate. Mary stayed for a few minutes to help Beth clean up the table and carry the remaining food inside; then Mary said she was going to take down a pitcher for water and a few cups. She added a couple washcloths in case they needed to wet them and place them on the boy's head. She thought his fever might climb during the night.

"Beth, I didn't think that the boy was that sick. Why is Jed acting like he is?"

"Mary, when he was a teenager, his grandfather, that he lived with, got sick in the chest and the doctor that came just gave him cough medicine. He died and Jed was alone. He vowed that he would learn all he could about healing medicines so he could help people. He didn't want to lose anyone else that he loved because of sickness."

"Somehow I never knew about that. Thanks for telling me. I think I want to take the wagon down with this stuff and then I'll go on home. My little boys are tired and so am I tonight. I don't like it when Ben is gone. Do you need any blankets or anything? Jed will probably be back with Father Bob and Brother Tim, before long."

"No, I think we have plenty. It is a warm night and I will put Tim on the couch. See you in the morning."

CHAPTER THIRTEEN
SOME REVELATIONS

The men had worked hard and so had the horses. All of the four work horses purchased by David from Lucas Donner proved to be good animals. When they were treated kindly they were willing to do what was asked.

The walls were up and the roof was planked ready for wood shingles. Three stripped logs were placed to support the loft and fastened to the beautiful stripped big beams in the ceiling. David was amazed at the progress that many hands could make in just a few days.

Their evening meal was eaten in front of the cave. The chili that Sarah had made was thick and hot. The men enjoyed the crackers relishing their salty taste with the meal and then drizzling honey on them for a desert. David had brewed both tea and coffee and they sat and appreciated the evening, talking until late. They bedded down just as if they were on the trail, using their bedrolls.

David had kept his word and left food and water by the wolf den but didn't see them.

In the morning David took on the role of cook long enough to make cooked grain and added dried apples, sugar and cinnamon. Fresh coffee and tea satisfied the men and soon they were all back to work praising David's cooking skills.

"I miss having the women around. I hope they come back today," said Soren. "Cumae and I have never been apart since I chose her." The men started to tease him, but David spoke up and said he didn't like it when Sarah was gone either.

"If they stay at the ranch today, we could finish up and leave here mid-afternoon and surprise them before dark," suggested Debon.

"If you want to go, I will be more than happy with the work you have completed. I need to stay here to keep animals out of our supplies and we still need a water tight roof, windows and a door that closes, but send back my woman!" David said it in a joking manner and the men laughed.

Having Willow as my wife and taking care of Clover and her children has given me a family that I love, but I have to admit there are times it gets trying. Have you ever had two women telling you what needs to be done?" The men laughed again.

"You have two wives and don't know it," said Night Hawk. Then the men burst into such laughter that they couldn't stop.

"Two Feathers, maybe you should stay here and guard the supplies. You need the peace and quiet!" Debon was joking.

"That's not a bad idea. David and I could explore the cave. What do you think David?"

It sounds fine to me. I was wishing that I wouldn't have so much work so that I could take the time to go back in there and see where it goes. You men have done most of the work and I really appreciate it. I have no doubt now that our cabin will be finished long before winter."

"Maybe, we should all stay here and explore the cave, said Debon. "It sounds like a lot of fun."

When they thought about it, they all got excited and eager to do it. They stuffed their pockets with dried meat and took two water bags, ropes and the two lanterns.

"Let's all think for a minute. What are we forgetting?"

Two Feathers raised his arms and the rest of the men did the same. He stood for a moment gathering his thoughts.

"Thank you Lion of Judah, for allowing us this wonderful experience of exploring a cave that you have created and chosen as your place of peace. It is a sanctuary as holy as any church that men could build. We ask that as we move about inside that you watch over us and keep us safe. Please help us to find anything that you have put here for us."

"Amen." They said together.

Two Feathers picked up a small piece of chalk stone.

"We should each take a piece of this, so we can mark the wall or floor if we need to mark our path." The men responded immediately and scurried around to find pocket sized chunks of the soft white rock.

"I think we are ready. Two Feathers, would you like to go first?"

"Yes, thank you for the honor," he said and meant it.

As they moved back through the boxes and stuffed baskets belonging to Sarah and David, he stopped to add a large piece of hard wood to the fire. He couldn't guess how long they would be gone. He knew they would want a fire when they came out and its smell would keep animals away from the supplies. Debon carried a long clean branch with him.

"We can use this to test the floor if it becomes questionable."

"Good idea," said David. "There is a place not too far in that turns to the right. It slants down and becomes muddy and slick. Be careful."

"Two Feathers, watch the floor." He carried the first lantern and suddenly its light disappeared as he rounded the turn to the right. Two Feathers stopped and studied the marks on the floor.

"David, come here. Have you seen this?" It may explain why you can't find your wolf pups." The two men crouched and studied the small, dog-like foot prints in the mud. "Two turned around, but it looks like one broke through here. Debon let me use that stick."

All the men came where they could hear, but knew not to get into the wet area. Two Feathers gently prodded the area around the sandy, wet hole.

"There is running water under here. It has quite a strong force. I am afraid that one of the pups is lost to you David. It could never climb back up and out of there with the current of the water pushing it."

"Oh, that's awful. Sarah is going to be so sad. She loves those pups. I wonder where the other two are. I haven't seen them at all since she left."

"I am so sorry David, are you discouraged or do you want us to move on?"

In his mind, Two Feathers heard the old warning, "right is not right."

"Let's move back and not all walk so close to each other. We don't want to face the plight of the wolf pup. Let's go straight ahead and see where it takes us."

As he exited the little path to the right, David scratched a large X on the bottom of the wall with his piece of chalk stone. They moved forward cautiously.

"This part of the cave is dry and the floor is sandy underfoot." Two Feathers lifted the lantern and tipped it so that he could see the ceiling and then the floor ahead. He admitted to himself that he had almost expected to see sparkling crystals around and above him. There were none. The sandstone seemed to be changing color to shades of gray and soon they were climbing over huge jagged boulders that had fallen from the ceiling perhaps millions of years ago when the cave was formed.

"It looks like the cave ends up ahead." Two Feathers approached what he thought was a wall but saw that it was the start of a hand chiseled stairwell, curving down into blackness.

The men crowded around and peered down.

"Should we go down there? Soren had taken a step back. Debon looked at Two Feathers questioningly.

"This wasn't made by God, it was made by men."

"The men that made this are long gone," said David. "Two Feathers, maybe our far back ancestors made this for us to find."

"Where do you think it goes? Maybe it was rigged to collapse when their enemy walked on it," offered Night Hawk.

"I don't think that the Lion of Judah would lead us to a cave filled with dangers. The pup broke through because it is a baby and didn't know any better. That could be how God revealed a bountiful water source. I trust him, I am going down." Two Feathers took the stick and firmly tapped each step ahead of him as he moved slowly down.

"I trust him; I'm going next," said David. Slow down Two Feathers, it is hard for me to see."

They continued to go down until they reached a platform of rock that seemed to project out of the side of the solid rock.

"Do you think we should climb onto that? It doesn't appear to lead anywhere."

"No, I want to try climbing down the rocks. It looks like there are worn hand holds in the rock wall. Hold the lantern up high and take the stick for me." Two Feathers bravely began the climb across the deep darkness while the others stood silently praying that he wouldn't fall.

The wall that he had crossed was meant to discourage but they could hear his excitement when he completed the climb.

"There are more stairs over here! They go down a long ways. We are going to need the lantern, but how can we get it across without shattering it?"

Debon made a suggestion.

Let's tie it to the stick and then tie the long stick to someone's back so that it will be far enough away so it won't burn them and since it is my idea I will do it.

"We don't want to cut the rope, Debon, so we will have to wrap it around you and tie the end to your belt so it can't slip down and cause you a problem." Debon was a little jittery as he reached out for the first hand hold and carefully placed his foot on the first projecting rock.

"This is treacherous. Why would they make such a thing?" He was scared and just wanted to get across.

"Debon, watch where you put your hands and feet, and don't talk. Think about what you are doing," instructed Two Feathers. He could hear the fear in Debon's voice.

When he arrived at the side of Two Feathers the small group cheered.

"Send the rope and stick back so that we can bring the second lantern."

"Catch it David." It took several tries before they caught the end of the rope with the stick tied on it and then they were able to get the rest of the men and second lantern across to the top of the continuation of the stairs.

"Lead on Two Feathers, and use the stick to test every step," said David as he looked back at the faces of Spotted Feather, Night Hawk and Soren. They all were exhilarated by their climb and eager to continue.

"Has anyone else noticed that it is beginning to feel colder as we go? I have been counting the steps since our wall climb. We must be at least sixty feet down," said Night Hawk. "Remember that we have to climb all these to go back. My legs are getting tired already!"

Soren was the first to notice that the stairs were changing from the dark gray of the granite to an almost white color.

"Are these steps made of chalk stone?"

"No, I think they are salt, and we are nearing the bottom of the stairs finally." Two Feathers held the lantern high to light the entire area. As the men got to the bottom they stood in silent awe.

"What is this place? Whatever it is, it's manmade. Look how high the columns are and they are so big around that my arms only reach a fourth of the way."

"I don't see any tools or debris from creating it. How could they take it all out? There has to be another passage out that is easier and wider." Soren was sure that this was a temple, but he couldn't tell from where he was standing, which God the temple honored.

"Let's look inside," said Two Feathers. It took three of them pulling hard to open one of the huge doors at the top of six wide steps. It pivoted slowly and stood open. The space that it revealed was immense. The light of the lanterns bounced from the smooth, polished white floor to the walls. They could see that it was entirely decorated on the walls and ceiling with carvings of flowers and trees and animals. Realistic renderings of birds appeared to hover over water with every imaginable sea creature. Some of the things they were seeing, they had never seen before or heard of. "Are there really animals that look like these?"

"How did the workers light this to see well enough to do such beautiful work?"

"I don't know, David."

As they walked forward slowly on the shining floor; gazing at the carvings, their footsteps echoed loudly.

"This sounds hollow underneath," commented Night Hawk.

They could see an altar ahead. It was a huge rectangular block at least eight feet high and twenty feet long. On top of it lying beside each other were a perfectly carved, larger than life sized lion and a lamb. Each wore a heavy crown of gold and jewels.

Across the face of the altar they read the words, "Holy, holy, holy is the Lord God Almighty, who was, and is, and is to come." NIV Rev. 4:8.

"We are on holy ground," whispered Two Feathers. He quickly slipped off his moccasins. The others did the same.

"Thank you Father, for allowing us to see this," said Two Feathers. They stood silently worshiping Jesus, The Lion of Judah, and King of Peace.

Soren and Debon could not fully appreciate the significance as the others did, but the Holy Spirit spoke gently to their hearts and they were able to feel the very special, sacred peace of this place.

Behind the altar Debon noticed that he could see an opening in the wall.

"Let's see if that is another way out," he whispered. He gestured toward it. None of them noticed that directly to their left a panel angled out of the wall covering still another doorway.

Two Feathers pointed and nodded and they respectfully moved in single file toward the doorway behind the altar. The polished floor and beautiful carvings gave way to a rough surface beneath their feet. They slipped their footwear back on. Two Feathers reached down and picked up a small chip of loose salt. They each felt compelled to do the same. It was still hard for them to accept that such a place existed. The small piece of salt would be a proof in the harsh light of day, that this was real. The walkway they followed changed from white to gray and soon the sound of their feet had changed from the echo of the basilica to a typical gravel-scuffing tread.

Although it wasn't quickly apparent, they discovered that the floor was slowly grading up and they encouraged each other to continue. The men were getting tired from their strenuous adventure.

"I wonder where this comes out," commented David. Two Feathers noticed a faint light streaming in ahead.

"I think we can turn off our lanterns soon. I can see light coming in an opening up ahead. My legs tell me that we have been climbing a long ways."

As he stepped to his left around a huge boulder, Two Feathers could see sky filtering through pine branches and an opening large enough to easily walk out by bending down just a bit. Each man made his way carefully through the branches and loose sand stone scree beneath their feet.

At that point they saw that they were on the backside of the bluff which again appeared to be made of yellow sandstone, with one exception. To their right, a wide stripe of loose salt chunks, chips and pebbles had been carried up a trail and poured out at the top. The path that the ancients had used to remove their scrapings would not have been evident from below unless someone knew to look for it.

"I know where we are. This is where Growling Bear and I got our deer when we hunted. I think we have been moving in a wide circle. He and I took our horses between those big boulders over there. I saw that white color on the bluff then but I didn't realize that it was salt I was seeing. I thought it was chalk stone. That salt has high trading value. David, you and Sarah can make use of it." The men had carefully picked their way down the side of the bluff to the prairie below.

"That's a good idea Night Hawk but right now, the only thing I can think of doing is sitting down." David lowered himself to the grass and took a long drink from the water bag and then passed it to Soren. Two Feathers looked at the others and saw the expressions of wonderment on their faces.

"You must all realize that The Great Spirit has given us a rare gift. He has trusted us with the knowledge that this exists and with that comes a responsibility to protect and guard it. We must tell no one."

"We have to tell our wives!"

"No, you must take an oath. You will tell no one, especially the women. When we have figured out a way to live near enough to protect this treasure, then The Lion will show us His will and we will know who should be told.

"I won't tell anybody! Who would believe us? It is there but I can't believe it myself," said Night Hawk. Each man agreed that they would tell no one. They knew that it was a secret that would be hard to keep, but they all took an oath to hold the knowledge of the temple's existence in their heart until it was made clear that they could speak about it.

Once they were through the passable break in the bluff, they found they could see the start of the trees near the back of David's land and to their left was the face of the bluff that held "The Lion's Den".

"How can something so magnificent exist and people not know about it?" David was puzzled. Two Feathers stirred the embers of David's fire and added twigs to get the fire going.

"It's because they don't know about it that it can exist," said Two Feathers. We have been entrusted with the responsibility to guard this sanctuary. There are men that would steal the crowns. Others would try to pry the carvings from the walls to sell!"

"How can we guard it when we live so far away?" asked Debon.

Two Feathers felt the weight of their discovery heavily resting on his shoulders, but he didn't yet understand how he fit into God's plan.

"I am going to check our horses before it gets dark." Two Feathers moved away from the men and the opening to the cave. He glanced back just in time to see the fading image of the Lion, above the cave entrance. It caught him off guard and he stumbled into the branches of one of the big pines.

"Lead me my Lord and I will follow." His eyes were glued to the rocks above the entrance until he could see the image no more.

David and the others had a wonderful beef stew bubbling from dried meat and garden vegetables when Two Feathers finally returned.

"I hope it's alright, I took the work horses across the river and put them there in new grass. They had depleted any they could reach. The rest of the horses are fine until morning. We should move all of them then."

"Thank you, Two Feathers, come sit down, rest and I will pour you some coffee or tea. Which do you prefer? Our food will be ready soon." The men sat on their bedrolls together quietly. Their bodies were very tired but their minds were filled with incredulity at the things they had seen and the new strong fellowship they felt. This was a bond that years would never be able to break.

"David, I feel certain that the cave still holds mysteries that we have not discovered. I think that God has put us here to guard it but I feel there is still something else He will reveal when He is ready."

Two Feathers wasn't sure about any of it. Why should it need guarding now? I doubt if anyone has seen that temple in centuries, he thought. Why has it been revealed to us?

David was pleased to see Woof and his sister in the den when he set down a bowl of the hearty stew and filled their water bowl. He broke a large piece of dried meat into four pieces and left that for them, too. He slowly reached out and was able to pet first one and then the other.

"Your new mother will be back tomorrow, I think. I am so sorry about your sister. I know you miss her. First you lost your mom and now this."

After their meal the men lay on their bedrolls looking up at a cloudless sky. The stars seemed brighter than usual as they drifted off to sleep.

*****

Water Bug and Adam woke during the night when the little wolf pup crawled onto Adams covers. They tucked the baby between them and were giggling quietly when Sarah sensed that they were awake. She had insisted on sleeping next to Water Bug so she could care for him if it was needed.

"Water Bug, how are you," she whispered.

"I feel much better, but I am thirsty."

"Me too," said Adam. Sarah delivered two drinks from the pitcher and felt Water Bugs forehead. It was cool.

"Is it alright if I take this thing off my chest? It itches."

"Sit up and I will remove the cloth that is holding it on." The strong poultice had irritated his skin and he immediately started scratching it.

"Don't scratch. I will put some grease with mint and clover on your chest to sooth it. There, does that feel better?"

"Yes, thank you Sarah."

"I see you have won the heart of this little wolf girl."

"She likes me. Please let her stay here with us until morning." Adam was grinning broadly.

221

"I will take her out on the grass for a minute so she doesn't wet on your blanket. Stay quiet and don't wake the ladies and I will bring her back to you." He nodded. Sarah took the little pup out and sat on the steps for a long time. She hadn't intended to stay that long, but her mind wandered back to the happy events of the first day that she had seen that cabin.

When she went inside both boys had fallen asleep. She tucked the pup between them watching it snuggle and settle close to Adam.

As the women woke they were joyous to hear the news that Water Bug was feeling much better. Sarah insisted that he take one more dose of the bitter medicine after his breakfast, but everyone felt relieved that he had gotten better and not worse. Jed was the most exuberant of all. He whistled his way to the cow barn to start the milking.

The women cleared all their things from the little cabin and returned Beth's pitcher and cups. Each of them felt a new wish in their heart. They wanted a cabin to live in. It was so nice to sleep in Sarah's cabin. They wondered why she would ever move up river and want to live away from this beautiful ranch. Sarah was questioning the same thing when she heard the bell clang three times. She hurried to the crossing with Pili in her arms and the little wolf bounding along at her heels.

Everyone gathered at the crossing to greet Ben. He knew that Father Bob and Brother Tim were there before he saw them. The big freight wagon stood in the shade of the old oak tree and the team that pulled it was visible up stream.

Hello everyone, I have had a good trip to Silverville and I have a surprise for the children. Adam and Water Bug climbed down carefully from the lookout and Johnny ran from the chicken pen he was working on, glad to have an excuse to stop for a little while. Tim helped him ferry his little wagon across and was smiling as they hitched it back up to Sundown and he moved it up to the path where everyone stood waiting.

Bedded down in the hay was a very cute pair of miniature goats. Lily squealed with delight when she saw the little animals. Each wore a collar with a rope attached. She tried to hug one and it immediately started to chew on the edge of her dress.

"Don't do that, you dotty baby! You can't eat my dress!" everyone laughed. Josh and Johnny corralled the other one and agreed that it was the cutest.

"Dad, did you notice that this one has one blue eye and one brown one? I have never seen such a thing!"

"No, I didn't, but the man said that if we make a moveable pen, for them, they will eat anything inside it, and they will clean up all the fire mess along the river and keep the grass down very short. He said they are great at keeping things looking clean. Since the fire happened recently we will need to subsidize their feeding until the green grass starts to grow back in that area. Ben turned to the covey of women standing on the path and finally noticed Sarah and Mary standing together. He went to them and hugged both at the same time. He saw the wolf pup but decided to not make an issue of it.

"Pili, you are growing fast!" He kissed her head but didn't take her. Instead he turned and shook Father Bob's hand and then hugged him and then Jed.

"This is the best part of coming home, he said as he hugged Beth. "I get a lot of hugs." They laughed and then he turned Sundown toward the path to Sarah's cabin. "I'm glad that you ladies were able to return to visit. Did you all see our new foals?" They smiled and replied with comments of how beautiful they all are. "Most of the things in here are for the cabin." He walked Sundown very slowly. Freedom was in Tim's arms and Eli was laughing running along as they all walked beside the wagon.

"Mary, I was able to get the canning jars you and Beth need. I am afraid that I took nearly all that Sam had." He stopped for a minute and said that he had room for one on the seat and a couple in with the boxes and sacks, but no one took him up on the offer. Jed finally lifted Natty up and put him in the back of the wagon where he could stand and hang onto the back of the seat. Jed knew that at this slow crawl, if Natty lost his balance, he would just land on his seat in the hay where the goats had been.

Ben pulled the wagon close to the cabin door and everyone carried something into the empty cabin.

"Those four boxes are the canning jars. This one is the rubber rings and screw lids for the quart sized one. This one is the tops for the jam jars. Where do you want those put?"

"You can put them in either barn for now. It won't be long before we need them," said Beth.

"I'm so glad that you were able to get them," said Mary.

Well ladies, I think we should gather our things and get on our horses and head back. If we leave now, we will be there in time to make a good supper for our hard working men." Sarah looked back at the crossing to see David and several other men riding across the river. Willow and Clover spoke as one.

"Where is Two Feathers?"

David answered.

He stayed to guard my food supplies. He has been such a big help. All the men have worked very hard. I can't wait to show all of you our progress."

"Sarah, have all the foals arrived? Did you see Dart Away's offspring?"

"Oh David, they are so special, and Dash Away is so much like his father that in a year, when he fills out he will be exactly like Dart Away. Ben has three other beautiful foals in his barn. Two of them are pure white like Moon Boy and a little golden tan one that is Ginger's granddaughter!"

"You can show them to me." He took Pili in his arms and that's when he spotted the pup following Sarah. He reached down with one hand and scooped her up and plopped her down on Pili's tummy. She laughed out loud, which made all of them laugh. We found a spot in the cave where there were paw prints and one set went to the edge of a small spot that had collapsed. We could only find two pups. I thought this one was gone forever!"

"She was as near dead as she could be and still being alive. She washed out of an underground waterway into the lake over there and I pulled her out. Jed saved her. He got her breathing again." All the men that had come with David gathered around to hear her relate the story. They had all seen the place where the pup had gone in the rushing water. "Water Bug and Adam were hand-fishing and Water Bug investigated the muddy water. He ended up being rescued by Cumae. The current there is churning and very strong." Jed spoke up and said that he would have been in the water, fencing that area off, if they hadn't all arrived when they did.

Debon and Soren said they would like to help him.

"We are both good swimmers, we will be glad to help. Jed and his two volunteers walked toward the lake and Mary and Beth loaded the youngsters into the little wagon. Clover hopped up in the back and took Freedom and Cricket. Sarah thought it looked like fun and got in with Pili. The rest of the group followed the wagon back toward Beth's house. Ben, David and several others continued on to deliver the canning supplies to Jed's barn.

"Josh, ask Dad to please prepare a side of beef for the pit. We are going to have a feast tonight!"

Once again Beth's lawn was covered with blankets, babies, and women cooking big pots of delicious smelling food.

The young goats tied near the river were soon surrounded by a split rail fence that was wrapped on the outside with farm fence. They were freed, to run around inside it and eat anything they could reach. One corner of the fence allowed just enough room to extend over the river so they could drink but not exit. Everyone thought it good fun to walk over and pet them.

When Jed, Debon and Soren waded out of the lake, they came out near the willows at the back, not far from Jed's corral. They had found where the river exited the small lake and had also pounded thick branches into the bottom that stuck up from the water in a row against the bank.

"If one of the boys got pulled in there by the current, they would die! We didn't even know that was there. I am glad that Ben made the fishing platform on the other side and close to the front path." Jed was upset and he was restating what they had already acknowledged. The three of them sat down on the grass by the big campfire and took the cups of hot coffee that Beth offered them.

Jed patted the grass beside him and indicated that he wanted her to sit down beside him.

"Beth, the people will be going back to David and Sarah's in the morning. Would you mind if I go with them?"

"No, I think you will enjoy the fellowship and frankly, although it is nice to have the Indians here, I am tired. I think I will take a day off and just rest." She had leaned close to Jed when she spoke not wanting to be overheard.

The women were happy to be back in the company of their men and after eating and talking, they bedded down here, there and almost anywhere. Mary and Ben thought it a little odd with the hut and Sarah's cabin empty. They had offered but no one used them.

Ben had taken Sarah, David and Pili to their house as soon as the meal was over and insisted that they stay with them. Even the little wolf was allowed to come inside. She curled up with Adam on the bear rug and slept. Mary sat in the willow rocking chair crooning and cuddling Pili as they visited.

In the morning when the sun stirred the sleeping people they quickly packed up their belongings and prepared to head back up river. Father Bob and Brother Tim said they wanted to see the progress on the cabin and then they would be heading to the village. They had slept at Jed's and thanked everyone. Ben and Josh took on the duty of milking and Adam and Johnny started for the chicken pens. Lily went with Beth to the barn to freshen the stalls of the thoroughbreds and give them water and grain. She moved slowly. Beth knew she had been doing too much.

After saying goodbye to Sarah, David, Pili, Jed and the People of the Lion, Mary put Natty and Eli in the little wagon and took several baskets to the garden to collect produce.

The two little boys enjoyed playing with the many different types of animals that the men had carved for them. Mary had gathered the wooden farm animals from the toy shelf and placed them in the wagon before heading out. She stopped at Ben's barn just long enough to check the mares and foals. Their areas were clean and they had what they needed. I love them all, she thought.

A wave of nostalgia hit her as she passed the hut, continuing on to the garden. Parking the wagon in the shade she gave Eli the carved animals so he could play. Natty was napping beside him. The ranch was quiet.

CHAPTER FOURTEEN
A ROCK SOLID ASSIGNMENT

Tim drove slowly, leading the way for the caravan of people on horseback. Pili and Freedom were happy in their harnesses, riding beside their mothers. Singing Cricket and Water Bug rode near Clover and Willow. They were eager to see Two Feathers.

"Father Bob, look at the change in the church land! The downed trees have been cut and piled to the side. There is a clear path to the crossing."

Tim efficiently took the big team near the water and found them a comfortable place to graze and drink; the others used the crossing and went to the area near the cabin. The women went to the front of the cave and they immediately saw that all of Sarah's things had been pulled out of the cave.

They were met by the two growing wolf pups that danced with joy at the sight of their sister, when Sarah placed her on the ground.

"There you go, my water baby. You are home and safe." She and the other women laughed as the prancing wolves hurried off together in the direction of their own den.

Two Feathers came out of the cave as the returning people arrived.

"Everyone, please wait here," he said with a serious expression on his face. He walked straight to David and pulled him aside.

"There has been a change in the cave. Yesterday I followed the same route we took and it was open and clear. I found what appeared to be living quarters for many people. The doorway is to the left of the altar. It is all sectioned off by short walls separating what looked like family areas, but last night when I got back I went out to check the horses and there was a terrible rumbling and a huge cloud of dust came out of the mouth of the cave. When it settled I went back in and just beyond the opening to the waterway, some of the ceiling has collapsed. We can't go across the part that goes to the stairs anymore. It is all closed off. Your belongings were totally covered in gray dust, but I have spent the morning doing my best to bring them out and clean them off. There doesn't seem to be any damage to anything you had stored in there." Sarah hurried over to find out what was the matter. She could see all her belongings piled on the slate, outside the cave. Willow came and slipped her arm around Two Feather's waist. She was frightened. She had suddenly felt the impact of terror again as she had when she fled the cave in the active volcano. She was shaking.

"It's alright Willow. Just some rocks shifted and made a mess. I am fine and nothing was damaged." He held her close.

Tim could see at a glance that his view into the depths of the cave was stopped by a wall of rock rubble. I am glad no one was in there when that came down, he thought. Father Bob was thinking similar thoughts as he wandered toward the cabin to see what was left to be done before winter.

"Come on everyone," said Father Bob, "This is a blessing in disguise. We will all work hard to put the planks down for the floor and we can finish the shutters and doors. By dark we will be able to move all their stuff in the cabin."

Before many minutes passed, the women had a fire going and food cooking in the big kettle at the back of David's property. The men were hammering and sawing and laughter drifted through the trees as the many hands made light work of the remaining projects.

As Father Bob had predicted, the floor was down and sanded by dancing feet as merry singing celebrated the cabin's new floor and cozy feeling. The windows would soon be in and Calvin Briggs would build the fireplace and chimney before the first snowfall.

In the morning sunshine, the men carried the hand carved bed parts into the cabin and put it together. Clover felt it a privilege to wipe it down with an oiled cloth before the bedding went on. The cradle and rocking chair, the table and benches came in next.

Men were still hammering long nails through the boards of the cupboards, securing them to the wall when the slowly moving column of tired people was spotted. The Blue Stone People arrived at noon and it seemed that they were all talking at once. Hugs and hearty laughter filled the air as each person shared their stories of activities at the summer meeting.

Moonflower was pleased with the cabin and thought that she just might like living in such a place. She pushed the shutters open wide and said that if it were her home, she would only close them if the snow or rain was coming in. Sarah was hugged and patted by every woman as they came near. She was loved. These were her people. That would never change no matter where she lived.

That evening the fire in the cave opening was rekindled and as people bedded down, Chief Dark Wolf announced that they would leave for their village in the morning.

Two Feathers said quietly that he and his men would follow in a couple days, but that their women should go with him, back to camp.

Chief Dark Wolf felt a new independence in Two Feathers that had not been there. He wondered what had occurred to bring about the change. The use of the term "his men," had not slipped by unnoticed. The Chief got into his bedroll of soft furs and touched Moonflowers hand.

"The young men still have something left to do here. They will follow in a few days, but the women will all come in the morning. Since they are going to be here, would you like to stay and spend the time with Sarah and Pili while you can?"

"Oh, Dark Wolf, I would like that very much. Will you be alright? I won't be there to open and clean our tent or cook for you?"

"Yes, I am sure that someone will share food with me. Don't worry about a thing. Enjoy your time here."

"Thank you, my husband. You are thoughtful."

In the morning, Chief Dark Wolf looked around inside the new little cabin and nodded his approval.

"It is good," he said, patting David's shoulder. "It is as solid as a rock. He put his arm around Sarah and then scooped Pili into his big arms and lifted her high above his head. She laughed out loud and grabbed both hands full of his hair as he lowered her. He was smiling broadly as he handed her back to Sarah.

"Your mother has decided to stay until the younger men leave. She will ride back to camp when they do." He offered the news as a parting gift.

"Thank you, father, we will enjoy the time together." She was smiling, too, but already her mind was puzzling over why the men were staying now that the cabin was livable. She knew that something important had happened. She hadn't been alone with David to have a conversation for many days. She was eager to know what they had planned to do.

Father Bob and Brother Tim led the column through the prairie grass with their big team and slow moving wagon loaded with the rest of the supplies needed to build the school.

Snow star gave her another quick hug and smiled as Sarah placed a hand on her sister's rounded tummy.

"Not long now, and you will have a new little one to cuddle this winter," said Sarah.

"Yes, Flying Eagle is very happy. He has been saying that our tent feels empty since Spotted Feather has been living with the People of the Lion. A baby will certainly fill the space and Watching Owl needs to share me with a sibling. He is very spoiled. I would stay too, but I feel that Flying Eagle and I have been apart too much. Maybe you can come when the weather is nice in the spring."

"That would be good. God bless you, dear sister, stay well and have a healthy baby." Sweet Grass stepped close and said goodbye and assured Sarah that she would take special care of Snow Star and the baby. Sarah was glad that she had encouraged Sweet Grass and trained her to be the new healer of the people. Now that she had gained experience and confidence, she was a very good healer and Sarah was glad that Sweet Grass would be there for Snow Star, when she was needed.

Moonflower felt a bit strange watching the people leave without her. She couldn't see the slight smile and satisfied expression on Chief Dark Wolf's face as he headed out. He was already planning on holding off on the first communal fire after their return to camp until all the men had returned. He wanted his announcement to be heard by all the people at the same time. He hoped that the growing independence of the young men could be slowed and maybe he could keep them a bit longer if they had more than enough profitable work to do.

*****

"Come Grandmother; watch your granddaughter while I work in the garden. There are more weeds than vegetables!"

Her garden was definitely showing that it was planted later than the one at the ranch and much later than it should have been. Her rows of vegetables were shorter and the tomato plants were small but blooming. Only a few little green nobs showed the promise of a red tomato later on. Pili crawled all over Moonflower while Sarah bent pulling the weeds. Finally Sarah glanced over to see Pili sucking her two middle fingers and cuddling down in Moonflowers lap.

"She needs lunch and a nap, and I think we could use a snack and a break too."

When she took Pili in her arms and shuttled them across the river, Sarah realized that they were alone. All the men were gone. David had said that he was going hunting, but she hadn't thought that he meant all of the men were leaving. They had taken their horses and left so quietly that she hadn't even noticed.

As the day wore on and the men stayed absent, she began to worry. She and Moonflower worked inside the cabin putting things in order. They gathered great armloads of grass and sat under the trees working at making mats. They made one for the front step and one for just inside the back door. Sarah was very good at weaving and finished her larger, tighter woven mat for the front just as the men returned. David had a deer over his horse's back and he walked along beside Thunder. The antlers were large and covered in pink velvet.

"Look Sarah, this will be good meat for winter."

"Yes, he is big. Do you intend to make a cache in the floor of the cabin?"

"No, we are going to all work on building a storage room on the back of the cabin tomorrow and we will put a big cache in the floor of it."

"That sounds good, but I am wondering if Father Bob is missing all of these men. He needs their help to build that school."

Two Feathers agreed and told her that they would be staying only one more day.

"I like having you here. We missed all of you today."

"You have all worked so hard for us. I think while you are making the storage room tomorrow, that I will make something sweet as a thank you treat. Maybe I will make a cake in my new oven. Sheltah helped me make the last set of bricks while she was here and when we came back from the ranch she and Cumae put it together and plastered it. I have kept a small fire in it all day. It should be dry enough to use now.

"That sounds like a delicious idea, Sarah."

The men were hard at work cutting the wood to the right sizes as others dug the pit that would become the large covered cache. The dried meat from Growling Bear's hunt had been secured in the cave and some of it would go in the cache too when it was finished. The sun was high over the trees when Moonflower heard Soren ask if they had a pick.

"The ground has so many rocks. I wish you had built on the other side of the river, David."

"Here, let me take a turn digging and you can rest a bit," said Debon. "We may as well make it as big as we can while we are all here. It will be many months before we move here. They need to use it this winter."

Moonflower heard him say "move here." Her heart leapt.

"What did he say?"

"I think he was saying there are too many rocks where they are trying to dig the cache."

"No Sarah, after that, he said he was going to move here."

"Mother, I think you didn't hear him correctly." The men continued to work taking only a short break at midday for a meal. The drying racks were covered with the deer meat and the aroma of the apple cake filled the air as the evening breeze told the men that Sarah had made the promised cake.

"That cache is plenty big enough for meat, David, and maybe you can dig another one and turn it into a root cellar. By the time that garden starts producing you will have to have a place to stash all the winter vegetables."

"You are right, Night Hawk, that's what I will do."

"This is a delicious cake, Sarah. I hope that Willow knows how to bake one."

"Thank you Two Feathers. I can't thank all of you enough for all that you have done here. I am still amazed when I look at the cabin."

"We had fun doing it and we are looking forward to working on the school when we get back. I know that Father Bob will be glad to see us. I wish we didn't have to leave in the morning," said Spotted Feather.

David looked around at the group of men gathered there around the campfire.

"I know that you all have responsibilities and work waiting for you in the village. I just want to say thank you for taking the time to help us. We will feel joy in our hearts when you come back. Sarah and I will think of you often during the cold months ahead. Your hard work has provided us with a wonderful home."

In the morning, Moonflower was sad when it was time to ride out. She kissed Pili and handed her back to Sarah.

"I wish you could be there when Snow Star has her baby. We all love you and David and Pili and I know I will miss you every day until I can see you again."

"We will miss all of you, Mother. Stay warm and safe this winter and I plan to see you next spring."

Sarah and David waved as the men led the way through the trees heading out on to the prairie, following the trail left by the heavy wagons and the many horses of the people.

David turned to her and took the little girl.

"Sarah, I think it is time that we had a long talk. I have so many things to tell you. I am not sure where to begin." He strolled through the trees and sat down on a blanket near the campfire. He placed Pili beside him. Sarah poured them each a mug of tea and handed Pili a gourd with loose seeds inside of it. The baby was delighted and shook it vigorously then worked hard to move it from one hand to the other.

"Sarah, Two Feathers and his People of the Lion will be moving here in the spring."

"All of them?"

"Yes, all the young couples that have formed a bond with him. They are going to be here, as a new people."

"David, where will they stay? Now that the cave has closed up, they can't stay in there? Are they going to build cabins or put up tents in the trees? Tell me, David."

She didn't realize it but Sarah was speaking loudly.

"Calm down Sarah. Let me start with that day that all the women went with you to the ranch to see the foals. We stayed here and worked until late morning and then we decided to go in the cave and do some exploring. We found where the wolf fell in the water and marked the path. You still haven't explained how you ended up with her and were able to bring her back safely, but let me continue. You can tell me that story later. We back tracked and went through a lot of climbing over and across and found a curved staircase that was hand cut out of the rock. It was scary, but when we got to the bottom, we found something so beautiful that it is unlike anything that you can imagine. The bottom of the stairs came out onto an area that was all white, with big columns and two huge doors. It took three of us pulling to open one! Inside was totally breathtaking white. There is a temple down there that is entirely carved out of salt! It is decorated on all the walls and ceiling with animals and beautiful things. Some I didn't know what they were. There is a huge altar and on it is a carved lion and lamb. They both have crowns on their heads made of gold and jewels! Sarah it was so awesome that I can't begin to tell you how beautiful it is. It's there Sarah below this bluff and no one knew about it until we found it. There is an opening behind the big altar and we walked up a long way. Our legs were aching when we came out on the other side of the bluff. We came out and Night Hawk pointed out a streak of white salt that pours across the bluff and down where the ancients that made this must have poured their scrapings."

Sarah sat, still holding her tea.

"Oh David, now it is all lost to us. The cave is closed. Why did the Lion of Judah show you this and then close it up?"

Tears made their way slowly down her cheeks.

"Don't cry Sarah. There is more to the story. When the men and I went hunting we were looking for the exit we had used. It is still there and Two Feathers rode his horse down the ramp almost to the temple. He got off and walked down to the temple. He has found a large room that goes back into the bluff, with partitions that appear to have been used for dwellings, perhaps for the workers that made the temple. Or it could have been for guards. We don't really know. We were guessing. Anyway, the best part is that when the rocks blocked the entrance to the cave, they revealed small openings overhead that direct beams of light all the way down. He could see where he was going the whole time without a lantern! That is where they may live when they move here. No one will even know they are there, if they don't tell them. Sarah, you are the only woman in the whole world that knows about this. We all took an oath not to say a word to anyone, not even our wives. I am breaking that promise because I feel that you are special and the Lion has already shown His image to you.

"What about Brother Tim? He owns the cave?"

"He doesn't own the backside of the bluff. He doesn't know. In time if the Lion says the time is right, we will tell him and Father Bob."

"David, this all seems other-worldly. I feel like this is the start of something, but it is scary.

"Do you remember the story of Jonah and the whale?"

"Yes, but I don't know what that has to do with any of this," David.

"Sarah, think about how powerful God is. He directed that whale, to swallow Jonah, and later put him on shore uninjured, but even more important than that, I think, is to realize that God made the ocean and the world underneath the surface where the whale lives. No one really knows that world or even all the creatures that live there. I think we are small little specks compared to God's whole creation. I can't even think why he cares about us or what we do. When my mind gives me a tiny glimpse at a part of God's awesome being; I think it is really scary! I want to show you the temple, Sarah, but I am not sure that we are supposed to go back in The Lion's Den."

"Now that you told me about the temple, this all seems more sacred than before."

Just then the three little wolves came near and Woof sniffed at the meat on the drying racks. "Are you hungry? Meat on drying racks is off limits, but I have saved a pile of bones with a generous meal on each one. Here Woof, take your pick." She showed him the pile. He pulled a leg bone from the pile and moved away from the fire and settled in the grass beside Sarah. "Water Baby, are you hungry?" She handed her a meaty bone and gave another to their sister.

"Is that the name you have chosen for her? It's appropriate I guess. Let's call this one Tip Toe. She moves so softly that you can't hear her walk even in the grass."

"Yes she does seem to move very quietly and she has white on her toes. I like that."

Sarah told David the story of the waterway and that she wondered how a river could run underground so near a temple made of salt without harming it.

As they lay in the cabin they finished a prayer of thanksgiving with a request for no rain until they could get a roof of shingles on the cabin. David was astounded when two days later, Calvin Briggs arrived with Ben's largest wagon overloaded with shingles tied on and looking like they would cascade off at any minute.

The two men worked nailing shingles on the new cabin and storage shed for the next two and a half days. Sarah told them that she was glad that the roof was on because she knew that God was just holding back the rain for them to finish.

"I know He will water the garden tonight. He almost did last night, but I prayed and told Him that I didn't mind carrying water one more time."

The air was damp and cool as the early morning sun warmed the droplets clinging to a spider's web near the fire pit.

"You are as good at weaving as I am little spider. Your web is beautiful this morning." Sarah always noticed and appreciated the little things.

Today she had walked out the back door of the cabin, praising God for the snug house and for Calvin's help. He and David were cutting the logs, to open the back wall for the fireplace and chimney.

"These are good rocks. Ben knows what to gather. He helped with Jed's and then his own fireplace. It will help a lot to have them here," said Calvin. The men worked steadily until Sarah insisted they stop to eat. "It looks settled in here. You have all the comforts of home already. I like the way you planned the inside."

Thank you, Calvin. Everything in here came from the cabin that Ben and Jed built for me on their ranch."

"That's a good thing. I like to hear about families taking care of one another. Sarah, it takes a special touch to make a house look and feel like a home. You have that. It feels good here. Peaceful, you know what I mean?"

"Yes, we do Calvin. I feel it, too," said David.

The two men went out the back door and returned to their work. Sarah was glad that they were not pounding nails. She tucked Pili in her crib and sat down in the rocker. She felt tired. The shutters in the front wall were wide open and she remembered what Moonflower had said that she would keep them open unless the rain or snow was coming in. Sarah smiled as she listened to the soft tap, tap, of Calvin's work, settling another stone in the mortar.

"Everything here is new and different and yet it is as old as time itself. How old are the huge logs that make this new house? How long have the rocks watched the Hickory flow?

How many men built the hidden temple and how long has it been there?" Sarah spoke her thoughts softly to the scene out her window as she picked up the knitting needles in the big basket beside her and looked across the room at her sleeping baby and whispered. "We have such an awesome God. It feels like this is "**Just the Beginning**."

AN INVITATION

If you do not know Jesus, as your savior but you would like Him to be, please pray the following prayer. Invite Him into your heart. Commit your "New Life" to Him. He will be your constant companion, counselor, comforter, and protector, The Holy Bible tells us that He will never leave you or forsake you.

"Dear Jesus, please forgive my sins. Give me grace and strength Lord, so that I will not commit them again. Come into my heart so that I can start a "New Life" with you as my companion and Savior. I want to live according to your will and commandments. Bless me Lord and lead me in a life that is pleasing to You. In Jesus' Holy name I pray. Amen"

If you prayed that prayer, you are saved. You are born again. Your soul is whiter than the snow on the tallest mountain top. The angels in heaven are rejoicing as they write your name in The Lamb's Book of Life.

Get a Holy Bible and begin to read it. Find a good Bible believing church and start attending, so that you can learn more about Your Heavenly Father. What a wonderful God we have. Tell someone about your new life.

I will pray for you. God bless you. Louise Bouck

ABOUT THE AUTHOR

Louise Bouck is a follower of Jesus Christ. She and her husband, Dale, live in Arizona. Together they have raised six children.

Until an early retirement from her fulltime job in 2000, time was not available to allocate to writing or art. Along with many other interests, Louise enjoys painting on location. The lush greenery of Michigan, her home state and the abundant flowers in her grandmother's greenhouses and flower shop all encouraged her eye to appreciate the colors and beauty of nature.

After moving to Arizona, the rugged landscape of the mountains and desert stole her heart and took her artistic soul in a new direction.

Paintings in many media cover the walls of her studio as she has deliberately turned her creative side more to the discipline of writing.

Hesitantly she withdrew from the art gallery where her work was sold and left the position of resident artist at the local Historical Society Museum. Louise has written a ten book series of Christian; Bible based novels that she is now starting to release for the first time as she works on still another story and another painting.

BOOKS IN **"The New Life Series"**

1 MORE THAN SURVIVAL

#2 LIFE'S MANY JOURNEYS

#3 THE LAND'S HERITAGE

#4 THE STORY OF SARAH

#5 TOGETHER

#6 THE BLUE STONE PEOPLE

#7 TEEWAHPANYEE THE BOY, TWO FEATHERS THE MAN

#8 THE PEOPLE OF THE LION

#9 THE LION'S DEN

#10 JUST THE BEGINNING

www.ingramcontent.com/pod-product-compliance
Lightning Source LLC
Chambersburg PA
CBHW050735180626
46814CB00002B/764